The Last and Final King

The Last and Final King

by

Larry Redmond

Penknife Press   Chicago, Illinois

Copyright © 2003 by Larry Redmond
All rights reserved under International and Pan-American Copyright
Conventions.
Published in the United States of America by Penknife Press, Ltd., Chicago,
Illinois.

The Last and Final King.

ISBN 978-1-59997-031-8

Manufactured in the United States of America

BOOK I

I Will Send a King
For thus saith the Lord God;
Behold, I will bring upon Tyrus
Nebuchadnezzar, king of
Babylon, a king of kings, from the north, with horses, and with
chariots, and with horsemen, and companies, and much people.

The Holy Bible
Ezekiel 26:7

I

Life is a fuck. In and out, in and out, over and over again. Like a sine wave. Like a wave good-bye. It feels good to push it in, but the feeling doesn't last. It fades like the sound of a plucked guitar string, or a train whistle breezing by the station. Good-bye! You have to pull it out just so you can push it back in, just so the feeling will be intense again. And there you are again as the feeling fades, and you want it to last forever, so you pull it out again. Your rear end is bobbing in the air, and to what end? The feeling that fades and keeps you bobbing? Is this what forgetting history is like? What about your own personal history? In and out, in and out, over and over again.

I want to forget, but I can't. The blood, the fire. Was it right? Even if it was, should I have done it? There is no right or wrong, remember? There is no good or evil. Ida forgot, because she couldn't forget. It drove her crazy, what the two of us did. It cost her the baby. It woke her up at night crying. She wanted to talk about it but she couldn't, because talking about it meant jail or worse. The tears she cried were drops of her soul. Each time she cried, a little piece of herself spilled out and got wiped away. Eventually, there was nothing left. She stopped crying, and she was all gone. Mopped away in countless tissues and handkerchiefs. Evaporated into the air. Blown from her nose in one quick burst, hocked up and spit on the ground, leaving only the salty shell, skinny, hollow-eyed, staring into space. In and out, in and out, over and over again. Fuck it.

"Are you the one?" he asks.

I answer, "What turns on the answer? Am I the one what?"

"Are you the one?" he asks again. Staring him in the eye, I turn my head to the left, then to the right. I nod it up and down. Left and right, up and down. Left and right, up and down. Does he know who I am? Or is he just hoping and guessing?

* * *

My body and I are distinct, much as a CD and the music that is on it, or this book and the story that is in it. My body has characteristics that are similar to those of many other male bodies. It is tall and narrow across the shoulders, and it has a thin neck. Muscles protrude and roll under the russet brown skin like mice stuffed in a leather pouch. The face is long with shallow cheek bones and lean as if a minimum of flesh and skin were used to construct it. The hair is short and black and kinky and rough to the touch. The eyes are light brown, and have an asynchronous blink.

I, on the other hand, simply am. And I always have been. I live in my body. Living in it is like living in a computerized robot. The computer itself is in the robot's head, and it makes the robot function. The computer gets information about the robot and the robot's environment from a network running through it. The computer tells the machine what to do. And to give you an example of how complete the robot is, it can even feel and express emotion. It expresses emotion so well that I sometimes think it thinks it is me. I rarely have to tell the computer anything. It functions independently of me if I let it. And most of the time, I do. It talks to people, smiles, eats, cleans itself, makes love, everything. Sometimes I am in it, and sometimes I am gone. I enter and leave by way of the spaces between the molecules at the crown of its head. Right now, I am in it sitting under a cottonwood tree in Rainbow Park on Chicago's south side.

A bronze plaque at the park's entrance states that it was "named to commemorate the famous 42nd Rainbow Division of the United States Army by order of the Chicago City Council April 22, 1918." The division was led by a young Douglas MacArthur in some 13 battles in Europe from February 22, 1918, to April 1, 1919. The plaque goes on to say that its "accomplishments are a living part of the glorious heritage of the American people." I used to wonder sometimes whether or not my grandmother's brother, Uncle Buddy, ever served in that division. But then I thought about it. A black man? In MacArthur's division? Hardly.

I spend a lot of time in this park now that it is nearly summer. In fact, I have been here for days, lots of days, just waiting. People think I'm just a bum or a street person or something, just because I don't have a place to live. I don't spend any time on the beach as a rule, unless I want to get clean. Then I just dive in the water with my clothes on. That way everything gets clean at once. But usually I just sit in the grass under a tree and look. Usually, it is the same tree, a big cottonwood with a thick, black, rutted bark and countless little green heart-shaped leaves about the size of the palm of my hand.

I sit and look and write. My hand moves evenly. The words flow from the pencil tip like pictures in a Peter Max cartoon. Occasionally, I sit back and look around me to let my mind gather more images, then I go back to it. I sit back and see the brilliant yellow of the sun burning like a giant torch in the middle of a perfectly crystal clear deep blue sky. Then I write a few more lines. I sit back and see a honey-colored sister in a yellow bikini, her skin smooth and brown and shining in the sun as if she has just oiled it. Then I write some more. I see a bee hovering over a blade of kelly green grass like a tiny yellow and brown striped spaceship, then dart out of sight. And I write. I see the sister again, her close-cut yet full-bodied natural black and lustrous, her gold treble clef earrings shining. I write. I see a tiny red sailboat out on the lake bobbing like a toy as it drifts north. I write. I see the light of the sun flickering through the leaves of a maple tree as the hot wind stirs. The leaves glitter as if they were tinsel. I see clusters of tiny purple flowers on a bush like pearls placed in a young sister's hair. I see a little brown sparrow drinking from the puddle at the base of the drinking fountain. It throws its head back as though gargling, then hops onto the fountain itself. It hops around up there thrusting its chest forward like some of the strong men out on the beach. It flies away. After each of these, I write. I write my life, and I must write fast before it is gone.

Go in and out the window;
Go in and out the window;
Go in and out the window;
Sweet Mary came today.

Across the way in the parking lot, I see some boys spinning tops, and one of the boys is me. We've drawn a large chalk circle on the tar pavement. A black chalk circle? And as one of us spins his top in the circle, the others try one at a time to spike it.

Eddie Bunton is short and skinny with sandy colored hair. He spins his top first. It's metal with holes in it, and it whistles as it whirls, suspended in one spot like a gyroscope.

My top is new and fat and bright yellow. I just bought it this morning. I wrap the string around it, grasp it firmly between my first two fingers and my thumb with the point up and the button tight behind my fingers, and throw it down hard at Eddie's top sitting there like a duck. I turn my hand over as I throw it so the sharp metal point comes down first like a lightning spike. I hit Eddie's top and his top goes rolling under a parked Buick, one of the ones with the dynaflow holes. My top moves around the circle as it spins and will be hard to hit.

Eddie's twin brother, Richard, has a thin red top with lots of nicks in it. He rears back and flings his top point first at mine. He hits it right in the middle, and splits my beautiful yellow top into two ugly pieces. He and Eddie laugh. I try to smile. But water wells up in my eyes as I turn to leave. And though the world looks distorted through my tears, I see the twins' big sister spinning a diabolo on a string. She pulls each end of the string alternately up and down to make the diabolo spin while balanced on the string. Then she yanks the string taut. The diabolo sails about ten feet into the air, and she catches it again on the string. And in one fluid motion, she bends forward with her tightly curled fists together, then yanks herself over backwards as she raises up on her toes and snatches the string tight again. The diabolo zooms into the air and disappears in the perfectly crystal clear deep blue sky. The girl stuffs the string into her pocket and walks away.

One kiss before you leave me;
One kiss before you leave me;
One kiss before you leave me;
Sweet Mary came today.

I notice a little fat boy walking towards me. He is wearing a full length, black silk cape, one like a magician might wear. I am reminded of the way Ruby imitated magicians that day in Germany shortly before she was killed. How did she get out of that dress so damn fast? The little boy appears to be bald, and I am reminded of Tank, muscle-bound Tank.

As the little fat boy draws closer, I see that he isn't a little boy at all, but a dwarf. I smile. It is the dwarf who rifled our apartment five-- fifteen-- I don't know-- forty years ago. He looks older now. There are deep crows' feet at the corners of his eyes, and the skin on his cheeks and brow and neck is crepe. Was he the one in the hospital as well? He sees me and approaches. "Hi," I say.

"Mighty Red sent me," he answers. "I've been looking for you for a long time."

I recognize his voice as that of the man who rummaged through Red's kitchen the day I bolted for Spain.

"I know," I say. "I've been waiting a long time."

The man pulls a gun from beneath his cape. The silencer is as long as the gun itself. He holds his cape in such a way that the gun is hidden from the view of all except us. "What kept you?" I ask as I seep out of the robot's pores, and hover above its head.

The man steps closer, close enough so that the robot could easily kick the gun from his hand. "Are you the one?" he asks. "Lillian is spreading the rumor that you are not he."

"I thought Lillian was in jail."

"Are you the one?"

II

I graduated from high school in June of 1960, shortly after Grandma Daughter died. I enrolled at Wilson Junior College two weeks later. And I suppose the only feeling I had that I could identify as I walked up the concrete steps toward the heavy green doors on the west side of the building was one of disenchantment, disillusionment with life. The one person in the whole world who meant anything to me was dead, and the only option apparently available to me after having graduated was to continue studying subjects that I neither wanted to study nor could imagine would ever be useful to me. What in the hell was this thing called life all about anyway? Was this it? Was it limited to going to school, then someday getting a job and a wife and raising kids and dying like my grandmother had died without even having adequately addressed the question, let alone having answered it? I wanted answers to some pretty abstruse questions, questions for which I was not sure answers even existed. Even the building as I entered it looked unrevealing, cryptic, like a tomb.

I climbed the grime-encrusted steps to the second floor and dragged myself to the gymnasium where registration took place. The Fs through the Js were to report on the fourth day of registration, after the Ps through the Ts, who registered on the first day, the Us through the Zs, and the As through the Es. The line to the English table where I had to sign up for two required courses wound out of the gym and by a glass case hanging on the wall in the hallway. Behind the glass was a neatly accordioned canvas fire hose, and superimposed on the hose was my reflection in the glass, transient and meaningless, like a wraith. Then, in the half-light cast through the skylight, I saw Grandma Daughter in my face.

Grandma Daughter was a stout, buxom woman and I was a thin boy of eighteen. But the similarity between our features was uncanny. I wondered why I had never noticed it before. I felt guilty for not having noticed while she was alive, as if my noticing would have somehow prolonged her stay. And as if to redeem myself, I strained to see the curve of my pointed chin and shallow cheek bones, the full lips and bony, angular nose, features I had in common with Grandma Daughter. I studied with equal intensity the features I had that were dissimilar to hers, the close set, light brown eyes, the widow's peak, and the short, black, kinky hair. I felt closer to her now somehow. I felt as if we were one, and I felt myself mimicking an expression of hers, a smile that she smiled whenever she felt affectionate and wanted to hug me.

Grandma Daughter was my maternal grandmother. Her father called her Daughter although her name was Betty Lou. "Come help me haul this wood, Daughter," she would mimic him. Her younger brother, my Uncle Buddy, called her Daughter as well. When she had a child of her own, my mother, she made her call her Mo'Dear because that is what she had called her own mother. But when I was born, she insisted that I call her Grandma Daughter.

She came to live with us right after my grandfather, Paw-paw, got killed in an accident at a sawmill in Memphis, Tennessee, and to this day she remains a mystery to me. My remembrances of her are divided into two categories. The first category contains images of her working around the kitchen in blue flannel house slippers that slapped the bottoms of her feet as she walked, and of her stirring cornbread batter with a big wooden spoon as sweat beaded on her nose and the batter clapped together with a muffled thud.

Grandma Daughter moved more gracefully than her size would suggest. Her calves were thick boles of flesh, and her buttocks rose up on each side like bags of laundry strapped around her waist. She walked, however, like a much lighter woman. In fact, she walked on the balls of her feet with a deliberate controlled rhythm, like a dancer.

She was as dark as molasses. The skin on her face was soft and smooth and downy like rich, brown velvet, and I liked it whenever she rubbed her face against mine. I got my skin color from her, too. Sometimes she would kiss me all over my face. And I would get so excited, I would hug her around her neck as hard as I could. Then she would hold me away from her and look at me. And I would look at her. And her eyes were dark brown and fluid as she narrowed them slightly when she smiled at me. They were bottomless and mysterious like a crystal ball resting on deep brown velvet. I used to stare at her face, up close, and just look into her eyes trying to see what was in them. I asked her once, "Grandma Daughter, what's in your eyes?"

"You are," she answered.

I looked closely, and sure enough, my reflection was there. But there was more. Deep down there was much more. Grandma Daughter had the kind of eyes that were not afraid to look at people. Her eyes held power. Their movements were steady and deliberate. And most people who looked her in the eye looked away after only a few moments. If she were mad at me, she could make me tingle with fear simply by staring at me. And after seeing me hurt, she could soothe me long before she was close enough to touch me. I never told her what I saw in her eyes, but as I looked at the rest of her face with its shiny cheeks, its long, angular nose and flaring nostrils, its wide, thick lips that turned up slightly at the corners with an inborn smile, I suspected that she knew what was there.

The second category of remembrances is less lucid than the first. It is also the more interesting of the two. The images in this second category are only half-images, though, the result of glimpses of Grandma Daughter crying at times as she read the Bible, and smiling an almost wicked smile at other times as she read it. Whenever she caught me watching her, she would either close the book or tell me a story about the life of Jesus. I never knew which she would do, and whichever one she selected always surprised me because invariably I had guessed the other. These images are of her burning candles and incense, and making a series of strange hand gestures as an ambulance or fire truck would roar by. It was like Catholics crossing themselves, but different. She would put the palm of her right hand to her forehead, then to her heart, then to her navel. She would say that the noise upset her stomach and gave her a headache, but I knew it wasn't true because the noise never bothered anybody else. In fact, nobody else would even notice the noise if the sirens were at a distance. But Grandma Daughter always heard them and always palmed herself. She later told me she palmed herself to acknowledge God's intervention on Earth. I'm not sure I believed that either.

The day she arrived, Mama and Daddy and I stood shivering on the platform at Englewood Station waiting for a train called the City of New Orleans to arrive from down south. I was three then, and it was just after Thanksgiving.

It was snowing. Thick, heavy, white flakes dropped out of the sky so hard, I could almost hear them. They clung to everything they touched, and everything they touched turned white. The trees off in the distance looked like white scarecrows, their branches drooping under the weight of the accumulated snow. No wind to amount to anything blew, but once in a while the air stirred and shook the snow off one or two of the branches. The branches were black. And as the snow fell off, the branches sprung back up an inch or two as if they were skinny black arms.

I looked over at Daddy. He was humped over against the cold. Or maybe the snow piled on his head and shoulders was getting heavy. The snow was cold and clean and white and new. Especially the snow on his head. The wide-brimmed, gray felt hat he wore was piled high with it, and he looked as if he were tired of carrying it. I wondered if he would spring back up like a branch if he took all that snow off his head. But he didn't. He just let it sit up there, and he grumbled.

"Goddammit," he said, "where's that train?"

"Honey, don't cuss in front of the baby."

"Why not?" He said, "It'll make him a man. He ain't nothing but a sissy the way you treat him. And with your mother around, he'll sure 'nough be a little girl."

"He won't, either," Mama protested. She picked me up and held me close to her. I liked it whenever she did that. It made me feel warm.

"Hell he won't," Daddy scoffed. He lit a cigarette, and blew out a thick cloud of white smoke.

Daddy was a tall, muscular, light-skinned man with a big lumberjack's neck. Whenever he turned his head, the muscles in his neck stood out like heavy ropes. His Adam's apple protruded like a sparrow's head caught in his throat, and it bobbed up and down whenever he talked or swallowed. His big neck made his head look small. A lot of people thought he was good-looking because he had curly hair that was almost auburn and almond-colored eyes. I got my eyes from him. And with his small, turned-up nose and thin lips, he looked almost like a white man.

His hands were big, too, big and knobby. The skin on them was rough and chapped and callused. The first phalanx on each of his fingers and thumbs was thicker than the other phalanges so that his fingers looked like a collection of little mallets or pendulums. His fingernails were like little, flat plastic shields, chipped and broken and dirty around the edges. The nail on the index finger of his left hand was purple from where he had hit it with a hammer.

"I sure hope that woman knows the trouble I'm going through for her." Daddy's voice was real gravelly, and sounded almost hoarse.

"Honey, don't say that. Mo'dear love you, and you know it."

"The hell she do," Daddy scoffed.

"Why you say that?" Mama's voice sounded pleading.

"What do you mean, why do I say that? She did everything she could to keep you from marrying me. Said I'd never 'mount to nothin'."

"But that was five years ago."

"Yeah, and ain't nothing changed. A job at the steel mill don't make me no less a bum in that woman's eyes."

"You just got to try to understand her."

"Why should I? She don't try to understand me!" Daddy spat on the ground, and the spit made a hole in the snow like a bullet hole. "The bitch."

"John Henry Bodie, don't chu call Mo'dear no name like that." Her voice was stern now.

"Shut up, woman."

"And I told you 'bout cussing in front of the baby."

Daddy looked at Mama, then at me, then back at Mama. His eyes were narrow slits, and I knew that meant he was mad. I started whimpering, because when Daddy got mad there was usually trouble.

His eyes fixed on Mama. "I said shut up. Don't let me have to tell you again." Mama heard me crying, and began rocking me in her arms. I could feel the tension in the air.

When Daddy said don't talk, he meant it. I remembered that previous summer. It was hot outside, about ninety degrees, and hotter than that inside. Daddy told Mama not to talk and she talked anyway and Daddy knocked her down. I cried as loud as I could trying to make him stop, but he didn't. He hit her again with a strap. She cried; I cried; and he hollered and hit. And as we stood on the platform waiting for the train, I could feel Mama taking a deep breath getting ready to say something else. I started crying louder. I knew daddy was going to hit her. But then she must have remembered that past summer, too. Because she exhaled slowly. I could tell from the rising and falling of her chest that her breathing was almost normal again.

We stood there about five minutes before we heard the train off in the distance. I had stopped crying by then, but when I felt Mama tense up, I got scared again. But before I could start whimpering or anything, she blurted out, "John, please be nice to Mo'dear." Her voice sounded pleading again.

Daddy had probably relaxed a little, too. But when Mama asked him to be nice, he snapped his head around at us, shooting darts with his eyes. And as the train churned into the station with great bellows of white steam shooting from its wheels, I knew there was going to be some trouble. Mama knew it, too, because I could feel her heart pumping harder in her bosom. But she didn't say anything else. She simply cuddled me and whispered, "It's Ok, baby. It's Ok," in my ear to ease my whimpering.

Mama was the very antithesis of Grandma Daughter. Where Grandma Daughter was big, yet agile, Mama was frail and clumsy.

Where Grandma Daughter was cryptic, Mama was transparent. Yet her transparency was her primary redeeming characteristic. I never had to wonder whether or not there were any hidden meanings in anything Mama ever said. Like Grandma Daughter, Mama read the Bible often. But unlike Grandma Daughter, she read it with the eye of a pragmatist. She was not interested in the deep and the subtle. She wanted right and wrong spelled out in plain English, and spelled out in plain English was the only way she would accept them.

In all fairness, I should point out that Mama was not so much clumsy as she was weak. When she would fall, it would never be because she absent-mindedly caught her toe on the edge of the curb. It would more likely result from a chronic weakness in her knees. She would not spill things by bumping into them, but by attempting to pick them up with an anemic grip. She was perpetually short of breath. She woke up tired, and dragged herself through each day.

Mama was beautiful, though, despite her infirmity. Her face was round like a peach, and she had the clear, brown and ingenuous eyes of a child. And though her skin was as dark as Grandma Daughter's and mine, it had an almost translucent quality, the result, I suppose, of a lack of blood in her cheeks. She had a narrow mouth and well-defined lips like Paw-paw, and she always looked poised and composed and genteel. Her ethereal beauty reminded me of the tragic heroine in a sad movie.

The train ground to a stop. I smelled the odor of steam and hot steel wafting from beneath the coach. Mama squinted up and down the length of the train while Daddy simply stood with his shoulders hunched up against the cold and shifting his weight from one foot to the other.

The doors slid open, and a uniformed porter stepped off the train right in front of us. Grandma Daughter was the first person he helped off.

"What took you so long getting here, woman?" Daddy snapped.

"The snow, honey," Grandma Daughter answered. "The train had to slow down because of the snow."

"Well, you should have taken an earlier train."

"John," Mama cut in, "she couldn't know the train would be late."

Daddy threw another dart in our direction with his eyes, and nobody said anything for a long minute.

"Get your bags and let's go," he said at last leading the way to the exit and limping slightly as he walked.

Mama was going to try to ask him to help Grandma Daughter with her bags. She had two big, old, brown leather ones. But Grandma Daughter must have seen the dart he threw and grabbed Mama by the arm and made a funny face with her eyes narrowed and her lips drawn into a tight pucker that meant, "Don't ask him; we can manage the bags ourselves." And they did. Mama put me down, and they struggled with those bags all the way to the taxi stand. Daddy had planned to take the bus. So when he saw us getting in a cab, he shouted, "Goddammit, woman, I ain't got no money for no cab!"

Grandma Daughter smiled real wide, almost too wide, and said, "Oh, that's all right, John. I still got a little of my ticket money left, so we can take a taxi, and I'll pay for it."

"And I guess you was gon' let me just take the bus?" Daddy snorted.

"No, John," Grandma Daughter smiled, "I was going to say for you to sit in the front next to the driver."

"Humph," Daddy said as he slid onto the seat next to the driver, and slammed the door. "Humph," he said again.

The driver hit the gas so hard when we took off that the car seemed to move away from the curb in a sidewards motion. I thought we were going to sideswipe the walls of the little tunnel we had to go through to get to the street. Because the little tunnel was on such a sharp incline, we began sliding down when the driver hit the brakes, and we slid right into the middle of 63rd Street. In fact, we almost hit one of the supports that held up the massive viaducts over 63rd Street. But he turned, and we got enough traction to move on into the traffic.

Mama and Grandma Daughter began to relax a little. I suppose they figured that now the driver had to know for sure that the snow made driving dangerous, and that he would slow down some. But he didn't. He slipped around slow-moving cars and buses like he owned the road. Mama tightened up so stiff, I thought her fingers would leave permanent impressions in my chest from holding me back against the seat. Grandma Daughter was tight, too. Her lips were drawn in, and the muscles in the front of her chin were so hard that the skin over them looked lumpy. They both breathed a lot freer when the driver slid to a stop in front of our building on 58th and Michigan.

As Mama and I got out, Grandma Daughter paid the driver. Daddy got out, too, and headed straight for the house. The driver took Grandma Daughter's bags out for her and carried them to the door. Grandma Daughter thanked him. The cab driver drove off kicking snow behind him like smoke from a Flash Gordon rocket.

Grandma Daughter was a stout woman, as I said before. And sometimes her strength and beauty would reflect in her eyes. Sometimes I would look into her eyes and see tender sprouts pushing up through sweet black soil and gentle water flowing over smooth rounded rocks. I would see rolling green hills resting in the shade of mountains, black mountains, purple mountains, big, strong and proud. I would see huge stone pyramids or fishing boats with yellow, green and orange sails highlighted brilliant gold in the summer sun. I would see people, black people, planting seeds and harvesting millet and rice and barley. I would see little children laughing and playing games in the sand by a wide and deep-running river.

But at other times it seemed, when I looked in Grandma Daughter's eyes, as if that river were dry. It seemed as if the black soil were hard and dry with deep cracks etched in a crisscross pattern over its surface. It seemed as if the seeds, the crops, the fishing boats, the people, even the sun were gone. Only the pyramids remained. And they looked as if they had been eaten away by maggots, with deep holes reaching into their bowels. Yes, at times, Grandma Daughter's eyes really looked-- tired. That is the only word for it, tired.

They had that tired look as she and Mama dragged those two heavy bags into the living room and set them down. She seemed to force herself to look around the room-- at the blue and gray garlands on the wallpaper, at the old mahogany tables and mantelpiece covered with little pink china ballerinas, vases, mirrors and glass elephants, at the worn green flower print rug, at the thick sagging red sofa with the curved arms, at the white lace curtains that Mama had spent all morning washing and putting on wooden stretchers to dry. Grandma Daughter had seemed to have some spunk while wrestling with her bags at the station, but now that spunk was gone. Now she just plopped down in the heavy, bowed red chair by the window and began loosening her shoes. The chair squeaked loudly as she pulled at the laces. That was when Daddy began annoying her.

"Look at you," he said, "sitting around already."

"But she's tired," Mama said, her voice whining as she tried to make it sound as if she were not shouting. "She's had a long trip."

Grandma Daughter must have known that Daddy would resent Mama taking sides with her against him, because she quickly drew her lips in tight as she looked back and forth between them. Before Mama even finished what she was saying, Grandma Daughter began pulling herself up out of the chair while mumbling something about Daddy being right and her having to unpack her bags. But she was too late. Daddy jumped down Mama's throat.

"Woman," he said, "I told you at the train station to shut your damn mouth, and I meant it."

Almost at the same time Daddy started shouting, I started crying. I knew that Mama was not going to shut up, even with Grandma Daughter trying to signal her to be quiet.

"But, John," Mama said. Her voice sounded pleading as if she were going to try to reason with him. Daddy, however, was not going to be reasoned with. In fact, he didn't even give her a chance to finish what she was saying. He smacked her with the back of his hand, his left hand, the one with the purple fingernail on the index finger. Mama cried out once and staggered backwards while cringing and holding her mouth. Her eyes welled up with tears. By now, I was crying so loudly, I could hardly hear anything else going on in the room. I thought Daddy was going to keep hitting her the way he had last summer. But he didn't. He snapped something about already being late for work. Then he shook his finger in her face as he stood over her, promising to finish with her when he got back. He looked over at Grandma Daughter, the muscles protruding in his bullish neck. His teeth were clinched and his lips barely moved as he said, "And you can expect some of the same, old woman."

He snatched up his hat and stormed out of the door, slamming it so hard that a piece of plaster broke loose inside the wall and clattered to the basement. The radiator in the corner hissed and clanked for a long minute after he left.

Mama turned to Grandma Daughter with water streaming down her cheeks, "Mo'dear, what am I gon' do?"

Grandma Daughter got down on the floor with her, and she held Mama's head to her bosom. Mama sobbed, then began to cry harder.

"It'll be all right, daughter. God will see to it." Grandma Daughter rocked slowly while staring blankly at the blue and gray garlanded wallpaper.

At dinner that night, there was nearly total silence, and it bothered me. Usually Mama and I played little games while we ate. Like sometimes, I would point to the buttered bread in her plate and ask her to give me a bite. She would shake her head no, and tell me to eat my own. "But I want some of yours," I would say. She would still say no. Then I would fake crying until she gave in and offered me a bite. But then I would refuse to accept it, saying in a sing-song voice, "Sorry, Miss, you took too long, I'll eat my own." We would laugh and I would let her 'stuff' the bread into my mouth. We sometimes went through whole meals playing our little game. But that night there was only silence, silence and the occasional tinkle of someone's fork on their plate, or the thump of their glass on the table as they placed it back down.

And I was the only one who ate anything. Mama ate one little piece of meatloaf and half of her peas and carrots. She didn't touch her mashed potatoes nor her buttered bread. Grandma Daughter didn't even eat that much. She just sipped slowly on a glass of buttermilk. They both stared into their plates for a long time. Once or twice,

Grandma Daughter's lips and the little muscles in her chin got tight. But then she would relax them slightly and sip her milk.

I pointed to the bread in Mama's plate and asked, "Can I have a bite?" She plopped the whole piece in my plate, and didn't look up even once. I left it there and went up front to color in my coloring book.

I had only been out of the kitchen a little while, only long enough to color the man's suit pink and green, and the lady's dress orange, when I heard Grandma Daughter ask Mama, "Is there a conjure woman in this town?" She sounded like she was trying to keep her voice down. But I guess Mama didn't get the hint, because she blurted out, "A conjure woman?! Wha'chu want a conjure woman for?"

"Don't ask questions, daughter. Just tell me where she is."

"There's one right around the corner, Mo'dear. But she's expensive." Mama's voice still had a shocked, questioning tone.

"How much does she want?" Grandma Daughter asked.

"A dollar just to burn a candle and tell some lies."

"She'll want more than that tonight."

"Why, Mo'dear? Wha'chu gon' do?"

"Never mind, honey, just get you and the baby ready so you can take me to her."

"But, Mo'dear . . ."

"Be quiet, child, and get your coat."

Mama complained all the while she put my snow suit on, but within twenty minutes we were standing in front of a two-story, brown brick building near 55th and Indiana. It was dark out, but the street lights gave enough light for Grandma Daughter to read the little cardboard sign in the window, "'Sister Theresa, Reader and Adviser.' Hmmm, I wonder if she's the real thing."

"She's a fake, Mo'dear, she don't . . ."

"Hush up, so I can think."

We stood there for two solid minutes. With a zero-degree wind whipping around us like knives, all up my sleeves and numbing my face and feet, Grandma Daughter stood thinking. I wondered what in the world she could be thinking about for so long. Then, finally, she said, "I guess we'll have to take a chance."

"On what, Mo'dear?!"

But Grandma Daughter didn't answer. She simply climbed the ice-caked stairs and rang the bell. Mama and I followed her. But nobody answered. Grandma Daughter rang again. I heard it myself this time, so I knew it was working. But still no one answered. Grandma Daughter rang a third time, and we stood. Then Mama said, "Let's go, Mo'dear. The baby is getting cold. Besides, it's dark in there. She ain't home."

Grandma Daughter hesitated. Then she reluctantly agreed. "Ok, daughter, we can go. I know the way now, so I'll just have to come back later by myself."

"For what, Mo'dear? Wha'chu want from this crazy woman?"

Grandma Daughter still would not answer.

We eased back down the icy stairs and were about to head home when someone tapped on the window behind us. We looked around and, in the window, a woman holding a candle signaled us to come back. She was in the window with the sign in it. And as she held the white lace curtains back with one hand and the candle in the other, the light of the flame reflected off her face from only one side like rays from the moon. I got scared. All I could see were her head and hands. And it reminded me of the Headless Horseman in *The Legend of Sleepy Hollow*, except she had a head and no body. I started crying and straining against going back up those stairs. Grandma Daughter was excited.

"She's there, Mary Jane. We got to go back."

We climbed back up the stairs. Mama labored with each step because her knees were not strong enough to raise her body. She had to heave herself painfully onto each stair. And because she was trying to hurry, she almost slipped. Grandma Daughter had to help her.

Once inside, it was warm, and the warmth felt good. Sister Theresa turned a light on and my fear seemed to evaporate into the fresh scent of sandalwood incense, to be absorbed into the warmth and comfort of Sister Theresa's cozy little front room. Even the lace curtains I had thought were white were a warm pastel yellow, and their very color seemed to be a source of comfort like the yellow rays of the sun. The Sister's voice was comforting, too. It was low and soft, but most of all, it was calm. I detected not the first note of anxiety or fear. She said. "Come on in. I'm Sister Theresa," almost as if she had been expecting us.

She was a short woman. She didn't even come up to Mama's shoulder. And she was thin. In fact, she looked like a little girl in a grown-up's dress. Only, the dress fit, so that I knew it was hers, and that she was not a little girl. Even her face looked young. She was dark but not as dark as Mama. Her eyes were big and sorry looking like puppies' eyes, as if she had seen a lot of sick people, people that she could not do anything for, but whom she wanted to cheer up anyway with a smile. So she forced it. The thing that comforted me most, though, was not Sister Theresa or the yellow curtains or the candles on the mantelpiece or the little brass urn sending a thin stream of sweet smoke into the air or even the dozen or so pictures of Jesus on the walls. No, instead, it was Grandma Daughter. For some reason, Grandma Daughter seemed sure that this was indeed the right place.

She even smiled. I had not seen her smile all day until now, and her smiling made me glow with warmth.

"How do, Sister Theresa. My name is Mrs. Adams, and I need something done."

"Please, sit down, Mrs. Adams, and tell me what I can do for you." She sounded so calm, so confident and sure that I almost expected her to tell Grandma Daughter why we had come.

Grandma Daughter sat deftly onto one end of the little green couch across the room from the mantelpiece and fireplace, and Sister Theresa sat slowly down on the other end. Mama released her weight a full foot above the cushion of the easy chair in the opposite corner by the window. I sat in her lap and inspected the lace doilies on the arms and back of the chair.

"My daughter here is having trouble with her man, and . . ."

"Mo'dear, don't tell this woman my business."

"It's Ok, dear," Sister Theresa said softly. "I knew what the trouble was as soon as you walked in. And in fact," her voice was like velvet, "both of you are in serious danger."

"Danger?!" Mama scoffed, "What kind of danger?"

"If the trouble in your home isn't resolved, that man will kill you both."

"What?!" Mama shouted.

And at the same time, Grandma Daughter gasped, "I knew it!"

"It'll be an accident and he'll be sorry afterwards, but he can't control his impulse to lash out at whatever is paining him. And right now that something is you, your son and your mother."

"Well, what can we do?" Mama sounded bewildered.

"Can you help us?" Grandma Daughter asked.

"What do you want me to do?"

"Protect us," Grandma Daughter answered.

"I can't protect you. Only God can do that. But right now, you must decide what you want done, and I'll ask the spirits to do it."

For a long minute, nobody said anything. Then Grandma Daughter said, "Uh, Sister?"

"Yes?"

"Is there any way you can get him out of the house-- you know-- make him leave?"

"Oh, yes," Sister Theresa said matter-of-factly. "I can have him gone within two months."

"But Mo'dear, I don't want him to go," Mama whined.

"Daughter, that man will hurt you if you stay together."

"But how will me and you and the baby live?"

"Don't worry, we'll make it."

"But I love him, Mo'dear. I love him."

"Well, it's plain he don't love you, honey."

"Oh, Mo'dear, he loves me." Mama sounded agonized.

"Well, he sure picks a funny way of showing it. A man don't usually beat somebody he loves."

"He was right," Mama said. "You just don't understand him. You think he's a bum."

There was a pause in which Grandma Daughter just sat looking kind of complacent, her lips pinched tight and the flesh on her chin tight and ripply. Mama rocked slowly side to side as she held me, her raisin-colored hands folded in my lap. Sister Theresa simply sat staring at the flame on one of the candles on the mantelpiece.

Then Grandma Daughter cleared her throat and said, "Sister Theresa, is there a place where we can talk alone for a minute?"

"Yes'm, right back in my consultation room."

"You wait here, daughter, 'cause I don't want the baby to hear this."

Mama agreed to wait while Grandma Daughter and Sister Theresa went through the blue curtains at the doorway to the back part of the apartment. I heard the door to the consultation room click shut, and for about ten minutes, Mama and I waited. All that while, Mama sat and rocked and looked worried. Her eyebrows were drawn so close together that they would have touched if it had not have been for three little neatly creased rows of flesh between them.

Finally, Grandma Daughter and Sister Theresa came back. Grandma Daughter thanked the Sister several times before we left, and Sister Theresa encouraged Grandma Daughter in her controlled manner and satin voice to have faith. Grandma Daughter said she would.

The walk back home didn't seem nearly as long or as cold as the walk up, even though we walked in total silence. Mama didn't ask anything about the private consultation, and Grandma Daughter didn't volunteer anything. We simply walked.

I was in bed when Daddy got home, and the noise he made beating Mama and Grandma Daughter woke me up. He was talking all loud like he sometimes did on Fridays or after parties. "That's right," he said, "I drinks a whole *lot* of whiskey, and I am a sure 'nough man." I heard a bottle break in the kitchen sink. "And I don't take no shit from womens." I heard Mama scream, and I cried out loud. I cried all the while he was hitting them, and when he stopped, the house was quiet, and I dozed back off to sleep.

I had a strange dream that night, strange and spooky. I dreamt that a pair of long, steel-gray hands extended down from a black sky, slow moving, controlled, almost mechanical hands that wrote Daddy's name nine times using a crow's feather and red ink on a piece of dull gray paper. The hands then stuffed the paper into a split calf's heart, red and dripping blood, and closed the split back up using eighteen shiny steel needles. They dropped the heart point downward into a jar of acrid-smelling, dark yellow vinegar, and placed the jar on an altar on top of another piece of paper with Daddy's name on it again nine times in red ink. The altar was covered with a black velvet cloth, and a creamy white skull rested on the altar surrounded by nine burning black candles in crystal holders, and a black, thorny crown rested on the skull, and the jar containing the calf's heart rested in front of the skull. Grandma Daughter sat across the room from the altar, watching the altar and waiting, and the candles burned and burned.

The next morning's breakfast seemed like a continuation of dinner the night before. Only now, Mama's lip was fat and had dried blood on it, and Grandma Daughter's left eye was closed. But as before, we ate in silence. Mama gave me a bowl with an egg and grits and a piece of sausage and a slice of toast, and I ate. I knew not to ask anything, because Daddy was still asleep, and Mama and Grandma Daughter wanted him to stay asleep a little while longer. So we tiptoed around and whispered and listened for noises from the bedroom.

I dreamt a weird dream that night, too. In fact, it was very similar to the dream I had had the night before. But this time, the steel-gray hands carved a little six-inch coffin out of an old two-by-two-by-six piece of pine. And they cut Daddy's name inside it. The hands then dressed a little stick doll in black pants and jacket, put the doll in the coffin, and placed the coffin open on the altar beside the jar with the noisome vinegar and calf's heart. With ceremonious grandeur, the hands wrote Daddy's name on another piece of paper, and soaked the paper in a half a glass of Seagram's Crown Royal Whiskey. Then after forcing a black chicken to drink the whiskey, the disembodied hands stuffed the chicken and a black tomcat, both alive, into a deep hole, and buried them.

I woke up crying that night because the cat and chicken were struggling to get free, and the more they struggled, the more dirt got thrown on them. Even after they were completely covered, the ground still moved from where they struggled to the end to dig themselves out.

I told Mama I was scared by a bad dream, and she said, "Don't worry, baby, it's over."

"But what if it comes back?" I asked.

"It won't," she said, and tucked me back in and kissed me.

But the next night, I dreamed again. This one was short, though. This time, the hands lighted nine black candles at the bottom, and set them in an old rain barrel to burn. And a voice, a calm, controlled voice like Sister Theresa's, spoke to the skull on the altar, and the skull listened, and the voice said, "Vengeance is thine."

I didn't have another dream like that until about a month later. To be exact, I dreamed on Christmas Eve. And this one seemed worse than all three of the first ones. In this one, the hands opened the grave of the chicken and cat, and placed a white bouquet of roses at the head and foot of the grave. Later in the dream, the hands put a calf's brain on a plate on the altar where the little coffin had been. They sealed Daddy's name in another calf's heart, and buried it with the chicken and cat and coffin and doll. Then they burned more candles and more candles and more candles.

In each of the dreams, Grandma Daughter sat across the room in an old rocking chair rocking and waiting, with the light of the candles glowing on her grayish, pale, deadpan face, and the reflection of the flames flickering yellow in her eyes.

It was after this last dream that I noticed Daddy acting kind of strange. He became forgetful. For instance, one day, he was on his way to work. He had opened the door, stepped out, and was about to close the door behind him. Then he stopped. He cocked his head to one side, thought for a minute, then patted his pant's pockets, felt in his shirt pockets, and dug deep into his coat pockets. He didn't find what he was looking for, so he came back in, closed the door, and started looking around the house. He looked under the couch and chairs and tables in the front room, under the bed and dresser and chest of drawers in the front bedroom, in all his pants and shirt and coat pockets, in all the drawers, under my bed, in all my drawers, under the stove and refrigerator, and in all the cabinets. He spent over an hour pulling things down and taking things apart to look in them. Finally, Mama asked him what he was looking for.

"For my pass," he answered. "I can't get in at the mill without my pass."

"Is that it on your shirt?" Mama asked.

Daddy looked down at the silver metal tag clipped to the front of the gray work shirt and said, "Oh, yeah, that's it." He left without saying another word. Grandma Daughter closed the door behind him.

About four months later, he died.

His death was sudden. But then again, maybe not so sudden considering that for a month or longer before he died, he suffered from severe headaches, headaches that kept him up nights, that kept him home from work, that caused him, on occasion, to sink to his knees screaming, cursing and clutching at his temples. The company doctor never found anything wrong with his head, so when his sick days ran out, he was forced to return to work. On his first night back he collapsed and died after pulling a dolly load of steel tubes about ten yards across a loading dock.

Three days later, we had his funeral. Some of the people who came cried. Others shook their heads solemnly. But Grandma Daughter simply sat on a nearby bench and rocked from side to side with a deadpan expression on her face and that tired look in her eyes. She looked as if she were off somewhere, as if she were not really there. The sky was overcast and gray.

With Daddy dead, our lives began changing for the better, at least for a little while. We moved away from 58th and Michigan because that apartment reminded Mama too much of Daddy. She remarked at least once a week about feeling his presence, his coldness in bed with her at night. I remember the first night she felt it, she screamed aloud.

"Mo'dear," she called. "Mo'dear!"

My bed was in Mama's room now that Daddy was gone. This way Grandma Daughter had my old room, the one right off the kitchen, to herself. So when Mama shouted, I woke up instantly, because I thought she was hurt or sick or something. I couldn't see anything, though, because it was dark in our room. But I could hear. And what I heard scared me. I heard fear in Mama's voice. "Mo'dear," she called, and she sounded as if she were in a panic. My pulse quickened. I stood up in my crib and held onto the railing. I heard Mama fight with her covers, then lunge for the lamp on the table by her bed. But she misjudged it, and sent the lamp, the clock, the glass of water and the table crashing to the floor. The lamp cord or switch or something must have gotten wet during the fall, because as soon as everything crashed down, a hideous, pale blue spark flashed and lit up the whole room for a split second. And in that short amount of time, I saw Mama bolt straight backwards across the bed with her hands outstretched in front of her and a grimace on her face that twisted her mouth, pinched her eyes shut and forced cords of stress to protrude from her neck. She screamed as she bolted. When she landed on the floor on the other side of the bed, she began crying hysterically.

The flash scared me, too. I thought it had hurt Mama. So I screamed when she screamed, and started jumping up and down and yanking at the railing of my crib. My blood rushed hard in my head, and my heart felt as if it might burst in my chest. I wanted to climb out over the railing, but I couldn't see and I was scared and my ears rang from the noise and from fear.

It seemed as if we cried for an hour before I heard Grandma Daughter clicking the wall light switch by the door back and forth.

"What's the matter, daughter?" Her breathing was labored. I could tell that she was scared, too. But I didn't know of what. She kept clicking the switch wildly. "You all right?! What's wrong with the lights?!"

"He's in here, Mo'dear! I heard him! He touched me!"

"Who's in here, baby?"

"John, Mo'dear! John is in here!"

Grandma Daughter stopped clicking and gasped as she blurted out, "John," in a loud whisper. Then she was silent for a long minute. Even her labored breathing had stopped. All I could hear was Mama and me sobbing. When she resumed breathing, it was slow and deliberate.

"Find a candle and light it while I go see about the baby," Grandma Daughter said.

I could hear her feeling her way around the foot of Mama's bed on her way over to my bed. Before long, her breathing was so close, I could almost feel her reaching in to pick me up. So I raised up my arms and waited to feel her strong hands under my arm pits. Just when I could feel the heat of her breath on my face, she cried out, "Oh," and threw her weight against my bed so hard, it knocked me down.

"Mo'dear! You all right?" Mama's voice sounded calmer now, but concerned.

"I stepped on something and I think I cut my foot." She paused a moment. "Hurry up and find a candle."

"I've got a candle, but I can't find a match."

I could hear Mama rummaging through all the drawers in the dresser. "There's some kitchen matches on the stove," Grandma Daughter told her.

Mama eased out to the kitchen and lit the candle and came back.

The room looked eerie in candle light. Everything looked familiar, yet strange. The shadows of my chest and toy box weaved around and bobbed as the flame flickered. They almost looked alive. Grandma Daughter had made her way back to the foot of Mama's bed and was sitting there holding her foot when Mama got back. In the light of the candle, her thick, brown foot and fleshy, heavy looking hands were stained red with blood.

As Mama inspected the cut, Grandma Daughter said, "That must have been quite a dream you had."

"That was no dream, Mo'dear. John was here. I could feel him cold against my body."

"Did he say anything?" Grandma Daughter sounded worried. "He said that now he knew who killed him. And he said to ask you who it was."

"Ask me?!"

"That's what he said." She paused a moment.

I looked at the candle, and it looked strange and secretive. It looked as if it were alive there in Mama's hand, like a little man flickering all by itself.

"What do you think he meant, Mo'dear?"

"I don't know, daughter. Ask him when he comes back."

"I don't want him to come back. And I want us to move from this house."

Grandma Daughter slept in the bed with Mama for the rest of the time we stayed there, and Mama only felt Daddy around during the day when she was alone.

Six weeks later, we moved to an apartment on the second floor of an old yellow frame house in the fifty-five hundred block of La Salle Street.

It rained all morning of the day we were supposed to move. And it looked so cloudy when it finally stopped that we were afraid to take anything outside. But since it was the last day of the month, some more people were due to move in the next day. Besides, the movers and a couple of the local winos were there ready to work. So we moved as planned. Moving didn't help Mama, though. She was perpetually tormented by the Daddy's 'presence.'

"He's in here, I tell you," she would say.

"Honey," Grandma Daughter would answer, "John is dead."

"His body is dead, Mo'dear. But his spirit is in this house. Mama would look around as if searching the air for a wisp of smoke, a wisp that always evaded her.

In time, she became so obsessed with Daddy's ghost that she began to wither away to nothing. She stopped eating because Daddy had poisoned all the food. She sat up nights so he would not catch her off guard like before.

"It's the water," she explained to Grandma Daughter. "He contaminates the water in food."

Everything Mama ate was dry: potato chips, apricots, popcorn, peanuts. She bought water in bottles, and drank it down without removing the bottle from her lips. That way, Daddy couldn't get inside the bottle. She ate like that for a long, long time afterward.

All during this time, too, Grandma Daughter became more and more cryptic. It was as if she, too, were affected by Daddy's death, and felt his presence in the house, though she wouldn't talk about it. She stayed in her room a lot reading or something. And whereas she used to leave the door to her room open most of the time whenever she was not there, now she began closing it. I even caught glimpses from time to time of burning candles sitting on the little writing table she had by the bed. So one day I asked her, "Grandma Daughter, why do you burn candles like that in the middle of the day?"

"Because candles are magic."

"Magic? Magic how?"

"The magic of the candle," she said, "is in its ability to throw light in dark places." Her voice as she spoke was mysterious. It was soft and smooth and measured as if she were imitating Sister Theresa.

"Grandma Daughter," I said, "it's light outside."

"But it's dark inside," she countered.

"Even with the shades up?" I asked.

She smiled a smile that I recognized as the kind that people give you when they know something you don't, and they don't plan to tell you what it is. On some people, that smile looked smug. On Grandma Daughter it looked sympathetic, understanding. I dismissed it as something old people knew because they were old. And I knew that I would know what it was one day when I got old.

The only information I ever got on what she was reading came one day after school when I was sixteen. I ran up the stairs, threw my books and jacket on the couch in the living room, and headed for the kitchen. But I stopped short in front of the coffee table. Grandma Daughter had left one of her books on the table open to a page with a picture of the Egyptian Sphinx on it. It was a drawing rather than a photograph, and I was struck by the thickness-- the Africanness-- of the nose and lips, not like the shot-off nose the Sphinx has today. I was fascinated by it. I sat down and read the caption. It read:

On the Egyptian sphinx,
the human head represents intelligence and knowledge;
the lion's claws, daring and action;
the bull's loins, will power, perseverance and labor;
the eagle's folded wings, silence.
Hence the quaternary of the magi:
KNOW, DARE, WILL, KEEP SILENT.

The paragraph next to the picture tied the various parts of the Sphinx to the races of the world: the eagle to the yellow race, the human head to the black race, the bull to the white race, and the lion to the red race. I didn't read much of that paragraph, though, because my attention lingered on the words "know, dare, will, keep silent" in the caption. A strange feeling came over me as I pondered the questions. I wondered: Know what? Dare what? Will what? Keep silent when, about what? Or maybe it was not the questions themselves, but rather the notion that there was something to know and yet keep silent about. Then I wondered whether or not Grandma Daughter knew what was to be so mysteriously known. I remembered the burning candles in her room. Then I remembered asking Grandma Daughter many years earlier about the magic of the candle. Was that the knowledge to be known?

I was going to read further, but I looked up and Grandma Daughter had slipped into the room and had been watching me as I read. I felt guilty for being nosy. So I mumbled something about being on my way to the kitchen. I flipped the pages back to the cover, closed the book, and left.

Grandma Daughter died two years later. She suffered a massive stroke in her sleep one night, and Mama and I found her dead in her room the following morning.

Her wake and funeral were short. A few of the neighbors came, and a friend of hers named Mildred Parker came up from Memphis. It was early May. The grass as we stood by Grandma Daughter's coffin at the graveyard left our shoes wet with water from the morning's rain. But the sky was clear except for a few small clouds way off in the east. Mama cried long and hard those few days. And although I didn't cry, I felt deeply anguished.

I looked all around in Grandma Daughter's room about a week after she died for that book with the Sphinx in it. I wanted to know more about the Sphinx and candles and not telling what was known. The drawers of her chest smelled of mothballs and cedar. I found small jars of acrid-smelling ointments, bottles of cloudy lotions and tins of colored powders. But the book was gone.

III

The gymnasium was hot, owing to the increased number of bodies present and the lack of ventilation. By the time I got to the table for English classes, it was almost noon. My knees felt rubbery, and I was lightheaded from hunger. Out of the corner of my eye, I saw a tall boy wearing neatly creased blue gabardine pants step adroitly over the rope barrier. The boy swaggered histrionically over to me and tried to squeeze by me and the table where a fat girl with braces sat checking everybody's registration cards. Apparently, I didn't jump out of the way fast enough, or maybe I just resented his jumping to the head of the line without waiting. In either case, I didn't move to let him by. And in trying to force his way through, he kicked the table leg and put a crease in the toe of his polished tan wing tips.

"Move out, punk," he snarled. Then he looked down and saw the crease. Actually, it was more than just a crease, because at one end of the sharp indentation, the surface leather lay peeled back revealing the coarse, dry layer underneath. He flexed his toes to see the tear in a different light. Then, having seen, he paused a moment, removed his high-crowned, dark green beaver hat and placed it gingerly on the table. The girl behind the table bolted straight up, knocking the chair she was in over on the floor, and the crowds of people behind me began moving and pushing back in a great wave away from me and the table.

My pulse surged. "I . . . I'm sorry . . .," I stammered.

The boy reared back and swung. I, not knowing what to do, merely reacting, leaned out of the way. As I did, I grabbed his arm, so that I would know where it was, I guess. And I pulled him off balance. He tripped over my foot as he lunged by me, and toppled into another boy who had not gotten fully away because of the masses of people in his way. Both boys fell to the floor with the new boy on top. Now, the one who had swung at me must have thought that *I* was on top of him, because he instantly began kicking and wrestling. The boy on top was terror-struck, his eyes wild with fear. He threw a barrage of curled fists into my attacker's neck and head. The boy on top was bigger than my attacker. His shoulders were broad and heavy under his bright orange, pullover shirt. And the boy on top cried even as he hammered the other boy's head. The boy on the bottom, the one who had swung at me, was limp within seconds. But the boy in the orange shirt didn't notice. He simply continued to pound.

It didn't take me long to get into the crowd of people plowing to the other side of the massive skylit room. In fact, I saw most of the fight by way of glances over my shoulder as I pushed people and rope boundaries away before me. By the time I got most of the way across the gym, two male instructors, who had been pushing through the outward surge of scared students to get in towards the fight, finally broke through. When I last looked over my shoulder, they were struggling to pull the still-swinging boy in orange off the boy with the creased shoe.

I ran down the stairs, taking them three, maybe four at a time. The people in line waiting to get up looked at me as if I were a madman. But I didn't care. I stumbled down the last five or so stairs before I got to the doors leading outside. I hit the door with enough drive to knock it down if it had not already been half open.

Once outside, I stopped running. I stood leaning against a lamppost for five solid minutes panting like a horse. My chest and throat ached from breathing so hard. My legs ached, too. I wanted to lie down, but I could not. So I sat on the steps in front of the door with my head down between my knees, and listened to my pulse throbbing in my temples.

I didn't know how long I sat there, five, maybe ten minutes. While sitting there, I must have slipped into a sort of trance, because when I finally raised my head back up, spit was beginning to drip from my limp mouth. I slurped once, then wiped my mouth with the back of my hand and leaned back on the steps. I felt sick to my stomach, and I wanted badly to lie down.

As I sat there, a red and black fire department ambulance pulled silently up and stopped by the curb right in front of me. It didn't have its red lights or sirens on, so I thought they were just stopping to be stopping. But then two guys dressed in black shirts and trousers hopped out, ran around and opened up the back, pulled out a neatly folded stretcher, and headed straight towards me. I was just about to say, I'm Ok now, and get on up when they picked up speed and walked right on by me and into the building. They must have been inside for at least five minutes, long enough for a little crowd to form around the stairs and me, but to me it seemed like less than a minute passed before they were coming out again carrying my attacker on the stretcher. Only now, two more boys were with them. They were dressed in the same gouster style as the boy on the stretcher, long collar shirts, pleated pants, wing tips, but they wore different color combinations. I stood up and moved to one side. One of the boys, the bareheaded one with the shiny process, asked the one on the stretcher, "Who did it to you, Maurice? Point the punk out." Half of Maurice's face had been bandaged, and his one exposed eye looked glassy as he rolled it around apparently scanning the crowd. His eye stopped on me. My pulse quickened, and I almost shit on myself. The two boys looked at me. "Is that him, Maurice?" the slick-head boy asked. But Maurice just closed his eye as if he were asleep. One of the firemen said, "He's out, guys. He probably can't even hear you." Then they maneuvered through the crowd, tucked Maurice into the back of the ambulance, and sped away, this time with lights flashing and siren blasting. The two boys stood just off the curb looking after the ambulance as the crowd broke up. Slickhead looked around at me with one eyebrow raised and the corners of his mouth curled down. He spat in the street. I wanted to run. But I knew that he was not sure whether or not Maurice pointed me out. So I just stood there quaking. Finally, they left. I sat back down with a knot in my stomach and my pulse pounding in my head.

"You feel any better?" a man's voice said behind me.

I ignored whoever it was, because I didn't know he was talking to me. My head rocked back as I tried to stretch out a little, and I closed my eyes. I felt miserable. I heard the person come down and sit beside me.

"Do you feel any better?" he asked again.

I turned my head where it rested on the edge of the step, and opened my eyes slowly. It was one of the teachers who had broken up the fight. I recognized his horn-rim glasses and clean-shaven, pointed chin.

"I feel sick," I told him.

"Well, just lie there and breathe slowly," he said. "You'll feel better in a few minutes."

I closed my eyes for a minute or two longer, then sat up with my elbows resting on my knees.

"My name is Mr. Favor." He paused a moment, then asked, "What's yours?"

I told him my name.

I remembered having been this sick from hard running and being afraid once before. I was ten. I had this friend, Melvin Sadd, a little roly-poly, dark-skinned boy with a long stubbly head who picked his nose all the time and ate the boogers. He told me about this old house on Garfield Boulevard about six blocks from where I lived. He said he had been in it the week before and found a lot of old clothes and things, and he wanted to go back to look for some treasure. I said I would go with him. That evening, we sneaked in a broken basement window. I was scared as it was. It was almost dark, and the only means of light we had was a book of matches Melvin had gotten from home. He lit one. We stood there by the window looking around. Melvin was scared, too. It was daylight the last time he had been there, and he could see a whole lot better then than we could see now. We stood there huddled next to each other, each waiting for the other to take the lead. Then the match died. And as Melvin fumbled around trying to get another one lit, we heard something fall in the next room. It was probably a cat or something knocking junk over, but we never found out for sure. We scrambled back out that window in nothing flat and ran full speed back to my house. I stopped in front of my steps, but Melvin kept running. I felt that night as if my dinner would come up any minute.

"You left the gym pretty fast," Mr. Favor said.

I didn't know whether I was supposed to respond to that or not. I chose to ignore it.

"Did you get registered?" he asked.

"No," I answered. "I was right at the front of the line when this boy came up and . . ."

"Yeah, that was Maurice Martin. He likes to jump in front of people like that. It cost him a broken nose today, though. And he might lose an eye."

I was almost glad to hear about his eye, because in my fear, I simply knew he and his friends would come looking for me for having gotten him beat up. If he lost an eye, I imagined that maybe he would not recognize me.

"Do you still want to register?" Mr. Favor asked.

"Yes, sir," I answered, my voice shook. "But I lost my cards, and I don't . . ."

"Don't worry about it," Mr. Favor cut in. "I'll take care of that for you."

"Thanks," I said, and I meant it. I felt like a limp dishrag.

"What were you going to take?"

"I don't know," I answered.

"Have you been advised?"

"No, sir."

"What year are you in?"

"I'm just starting this summer."

"Oh," he said. "Then you had the wrong cards, anyway. You waited in that line for nothing."

I thought I would throw up for sure when I heard that, but I didn't.

Then he asked, "What would you like to be?"

"I don't know," I answered.

And I didn't. In fact, I had seldom even thought about it. When I was little, I wanted to be a junkman, because I always wanted to ride on one of those horse-drawn wagons they had. The man would come by every week calling, "Junkman!" as if he were singing a song. In the summers, the watermelon man used to sing the same kind of song. Only he sang, "Wah-der-me-lon." And he would hold the "-lon," then sing, "red to the rind." But I liked the junkman. I used to ask him, "Can I ride your horse?"

"Not today, sonny. I'm busy," he always answered.

I thought he was so important. I wanted to be just like him. There was a direct connection between my decisions and real life back then. Now it seemed as if there were no connection between real life and anything, let alone courses to be taken in college. College was simply a place to be until I got my life sorted out.

"Well," Mr. Favor said, "certain courses are required, like English composition and biology. So I'll sign you up for those." He filled in the blanks on a blue card that was just like the yellow one I'd had earlier. He had a stack of them in his pocket. "How about a poetry class? I'm teaching an introduction this summer."

"That's fine," I said. I tried to steady my voice.

He filled that in, too. After I gave him my full name and address and all, he told me to wait there while he went back up and had my name put on the roster for each class.

By now, I felt a little bit better, but not much. My stomach had stopped churning even though it still felt tight, and my pulse seemed back to near normal. But when I tried to stand up, I found my knees still shaky. I walked around a little, though, just to loosen up some. I walked over to the curb where Slickhead and his friend had stood watching the ambulance drive away with Maurice. I did a couple of deep knee bends, then just stood awhile looking up and down the street.

A few of the people who had been part of the crowd around Maurice and the ambulance still lingered near the front of the building, some of them walking, from time to time, to the bookstore across the street. So when this girl came out of the bookstore and loped back across the street, I all but ignored her until I noticed that she was heading straight towards me. At first I thought I was just in her way.

So I stepped to one side a little. But as she got closer, she slowed up and stopped.

"You didn't have to move," she said. "I wasn't going to run into you." She smiled and switched poses like a model as she spoke. Her tone was warm as if she had known me for a long time.

"I'm sorry," I said, "I just thought I was in your way."

"I understand," she said, "you probably have so many girls running after you that you just step aside out of habit." She went over and sat on the stoop by the stairs.

"Naw," I said, and I could feel myself beginning to blush. "It's just that I . . ." I didn't know what to say, so I simply hunched my shoulders up and down.

I must have looked awkward standing there, my hands stuffed in my pockets, so she gestured for me to sit down beside her. I sat on the steps, though, and looked off across the street.

The girl was beautiful. I guess that is why I didn't want to look at her. I didn't want to appear to be gawking. She was almost as tall as I was, and she was slim with a long neck. But even though she was slim, she had big, shapely legs and feet that looked too big for her body.

Her heart-shaped face was the color of bamboo. She had a round mouth and supple, animated lips that not only formed the words she spoke, but added an extra dimension of expression in their own right. She had a short nose and light brown eyes flecked with gray. She wore her long straightened hair pulled back into a ponytail. She reminded me a lot of Dorothy Dandridge. And although I later found out they looked very different, I always thought of Carmen Jones whenever I saw her.

"I saw you in the gym," she said, "and I was glad to see somebody knock that Maurice Martin on his behind."

My heart thudded in my chest so hard, I thought she would see my shirt moving.

"He tripped over my foot," I said.

"Where did you learn to do that?" she asked leaning forward. She sounded almost like a little girl.

"Do what?" I asked.

"Flip people like that."

"*Flip* people?! I didn't . . ."

"You were so smooth and strong and-- Ooh!!"

She sounded so enthusiastic, I thought she was talking about somebody else. And when she said, "Ooh," she sounded even sexy.

"Me?!" I asked.

"You, baby," she said. "And where did you go? I looked for you after they pulled that other dude off of him, but you were gone."

"Oh," I said, "I just kind of came outside."

"You were so cool."

I could feel myself blushing again, and getting all giddy. I wondered what was taking Mr. Favor so long.

"What's your name?" she asked.

"Noel. What's yours?"

"Ruby."

"That's a nice name," I said.

"I hate it," she said. "I wish my name were something like-- Adrienne. Adrienne Holmes." Her voice had a far-off, Alice-in-Wonderland sound to it. "That sounds good, doesn't it?"

"Uh-huh," I answered.

I sat there a long minute staring off across the street, and all the while, I could feel her staring at the side of my face.

"You don't want to talk to me?" she said hitting me softly on the shoulder. She spoke lightly, affecting indignation.

"Yeah," I said, "I like talking to you."

"Well, why don't you say anything?"

I hunched my shoulders and looked down at the ground.

"You're shy, aren't you?" she asked.

"Uh-huh."

She eased from the stoop down beside me on the stairs. She moved her foot down a step first. Then she shifted the rest of her weight. The red skirt she was wearing slid up, and for a split second from the corner of my eye, I could see the flesh of her yellow thighs all the way up to her panties. By the time she was settled on the step beside me, my blood was surging. I could feel the thickness in my crotch growing.

"I like shy boys," she said.

I forced myself to look at her and into those lucid tan and gray eyes. She didn't smile or anything. She simply stared back. It felt as if she were starting straight into my brain, as if she knew all the lustful thoughts running through my mind at that moment. I didn't want her to see them, so I looked away.

"What classes are you taking?" she asked.

I cleared my throat and tried to sound controlled. "English composition and poetry," I said.

"Poetry?! You like poetry?"

"It's Ok," I answered. I didn't want to commit myself one way of the other.

"Oh, I *love* it," she said. "'To see a World in a grain of sand, And a Heaven in a wild flower, Hold Infinity in the palm of your hand, And Eternity in an hour.' Do you like that?"

"Yeah," I said, "I like that a lot."

"What about this, 'When love beckons, follow him, though his ways are hard and steep. And when his wings enfold you yield to him, though the sword hidden among his pinions may wound you.'"

"I like that one, too," I said.

"I guess I've taken just about all the English classes they offer here," she said, "and of all the genres I've studied, poetry is my absolute favorite. Gwendolyn's father was a poet. I think that's why I loved him. Or maybe that's why I love poetry."

"Who's Gwendolyn?" I asked.

"That's my little girl."

"Oh," I said. Then I wondered how old Ruby was. And how old was Gwendolyn?

"That's why I'm still here," she said looking around at the building. "I had to drop out for a year to have a baby."

"How old is she?"

"Ten months. My mother keeps her while I go to school."

I thought about Grandma Daughter and how much she had wanted to go to school, but couldn't. She would have given anything to have been in Ruby's situation.

"How old are you?" I asked.

"Don't you know you never ask a woman her age?" She smiled and I felt ashamed. "But I'm probably older than you are."

"I'm only eighteen," I mumbled.

"I *am* older than you," she said. "But that's Ok. You're sweet, and I like you. Besides, you've got eyes kind of like mine."

"I don't have any gray in mine," I said, "only the light brown."

"They're pretty anyway." She smiled.

I looked away.

"Listen," she said, "I'm giving a party at my house Saturday night, and I want you to come."

"Where do you live?" I asked.

She dug around in her little black leather purse for a pen. "Over in Hyde Park," she said. She found a pen and a small notebook. "Here's my address," she said handing me the paper. "It starts at eight."

"I'll try to come," I said.

She stood up to leave, but then she lingered a moment. She shifted her weight to one leg. "Well, aren't you going to walk me a little ways down the block?" she asked.

"I have to wait here for somebody," I said. I didn't want her to know that my dick was hard as Chinese arithmetic and that I had been sitting with my legs crossed so she wouldn't see it.

"Aw, come on," she said, and she grabbed my hand and pulled me up.

I tried to crouch a little so it wouldn't stick out so much, but that didn't help. It pressed out against my pants as if it had a will of its own and was determined to get free. I tried to pull my hand from Ruby's so I could put it in my pocket to hold the thing down. But Ruby held on tight for a split second longer, before she let go. And when she did, I stuffed my hand in my pocket and sat back down. Boy, was I embarrassed.

"Well, sit there, then," she said pretending she had not seen it, "I don't care."

"I'll see you Saturday," I called after her, but she didn't answer. I guess she didn't hear me even though it didn't seem like she was that far away. I watched her until she turned the corner at the far end of the building, her round behind swinging from one side to the other with each step. And for a long while after she was gone, I felt intoxicated by the scent of her. I don't know what it was she wore, but I loved it. My dick pulsed every time I inhaled. I inhaled for as long as I could before I exhaled, at which time I forced the air from my lungs so I could inhale again. Mr. Favor came out behind me at the peak of one of my inhalations.

"Are you all right, Noel?" he asked.

"Sir?!" I said, "Oh!! Yes, sir, I'm-- fine."

"Good," he said. "One ambulance at the school today was enough." He sat down beside me on the step. "I got you in a ten o'clock poetry class. The only biology open was at three. So I put you in a Spanish 101 class at twelve. Is that Ok? I mean, you have to have a language, anyway. And if you ever go to Mexico, you'll be ready."

"That sounds fine to me," I said.

"Good. Now you can take these forms to the cashier, pay your registration fee, then see about getting yourself some books."

"Thanks a lot, Mr. Favor," I said. "I don't know how I would have . . ."

"It's Ok, son," he stopped. "I could see that you were new here and pretty shaken up."

"Yeah," I forced a chuckle. "I was."

He went back inside.

I sat there a few minutes longer hoping my dick would go down. But the longer I sat there, the more I thought about Ruby. And the more I thought about Ruby, the harder it got. So I just held it down with one hand in my pocket, stood up slouched over all cool, and bopped to the bus stop.

It seemed as if Saturday were an eternity away. The next day, Thursday, dragged by and I ate hardly more than two mouthfuls of food all day. Mama came home late that night because she stopped downtown to do some shopping. She ate dinner with some friends downtown, too. It must have been about nine o'clock when she walked in.

"Hi, baby," she said.

"Hi, Ma."

She put her bag on the floor and unfastened her shoes. "What did you eat today?" she asked.

"Nothing."

"Nothing?! All day?"

"I wasn't hungry."

"Well, what did you do all day?"

"Watched TV."

I didn't tell her this, but I daydreamed all day. I daydreamed about Ruby, and the party Saturday. But I think she knew. I had told her Wednesday evening that a girl I met at school invited me to a party. And she had smiled and said, "Got a new girlfriend, eh?" She liked teasing me about having girlfriends. "Is she pretty?" she asked. "Is she as pretty as Doris?" Doris was my first girlfriend.

"Yes," I answered, "but she's not my girlfriend."

She laughed and hugged me tight.

Friday went the same as Thursday except that Mama fixed dinner Friday evening and I ate two plates of fried catfish and coleslaw and spaghetti cooked in tomato sauce with lots of onions and green pepper and oregano and cheese.

I got a job on Friday, too. Mr. Macklin at the little Grocerland food store around the corner on State Street had been telling me for months that he would give me a job as soon as I graduated. I think he liked Mama and thought that by getting closer to me, he would be getting closer to her. So I went by his store and he told me I could start Monday from four to eight. But that was all I did all day.

Then came Saturday. And at first I was glad. In fact, as soon as I woke up, I knew what day it was. And I stretched and flexed my toes and thought about Ruby, and the way she said she liked me and the way she walked away, switching her behind from side to side. I hopped out of bed. I inhaled deeply, then cleaned myself up and ate a bowl of corn flakes and bananas. And right after breakfast, I went to my room-- I had Grandma Daughter's room now-- to decide what I was going to wear. I got my gray slacks out and pressed them. I brushed off my blue blazer, which had just recently been dry cleaned, and I polished my black shoes. After that, I flopped across my bed and daydreamed again about how much of a hit I would be at the party, how much I would bop and cha-cha and two-step, and how Ruby would swoon over me.

Then it came to me. Suppose she had a boyfriend already. She would have told me, I reasoned. But *would* she have? Suppose I went to her party and got squared? Suppose she didn't even remember me! I mean, after all, the girl was beautiful. She must have lots of dudes after her. It would be so crowded there, she would not even *see* me, let alone remember me. I sat straight up on the bed. Why had she done that to me? Why had she led me to believe she liked me? She had *lots* of boyfriends! She didn't want me. I flopped down on my back. That was it! I was not going to the party. She could not toy with me that way. She was not *that* cute. Doris had taught me a lesson: Do not allow yourself to be played with. Or better yet, I would go to the party and ignore her. All her other boyfriends could mill around her if they wanted to. I was going to be aloof.

And all the rest of the day, I practiced. Mama and I went shopping at A&P, and I walked slowly and with deliberation. My speech stayed controlled and devoid of emotion. I carried the bags of food with poise. And when we got home and unpacked the bags, I felt as stable as a rock and cool as a pimp. Mama even commented on it. "You seem so much more mature today," she said. "What's wrong?"

"Nothing's wrong," I said. "I'm just getting my game together for tonight."

I didn't realize it at the time, but I was practicing Grandma Daughter's technique. Grandma Daughter had always said to be controlled, emotionless. But I didn't hook my behavior and Grandma Daughter's advice together at all. Not even at the party that night.

I got to her place at about nine-thirty, an hour and a half late. She buzzed me in, and I ascended the stairs with slow, even paces.

"How you doing?" she said when I got almost to the second floor.

I didn't answer right away. I waited until I got all the way up. "Fine," I said. "And how are you?"

"I'm fine," she said. And she sounded almost as if she were singing a song.

One thing was certain. She *did* remember me. But I stayed in my act anyway.

"Would you like some punch?" she asked as I walked in.

"Yes, thank you," I answered. I didn't smile or anything. I felt like a real snob, and I liked it.

I walked on into the front room where something by the Impressions was playing on the phonograph in the corner. It was a fast number, and three couples were doing the bop in the middle of the floor.

The room wasn't big as living rooms go. But most of the furniture had been moved to another part of the house, and kitchen chairs had been placed along the walls. There were almost enough seats for everyone and plenty of space to dance. The room was lit by one blue light over the phonograph.

I found a kitchen chair by the window and sat down. I leaned back and folded my arms and crossed my legs. I mean, I was cool.

Ruby came back with a paper cup full of punch and ice. "Here you go," she said handing me the cup.

"Thanks," I said. I sipped a little punch, and it tasted rich and sugary and cold.

She stood there a moment waiting for me to say something. But I sipped some more punch instead. By now, the record had changed. I think this one was by the Coasters, but I'm not sure. Anyway, somebody asked her to dance and she accepted. I pretended not to even notice. And as soon as the record was over, here she was. "You like the punch?" she asked.

"Yeah," I answered, "it's nice." My voice wasn't cold or impolite. But it wasn't really warm, either.

Ruby looked at me with her head cocked a little to one side. "You've changed," she said.

"Have I? In what way?"

"I'm not sure," she answered. "But it's like I invited a boy to the party, and a man came."

My pulse surged! But I slowly uncrossed my legs and crossed them the other way. Then I leaned forward a little resting my forearms on my knee and said, "Is that right."

"Yeah," she answered, "and I like the man about ten times as much as I liked the boy."

"That's good," I said. Just then, a short boy wearing a tweed jacket came over from across the room and asked her to dance. She declined. Then the first boy she had danced with asked her again. And he looked almost smug as he put his hand out, as if he were certain she would say yes. But she turned him down, too. Then she looked at me. "Can you dance?" she asked.

"A little."

"Then why don't *you* ask me?"

"I'm waiting for something slow," I answered.

"Ok," she said, "I'll put on something slow."

I was about to try to stop her. But she stood up so fast that I didn't have time to think. She weaved through the people to the phonograph and rejected the cha-cha that was playing. One couple grumbled a little, but obviously Ruby didn't care. She put on one of those slow, belly rubbing numbers by the El Dorados. I think it was called *A Rose for You, Dear*. Then she came straight back through the crowd, refusing invitations to dance all the way, and stood in front of me with her arms akimbo.

"Yeah," I said. "That's about what I had in mind."

I stood up and led her onto the floor. I slipped my arms around her waist and she put both her arms around my neck. We stood right there in the middle of the floor for the entire length of the record grinding. We didn't take even one step. My dick was as hard as a broom stick. I was so warm in that blazer, I could feel sweat running from under my arms. But I didn't care. She felt warm and soft and good next to me, so good that when the record ended we stood for an extra few seconds just holding each other. Finally, I stepped away from her and led her back to where I had been sitting. Someone else was in that seat now, so we had to stand.

We stood there holding hands all through the next record. Just as the following record began, she said, "Come back here for a minute. I want to show you something."

She led me through the hallway that connected the living room to the dining room in the back of the apartment. But she stopped me at a door about half way down. "Shhhhh," she said as she eased the door open. We tipped in. She closed the door softly and turned on a small light. Then she led me over to the baby bed by the far wall.

"That's Gwendolyn," she said.

I couldn't really see the little girl because she lay on her stomach with her face towards the wall. She was twisted up in her blanket. But I said she was cute anyway, and squeezed Ruby's hand.

Then that girl did the damndest thing! She kissed me. Not just a peck on the cheek. I mean she *kissed* me! First, she put her arms around my neck. Since we could still hear the music and since they were playing another one of those slow numbers, I thought she wanted to dance again. So I put my arms around her waist like before. In a way, she did want to dance. But this time we stood grinding, and kissing for the whole record. We stood there for the next whole record, too, even though it was fast. Then she really did it. She broke our embrace slowly and said, "Wait here a minute."

I waited. I heard her go into the living room and ask if anyone wanted any punch. One or two people said yes, so she walked all the way back to the dining room or kitchen or somewhere to get the punch. While she was back there, I heard an older woman who I guessed was her mother ask how the party was going. Ruby said it was going fine, and added that the baby was sleeping through the whole thing. The woman said that was good.

Before long, Ruby had taken several cups of punch up to the living room. On what seemed like about her fourth trip to the back, she opened the door to the bedroom and slipped in. She eased her shoes off and turned off the little light. Before I even realized what was happening, she kissed me again and rubbed my dick through my pants. Now, I had never made love to a woman before. I didn't know what to do. So I just let her rub.

Then she stopped. "What's the matter?" she asked.

"Nothing," I said. But I could feel my act beginning to slip away from me.

"Well, why don't you do anything?" she asked.

I didn't answer.

A long minute passed before she asked, "Have you ever done this before?"

I still didn't answer. I was embarrassed and ashamed. And my act was all the way gone.

"You haven't, have you?"

Her questions were like knives poking around at my liver. I flinched. I hesitated. Then I answered, "No." I hoped she couldn't tell from my voice that the little boy had replaced the man she liked so much. But deep down, I knew that she could. One good thing, though. It was dark in there. She couldn't see how small and ashamed I must have looked. Another long moment passed. Then I felt her move closer to me. She held me. Her body felt warm next to mine, and I relaxed a little. She could tell it, too. She knew I felt comfortable again with her. Because then she took my hand in hers and moved it under her dress and eased it deep between her legs. My heart leaped. She shifted her weight to one leg and raised the other leg up by lifting her heel and put my hand right up between her legs. Her hair felt thick and curly. I could smell her body. She didn't have any panties on or anything. She probably took them off right after she turned the light out. She placed my finger tips right on the moist crack amid her soft hairs. "Now, feel your way around down there awhile," she said. "And when you're ready, we'll get on the floor. But don't take too long," she added. Her whispery breath felt warm on my face and smelled sweet like fruit punch. She put her arms around my neck again and pushed her pelvis forward.

At first, I just played in her hairs a little bit. After all, this was the first pussy I had ever played with, so I naturally felt a tinge of apprehension. But I noticed one thing. Every time I ran my fingers over the opening she tensed up. Every time I slid my fingers away, she relaxed a little. But she never relaxed to the point that she had been before I rubbed the opening. So that, by passing over the opening several times, then moving away from it, a kind of pressure got built up inside her. I could control the pressure by the way I handled her pussy. That was all I needed to know to build up my confidence. This big, fine woman responded to my every stroke. It was so amazing, I almost laughed. When I finally put my middle finger in her, she squeezed me tight around my neck and moaned in my ear, and her pussy got real wet. Then she kissed me on the neck and put her tongue in my ear. After that, I put my ring finger in, too. She hissed aloud as I rubbed harder. She sank slowly to the floor and moaned in my ear again.

I stooped down in order to keep my hand inside her as she eased to her knees. Believe it or not, I was wondering whether or not to get on the floor in my good pants. And just as I had decided to go on and get down with her, the door opened. A short, fat woman walked in and said, "Ruby?" I recognized her voice as the woman Ruby had talked to when she went to get the punch.

"Oh!" Ruby said and forced my hand out of her pussy as she jumped up. "Mother, uh . . .!"

The woman turned the ceiling light on. "What are you two doing in here?!" she shouted.

"Nothing," Ruby answered. I just stood there holding my hand away from me so as not to get come all over my clothes.

The woman looked just like Ruby except that she was short and fat and had cut her hair so short it looked like a skullcap. But they had the same light brown eyes mixed with gray, the same rounded jaw, the same wide forehead. She even walked something like Ruby as she came over and grabbed me by the wrist and smelled my hand.

"You call fucking nothin'!" she said, "you little whore! You already got one baby and the daddy ain't here! You want another one?!"

By now, the woman was in the closet pulling a heavy belt off a hanger, and the baby was woke and crying, and people had gathered at the door craning to see in.

"Mother, please don't embarrass me in front of my friends," Ruby said.

"I'm not embarrassing you," her mother said. "You're embarrassing yourself."

Her mother doubled up the belt and hit her with it across the shoulder. Ruby backed away and put her arms up to try to keep the belt from hitting her in the face. But then her mother swung at her legs. Ruby cried out once, then doubled up on the floor covering her head with her arms. Her mother hit her about five times across the back.

"I've told you time and time again about messing with boys," her mother said. "But you just don't listen, do you?" She hit Ruby several more times across the back. Then she looked at me.

"And you," she said. "You get the hell out of here."

She reared back and hit me with the belt right across the face. The whole left side of my head stung, but I was back into my act by now. I barely flinched a muscle except to close that eye. I was mad. Not so much because she had hit me, but because she had hit Ruby and made her crawl in front of her friends. I couldn't do anything about it, though, except let her know that I wasn't going to crawl. I simply glared down at her.

"Get out, I said!" She hit me again, this time across the chest.

I hesitated a moment still glaring down at her, then moved slowly towards the hallway. The people looking in moved aside to form a little corridor for me to the door leading out. I left without looking back.

IV

My face ached and burned, but I cooled off some once I got outside Ruby's apartment. The streets and sidewalks and cars were wet as if it had just stopped raining. The air smelled fresh one moment and foul the next, like a sewer backing up. At times, it was so foul it almost smelled good again-- something like macaroni and cheese if it hit you right. I headed for the bus stop.

I pulled my jacket off and flopped it over my arm, then stuffed my hands into my pockets. The jacket brushed against my leg with each step I took, and I just strolled along 53rd Street looking in shop windows. The first shop was a tuxedo rental place. The outfits in the window were so boss, I couldn't believe it. I had been by tuxedo rental places before, but I had never been in one. I didn't go to my junior or senior prom, so I had no reason. But now I looked in the window, and for the first time, realized that those clothes could belong to me.

The outfit I liked most was a maroon velvet jacket with tails and matching shiny maroon pants, black patent leather slip-ons and pastel ruffles at the cuffs and down the chest. That suit of clothes was bad!

A little farther down the street I came to a travel agency. It had one of those scale model luxury liners in the window. Above the liner, fishing nets studded with big pink seashells hung on the wall. Big color posters of London, Brazil and Hong Kong lined the inner walls of the office. The one I liked most-- maybe because it was the one closest to the window and the one I could see best-- showed a composite picture of Spain. It had a flamenco dancer in a black lace dress with a blood-red rose in her hair, a bullfighter wearing skin-tight gold pants and ballet shoes and waving a flashy red cape before a charging bull with little spears stuck in his back, bony brown hands playing a guitar, cathedrals, castles. Everything that anybody has ever said you ought to see in Spain was in that poster. And the poster did exactly what travel posters are supposed to do. It made me want to go to Spain.

I imagined Ruby and me on that boat headed across the ocean. Naturally, I was dressed in the maroon outfit I had just seen. And when we arrived, everything and everybody on that poster would be on the dock waiting-- castles, slobbering bulls and all. Then as I walked on towards the bus stop, I considered the possibility of Ruby and me being together like that for real. Maybe not traveling to Spain, but just together. Then again, *yes*! Together going to Spain! My pulse quickened at the notion. I pulled my hand from my pocket and smelled the scent of her pussy still strong on my fingers, and my blood surged. I had to put my hand back in my pocket to keep my dick from protruding too much as I walked.

Even after the bus came, I couldn't help thinking about her. It was the 55th Street bus, one of those big yellow and green propane ones that make a lot of noise and bounce you all over the seat as you ride. I rode from over in Hyde Park to La Salle Street where I lived, and all I could think about was Ruby, and how she held me when I felt ashamed for not having made love before, and how she almost pleaded with her mother not to embarrass her, and how her mother hit her anyway and hit me too with all those people watching, and I got mad all over again. I imagined myself marrying Ruby and taking care of her and Gwendolyn, and Ruby loving me for having saved her from her mother.

I got off the bus. As I walked from the bus stop to the house, I held an image of Ruby in my mind and chanted almost audibly, "I love you, I love you, I love you."

I had expected Mama to be asleep when I got in. But as soon as I closed the door behind me, she called me from her room.

"Noel?" she called.

"Huh?"

"I just wanted to make sure that was you, baby." She paused a moment, then asked, "How was the party?"

"It was all right," I answered. But I guess something in my voice told her more than my words. Because then she asked, "What's the matter, honey?"

"Well-- nothing," I answered.

I heard her rustle the covers and sit up in the bed. Then she clicked on the little lamp on her nightstand. I could see the soft light around the edges of the door to her room as she did. "Come tell me 'bout it," she said.

I hesitated a second. "Ok," I answered. "But I want to go to the bathroom first."

I didn't really have to pee, but my dick was uncomfortable from having been hard so long. I rearranged it and peed and washed Ruby's sweet smell off my fingers. I looked in the mirror and wondered if Mama would be able to see how I felt. There was a bruise on my face where Ruby's mother had hit me. I splashed some cold water on it and patted it dry and went on into Mama's room.

Mama and I always had been close. After Grandma Daughter died, we got even closer. What I mean is, we talked more. I suspect Grandma Daughter's death made Mama aware not so much of what they had had together-- which I believe was a lot-- but what they could have had together. I believe she wanted to make sure our relationship was as full as a parent-child relationship could be. She became more than just a really good mother to me. She became a friend. I think she realized, too, that I needed a parent-friend. Since Daddy was dead and she never remarried, she had to be it. She did a good job of it, too.

"Tell me 'bout it," she said as I sat on the foot of the bed.

"There isn't that much to tell," I said.

"Well, tell me anyhow."

Over the years, Mama had gotten fat, really fat, fatter even than Ruby's mother or Grandma Daughter. After not eating for years when I was a child, she suddenly changed one day and began eating excessively. In the beginning, her excuse for overeating was that she wanted to regain her lost weight. Not eating had caused her to wither down to eighty pounds. But even after she had regained the weight, she continued to overeat. Now she was close to three hundred pounds, and rising. Her features were the same. It's just that her face was fuller. She had the same high, shiny black cheeks; the same long nose and flaring nostrils; the same thick black lips. And looking into her eyes, I still saw the same warmth and ingenuousness I had always seen. It's just that now she was fat and wore tent dresses and muumuus all the time. Sitting there in her silky pink robe with the covers pulled up over her thick folded legs, she looked like a living black Buddha. Her hair was salt-and-pepper gray now, too. She wore it in a puffy little natural. It gave her a kind of sexless, ethereal appearance. I told her most of what had happened at the party. Naturally, I left out the part about all that grinding and kissing and digging in Ruby's pussy. So when I got to the part about Ruby's mother hitting us the way she did, it sounded as if she came into the room and started beating on us simply because we were looking at Gwendolyn. Well, Mama didn't go for the story in that form, and she started asking me a bunch of questions.

"Was the door to the room opened or closed?" she asked.

"Well," I answered, "it was kind of closed."

"You mean it was closed, but only part way?"

"Well, no," I said, "it was closed all the way."

Mama nodded slowly. Then she asked, "How long was y'all in there together?"

"I'm not sure," I said.

"About."

"Around fifteen or twenty minutes."

"Could it of been as much as thirty minutes?"

Then it dawned on me what she was getting at. She knew that Ruby and I had done something in that room to cause Ruby's mother to hit us that way. I answered softly, "I don't think it was that long."

"But it could of been," she said.

I hunched my shoulders up and down slowly one time, then nodded yes. I couldn't even look her in the eye. Before I knew it, my eyes were full of water and the water began streaming down my cheeks and my nose started to run and I sniffed and I sniffed again.

"Aw, baby," Mama said reaching out for me, "don't cry." She said it in such a say as to imply, do anything *but* cry.

I moved up to the head of the bed, and she hugged me close.

"You love her, don't you?" she said.

I nodded yes and blew my nose. Mama wiped my face with her hands just like she used to do when I was ten years old and came in crying with the palms of my hands skinned up.

"Did you kiss her?"

"Uh-huh."

"Did you do more than kiss her?"

I hesitated. Then I answered, "Yes." I felt better now that she knew, but I still averted her stare.

She leaned back and stretched out her legs.

"Young people love," she said, "so precious. *So* precious. I loved your father the same way when I was your age. And he loved me.

Mo'dear hated that man, though. John was just a low-life nigger to her, but I loved him.

"I met him while I was still in high school. He wasn't like any boy I ever knew. I guess what I mean is, he was a man. He was wild and crazy. Compared to the weak-minded boyfriends I used to have, he was somethin' new, excitin'. I saw men like him only in the movies, men that was strong and knew how to handle a woman. He lived by hisself in a little room he rented, and he made his own living as a porter. Honey, to a young high school girl, that was somethin'!

"Mo'dear always called him a coward because he got shot in the hip during the war. She always claimed he got shot in the butt 'cause he was runnin' the wrong way. He always limped from that wound. But he was braver than a lots of men, I tell you. He lied about his age and joined the army when he was sixteen years old, and then he did a man's job 'til his body was so broke he couldn't do no more. After that he met me. We got married and I got pregnant. We moved up here, and he worked in that steel mill 'til the day he died. Even I didn't understand it at the time, but your father was a real man. Oh, he was bitter in spells, 'specially near the end. But he had a right to be. He was a man with a dream. But it seem like fate kept knockin' him down 'til finally he struck out at everything around him. The sweetness of our young love died a slow hurtin' death. It was killed by the weight of everyday living, crushed by a bundle of bills that never got through gettin' paid, ends that wouldn't meet. I'd marry him again, though. Even knowin' about all the beatin's and all the cursin', I'd marry that man today." She sat for a long moment musing, I supposed, on the life she had had with Daddy, and possibly on how things might have been had he lived. Then she sighed and looked back at me. "Just be careful, son." She said, "I know she seem like the whole world to you right now.

I also know y'all want to hold hands and kiss and make love behind the house. But babies is love. And love makin' is baby makin'. And if you just a baby yourself, having chi'ren can make you old and bitter fast."

"Aw, Ma," I countered, "I'm almost a man now."

"I know. But some boys die and never get past almost. So try to wait. That girl's mama know how hard life can be. That's why she beat her and you the way she did. She was prob'ly a young mother herself."

I reluctantly agreed with her and we talked for a few more minutes and I told her I would be careful. Then I went to bed. But it isn't easy getting to sleep when you've got things on your mind. I had Ruby on my mind. So I must have lain on my back staring out into the darkness of my room for an hour before I finally dozed off. And even then, I didn't sleep soundly. It was as if I lay in a semi-conscious dream state all night. Again images of Ruby were the feature presentations. The next morning when I got up, I was tired.

It was a funny thing back then about me and girls. They had a way of making me feel apprehensive whenever they were around me. And Ruby was no exception. That's why I spent all day that Thursday and Friday just lounging around thinking about her. Part of the thinking I was doing was on how much more relaxed I would be once I knew for sure whether or not anything was going to happen between us. And if something was going to happen, I wanted it to go ahead and happen. I felt as if knowing for sure one way or the other would enable me to relax. But it never worked that way with any of the girls I dated. In fact, something already did happen between Ruby and me. I got closer to her than I had ever gotten to any girl. And I still felt miserable. Agony greeted me on both sides of the coin. Yet, I felt powerless to throw the coin away.

Anyway, images of me and Ruby in her bedroom and the scent of her pussy and the softness of her pubic hair filled my head all day, even in church. In fact, I was embarrassed to stand up and sing the hymns because my dick was so hard. Finally, at about four-thirty or so, I got on the Fifty-Fifth Street bus and rode over to Hyde Park. I didn't know what to expect or what I was going to do. All I knew was that I had to be closer to Ruby.

I walked over to Fifty-Third and turned towards the lake. It was hot out and sunny. So I pretty much strolled along the way I had done the night before. And I daydreamed about Ruby. I must have been almost up to Lake Park Street before I noticed the sound of police cars coming closer. But I paid no attention. Then, just as I got in front of the Hyde Park Bank, I heard what I believed to be two firecrackers from around the corner. A woman screamed and somebody yelled, "Run!" All at once, a crowd of about thirty people streamed from around the bank, and they started running back down Fifty-third Street. I realized that what I had heard were shots. Another shot sounded, and I got scared. What the hell was happening?! That same person yelled, "Run before they shoot us!" I couldn't tell who it was, but I didn't want to get shot. So I started running with the crowd, slowly at first. But after two more shots rang out, I surged up to full speed. I ran straight down the street dodging cars, weaving in and out of traffic. I looked over my shoulder once and saw two policemen chasing us. They both stopped, though, to pick up somebody who had tripped and fallen. Two blocks down the street, after people had ducked into gangways or hopped onto cars and sped off or gotten caught, the five of us who were left slowed down to a fast walk. Finally we stopped in an alley a block or so further down the street and panted like spent race horses. After a few moments, one of the fellows said, "We've got to split up."

He was about my height, but much heavier. He looked solid as a rock. He was black with a lot of pimples on his angular face. His T-shirt rippled and bulged from all the muscles in his arms and neck and chest and stomach. He even had muscles on the side of his clean-shaven head that knotted up and then relaxed as he gritted his teeth and looked up and down the alley with nervous brown eyes, and wiped his thick, stubby nose back and forth with the big knuckle of his index finger. Little arteries pulsed in his temples. He reminded me of a powerful, precision, well-oiled engine. "Jeff," he said, "you head north. You go west, Pete." He pointed to a tall, skinny brown boy with a red handkerchief tied around his head like a pirate and said, "You go south. I'm gon' double back by the lake. And be careful," he added. "This whole area is already crawling with cops." He looked up and down Fifty-third Street to see if the coast was clear.

"Where should we meet, Tank?" the boy with the red handkerchief asked.

"Up in the projects. And we'll figure that anybody who ain't there by nine got caught. Ok, hit it," he said, and everybody fanned out.

But just as soon as everybody made their move, two police cars squealed around the corner as if they knew where we were. They didn't, of course. They just happened to be at the right place at the right time. But sheer pandemonium resulted. Three of the boys broke across the intersection in different directions. And the police bolted from the cars after them. Tank hesitated, though. Then he broke back down the alley. I jumped back into a gangway to get out of his path, and fell back against the old gray-painted wooden door to the basement of one of the big apartment buildings on the alley. The door creaked once, then just opened right up. It had a big padlock on it, but there were no screws in the hasp. It looked secure. That was enough to keep anyone from trying to get in. By now, Tank had doubled back again because another police car had turned into the alley from the far end and was headed our way. Tank turned into the gangway and ran right by me.

"Tank!" I shouted in a loud whisper.

He looked back, and I indicated for him to hop into the basement. He did, and I hopped in behind him and closed the door. Tank saw a chair and propped it under the knob. We stood holding our breath.

Outside, we heard the police stop the car and run down the gangway in chase. A few minutes later, they came back. One of them tried the door. It didn't open because of the chair.

"I *know* he's not in there," one of them said. "He'd need a *sledge*hammer to break that lock."

They got in the car and drove off.

"It's clear," I said. "So we'd better go."

"No!" Tank said, "Let's wait a while to be sure." He was right. It was better to wait. After all, the police knew he was in the area somewhere. And they would probably be patrolling all evening and most of the night. So we waited. We each sat on the concrete steps leading down from the ground level, and relaxed as much as we could. But we didn't say anything. I kind of let my mind wander as I sat there. It occurred to me that I hadn't thought about Ruby since this whole thing happened. Then for the first time, I wondered what in the world *was* happening. Who was Tank? What had he and those other boys done to be getting chased by the police? And the big question, what ever possessed me to help him get away? I sat up straight on the steps. Granted, it was exciting, and I had never done anything like that before-- I mean, running from the police and all. But that was no reason to help him get away. I could have messed around and gotten my own self in trouble. And it wasn't over yet. Suppose those two cops decided to come back and check that door good? I shook my head slowly. Potentially, I was in a real mess. Yet, I knew I wasn't going to do a thing right then to get out of it. This situation was almost fun.

I looked around at Tank.

"What was all that commotion over there by the bank about, anyway?" I asked.

"Freedom, little brother. The commotion was about freedom." His words came out neat and clipped, like little individually wrapped packages.

"What were you having, some kind of a rally or something?"

"Not really a rally. More of a service to the people kind of awareness session."

Tank outlined little circles in the air with his thick arms and taut fingers as he talked. I noticed that his fingernails were short and stubby with no outgrowth on them at all. And when he finished talking, I saw why. He instantly began nibbling at the nail on his left middle finger.

"But why were the police shooting?" I asked.

"It was a raid."

"A raid?! What kind of raid?"

"A drug raid. You see, we were trying to get the people to write their congressmen to legalize reefer. And we had some samples for people to test to prove that the stuff ain't no more harmful than cigarettes. But I guess somebody called the cops on us." Tank shook his head. "All that good reefer," he said, "gone."

"But you should have known somebody would call the man on you," I argued.

"Well," he said, "we knew somebody *could* call him, but we figured that over here in Hyde Park, nobody *would* call him. It was a chance we took."

A long minute passed before I said, "I think your friends got caught."

"Yeah, I think so, too. But we got a lawyer. He'll get them out." He spoke with a matter-of-fact tone. "He'll get them out on bail, and we'll skip the country for a while."

"Just like that?!"

"That's right, just like that."

Tank pulled a Prince Albert can out of his back pocket. "You blow?" he asked.

"Huh?"

"Do you blow?"

He pulled a thin homemade cigarette from the can and lighted it.

"Do I blow what?" I asked.

"Dicks, sissy!" His tone was sarcastic. He dragged deeply and held it.

"Hell, no," I answered.

"Try this," he said still trying to hold his breath.

I had never smoked before. I took the reefer and puffed on it like a cigarette without inhaling. Actually, I was imitating people I had seen smoke cigarettes. Tank stopped me, though, in pretty short order.

"No, man," he said. "This ain't a cigarette! This ain't something you just puff on. You inhale and hold it in as long as you can."

I tried to inhale the smoke, but I couldn't. Instead, it made me cough so hard and long I nearly vomited. Tank laughed. "You're a real square, ain't you?"

"I just never got off into smoking, that's all," I said in my defense.

"Well, just take a little bit," he said. I drew lightly on the reefer. I had wanted to try inhaling again. But I guess I was afraid of getting choked again. So I inhaled deeply through my nose. And to my surprise, I drew the smoke into my lungs by letting it mix in my throat with the air rushing in through my nostrils. I hardly even felt it. I held the smoke in like Tank had said, then exhaled slowly.

At first, I didn't notice any change. Then I felt a sensation as if someone were gently trying to gather my scalp to a point at the base of my skull. And my eyes felt gritty. I told Tank how I felt, and he laughed. He giggled uncontrollably for a whole minute. When he was about to stop, he noticed something I was doing and burst out again.

"Check yourself out," he said still laughing.

I hadn't noticed it before he pointed it out to me, but I was scratching myself. For some reason, both my arms itched. And I was scratching them incessantly. When I saw what I was doing, I stopped and felt embarrassed as if I'd been caught masturbating or something. Tank saw my embarrassed look and almost rolled off the steps laughing. Then I started laughing. I guess I began by laughing at him. But after a while it didn't matter. After a while, everything I saw was funny. I laughed so hard, my stomach muscles ached.

We finished off that joint, and Tank lighted another one. But I couldn't smoke any more. So he smoked it by himself. And by the time we came down, it was nearing dusk.

I hadn't told Mama where I was going. I guess I didn't want her to know. And usually when I left the house, I would be around the corner at Melvin's house. Melvin was the boy who had taken me treasure hunting some years earlier in an old abandoned house. She knew Melvin's phone number, and she called his house to check to see if I was there whenever I wasn't home. His mother did the same whenever he visited me. Sometimes, though, I would get back home before she'd get a chance to call. And she'd ask me about Melvin or his family to confirm in an indirect way that that's where I'd been. The questions became stock questions after a while. "How's Melvin?" "How's Melvin's folks?" and the answers became stock answers, too. "He fine." "They're Ok."

I'd been gone long enough now so that I knew she had called Melvin's house and knew I wasn't there. That meant she would be worried about me.

"Look here, Tank," I said. "I've got to go."

"But it's not dark yet."

"They're not looking for me," I said. "They're looking for you. And it'll be dark enough for you to leave soon."

"Yeah, Ok," he said. "But give me your phone number so I can contact you. You've got a lot of heart, and I might be able to use you in my organization."

I gave it to him, and left. Once outside, I could hear him propping the chair back against the door to jam it shut.

I looked up and down the alley. It was clear. Then I pretended that I was just leaving an apartment in that building and skipped out into the alley as if nothing were wrong. I even whistled. But as soon as I got to the street, I got the shock of my life. The police were sitting there in a car waiting! My act was good, though. I glanced at them, and kept walking and whistling. But my heart bounced around in my chest like a ping-pong ball. I wanted to run. And for a short moment, I thought I might piss on myself. I turned the corner and walked to the drug store on Hyde Park Boulevard and Blackstone Avenue.

The question was, should I go back and warn Tank or should I simply get on the bus and go home. Now, if I went back to warn Tank,

I would have to spend my carfare to buy a paper or something and to call Mama. That meant I would have to walk home. But on the other hand, if I just got on the bus and went home, Mama would stop worrying and I wouldn't have to walk. But what about Tank? What would I tell him when he called me next week or next month or next year?

The balding old man behind the counter looked at me over the top rim of his glasses as they rested near the tip of his nose.

"What'll it be, son?"

"Let me have change for a quarter," I said. "I want to make a phone call."

The phone was by the big plate glass window that faced Hyde Park Boulevard. I hesitated a moment before dropping the dime into the slot. I still wasn't sure of what I wanted to do. And in that moment I looked down towards Lake Park Avenue and there was the yellowish glow of the destination sigh on a bus headed my way. Damn it! What should I do? Go home or go back? I decided to let fate handle it. If the bus got stopped at the corner by the traffic light, or if the driver stopped to let anyone on or off, I would run out of the store and get on. Otherwise, I would make the call to Mama, then go back to warn Tank.

The traffic light was red. And even though the bus was still halfway down the block, I began to feel confident that the bus would have to stop. I felt relieved. I would be going home and I wouldn't even have to bear the weight of having made the decision. When Tank called, I would tell him that I hopped on the bus without thinking, almost out of habit. A man stood waiting by the bus stop, too. Without a doubt, the bus would have to stop.

I eased the dime back into my pocket. And before I dropped it, I rubbed my thumb over its smooth, slippery surface. I turned to leave.

As I did, I could hear the dime hit the other small coins in my pocket. It made a tiny clink. I approached the door to leave, and I saw 'pussy' scratched in jagged letters along the top edge of the silvery plate that I used to push the door open. I put the base of my hand over the word, and pushed hard on the door.

I got outside just in time to see the bus roaring through the intersection. And as it passed, I could smell the foul odor of spent diesel oil. The bus hadn't stopped at all. The light was green. The man was still on the corner, and the bus was gone. Hell, I was right back where I was before. I sniffed, hocked and spat a wad of snot onto the sidewalk. The only difference was that now I didn't have to make a decision.

I went back into the drugstore and called Mama.

"Where you been, boy? And where you at now? I've been worried sick about you," she said.

"I'm over in Hyde Park," I said.

"Well, you get your behind home right now," she said. "And when you get here, we gon' get an understanding on where and when you go. You hear me?"

"Yes, ma'm."

"And you better get here quick."

"But I have to walk," I said.

"Well, get started," she said, and she hung up.

I felt as if I were committed to warning Tank about the police car waiting by the alley, and I acted without thinking. It was as if my mind were almost locked on doing what I had to do. I hung the phone up, looked around the phone to make sure I wasn't leaving anything by it, and, confident that I was ready, I left. My attention was on the traffic light as I burst into the hot summer air. I could feel that my steps were long, loping strides, and I wanted to get across the boulevard before the light changed. The light turned to yellow and I was just about to raise my pace up to a jog when I heard someone call me from behind. I stopped and turned around. It was Ruby.

"Hi, baby," she said as she walked towards me.

She wore a yellow cotton dress with a full skirt and yellow sandals. She looked good.

"What are you doing over this way?" she smiled and took my hand.

I felt all loose inside just touching her, but the importance of warning Tank prevented me from becoming totally engrossed in her.

"Listen," I said, "there's something I have to do over on Fifty-third Street that can't wait. In fact, that's where I was headed when you called."

"Can I go with you?" she asked.

I hesitated a moment thinking that it might be dangerous for her. But at the same time, I wanted her with me.

"Well, you can walk part of the way with me," I said. "But if I tell you to wait, I want you to wait. And if I tell you to get away, I want you to pretend you don't know me and go home. Do you hear?"

"What's the matter?" she asked. Her tone was serious.

"Maybe nothing," I answered. "But whatever happens, do what I tell you."

The light was green for us, so I pulled her after me across the street. I walked at a fast pace without saying a word. It was as if talking would sap my enthusiasm, take the edge off my determination. So I kept quiet. But as we neared the corner of Fifty-Third and Blackstone, it occurred to me that I hadn't gotten anything at the drugstore. And since I still wanted some visible reason for having left that building and returning to it, I decided to use Ruby. I stopped before rounding the corner.

"Listen here," I said. "I want us to play the part of lovers when we get around this corner."

"That'll be easy," she said.

"And if you see any police around, I want you to be cool and keep up the front."

She was about to question me again, but I grabbed her around the waist and pulled her around the corner. And I have to give it to her. She handled it well. She put her head on my shoulder and walked so close to me my dick began to swell. In fact, I was almost disappointed that the police weren't still parked there by the alley. I didn't have time to dwell on it, though. So I broke her embrace and ran across the street pulling her by the hand behind me. But when we got to the gangway, the door to the basement was wide open. I looked in. Tank was gone.

I stepped in and sat on the stairs. Ruby followed me. It smelled wet and musty down there.

"What's the matter?" she asked.

"Close the door," I said.

She closed it.

"What's wrong, Noel?"

I looked up at her still standing by the door. Tears welled up slowly in her eyes, and I could see that she was fighting to keep from shaking. She must have really been scared! "Are you in trouble with the police?"

Tears began to stream down her cheeks. I reached up and pulled her by the hand, and she sat next to me. Leaning over to kiss her, I said, "You ask too many questions."

Her mouth felt warm and eager. We kissed for a long minute before I slid my hand under her dress. I thought she might protest because I hadn't answered her question. She did tense up a little. But then she relaxed, and I pushed my hand between her thighs and worked my fingers, and middle two, deep into her pussy. It was late by the time I got home. Mama was sitting up waiting with her arms folded under her breasts. She was pouting, too.

"Who's Tank?" she asked as soon as I walked in.

"Did he call here?" I asked.

"You just answer the questions, son," she said. "I'll ask them. Is that clear?" She sounded serious.

"Yes ma'm," I answered.

"Now, who is Tank?"

"A dude I met today over in Hyde Park."

"And how'd you meet him?"

I told her about the crowd of people running and that some of them got arrested. But I didn't tell her about the shooting. Then I skimmed over the part about us hiding in the basement together. The little I did tell her, though, was enough to get her pretty upset.

"You *hid* in a *basement* with *him*!" Her voice rang out.

"Yes, ma'm." I tried to make it sound as if it were nothing.

"Noel," she said, and her voice was sterner than I had heard it in a long time, "wha'chu two do in that basement?"

I got scared now, though I tried to hide it. Something was wrong, and I wanted to know what it was.

"What's the matter, Mama?"

"Answer me, boy!"

I hesitated. She was *really* upset. I could see little beads of sweat forming on her forehead the way they used to form on Grandma Daughter's nose. Mama had *never* used a tone that severe with me before.

"Nothing," I answered weakly.

"Don't lie to me, son." She looked me straight in the eye and said, "I'm gon' ask you one more time. Wha'chu two do in that basement?"

"We talked for a while. Then I left."

"Wha'chu talk about?" she asked.

"Well, nothing much," I answered. "We just kind of . . ."

"Noel," she cut me off, "don't make me have to get mad with you. Now, wha'chu talk about?"

"Mama," I said, "I don't know what you want me to tell you."

After I said that, I was surprised. I had never talked up to Mama before. Maybe it was because I never really had to. But whatever it was, I shocked myself. I even surprised Mama, because she softened her tone a little and changed her line of questioning.

"Did he tell you what he was doing over there today?" she asked.

"He said he was trying to get people to write their congressman to legalize reefer."

"He lied," she said. "That boy was selling dope on the street corner in broad daylight."

"Who told you that?" I asked in amazement.

"The police told me that!" she answered with an indignant tone of voice.

"They caught him?" I asked.

"They caught him," she confirmed. "And they found our phone number in his pocket."

"We've got to try to help him, Mama," I said.

"Help him?!"

That shocked her even more.

"He wasn't selling reefer," I said. "He was *giving* it away so people could see for themselves how harmless it is."

"Harmless!" she shouted. "Noel, drug addiction ain't harmless."

"Mama, reefer ain't drug addiction."

"How you know that, son?" she asked. Her voice sounded calmer.

"Tank told me."

"And I guess Tank know more than all the scientists at the police department?"

"Mama, the stuff is harmless," I asserted.

"Noel," she said, "it sound to me like you talking more from experience than from hearsay."

At that point, I guess I still felt kind of cocky from having talked up to her before and having gotten away with it. Because right then, I blurted out, "I *am* talking from experience." Having said it, I felt good. I felt a sense of poise, of power that I'd never felt before. But the feeling was short-lived. Very short-lived. With no hesitation, Mama jumped up off the sofa where she had been sitting and shouted, "What!!" Her eyes burned into mine with such intensity, I was petrified. I wanted to look away, but I knew that I had better not.

After a long minute, she narrowed her gaze. Her eyes looked like Daddy's used to look when he got mad. She moved closer to me and asked in a voice so low it sounded like a hiss, "What did you say?"

"I . . . I tried a little . . . once," I stammered.

Then she hit me. I mean that woman drew back, balled up her weak little fist and hit me so hard up side my head, I saw stars. When the stars cleared away, I was lying flat on my back looking up at her standing over me with her arms folded.

"Get up," she snorted.

I made an effort to sit up. But the stars came back. When they cleared away this time, I was still lying on the floor. Only now, I lay with my head and face soaking wet. Mama had thrown a glass of water in my face. I remembered having seen John Wayne and Roy Rogers get water thrown in their faces countless times on television to revive them after being knocked out. I used to identify with them. And the idea of being knocked out and having water thrown in my face had always seemed appealing. But in real life, it was no fun. Being knocked out hurt. And having water thrown in my face afterwards was like being thrown in a pool while asleep. I thought I would drown.

I rolled over on my stomach and tried to raise myself up. My arms felt rubbery, but I managed to get myself sitting in an upright position.

"From now on," Mama said, "as long as you live in my house, you will tell me everywhere you go before you leave here. Is that clear?"

"Yes, ma'm."

"I thought you could be trusted, but I see you can't. And I ain't gon' have you turn into no junkie."

Mama walked over to the phone and dialed.

"Lieutenant Williams," she said, "this Ms. Bodie, Noel's mother. Noel is home."

She stood there a minute listening. Then she said, "Tomorrow morning at eight will be fine. We'll see you then."

After she hung up, she told me to go to bed. Naturally, I did.

I didn't sleep, though. For one thing, the spot where Mama hit me upside my head throbbed like a toothache. She had hit me just above the spot where Ruby's mother had hit me the day before. I was also upset because of Mama's over reaction to my having smoked reefer. After all, she had never talked to me about it before. How was I to know her feelings about it? And I guess that night was the first time I ever considered leaving home. But it was more than just a consideration. I knew I would be leaving. And I also knew that it would be soon.

V

On the day following the Hyde Park incident, everything was all right again-- almost. Tank and his partners got bailed out during the night. His slick lawyer did it. And since his lawyer was present, Tank was able to talk and clear me. Lieutenant Williams called Mama and explained that I wasn't in any real trouble as long as I stayed away from Tank and similar company. He also explained that I wasn't a junkie from having smoked reefer just once, and that I wouldn't be so long as I never smoked it again. Mama vowed that I never would and that I was a good boy and that I got good grades in school. But my plans to leave were unchanged. Of course, Mama didn't know about my plans yet. And she wouldn't for awhile. I did what I had to do in secret up until the last minute.

The first part of my plan was to get some money. I started working in Mr. Macklin's store that afternoon. But I knew I would need more than he would pay me, especially for just part-time. So I started thinking of what I could do for more money. But understand, it wasn't just money for its own sake. I wanted to leave home. So that, when I saw the sign on the bus one morning on my way to school inviting me to travel with the Air Force, I was interested. In fact, joining the Air Force seemed like the solution to all my problems. I hesitated to join, though. I didn't notice the sign until I had been in school for a month, and I wanted to finish the summer session out. That was important to me I guess because I wanted to finish that poetry class. Ruby always asked about that class. I didn't want to have to tell her I dropped it.

Meanwhile, Ruby's mother was on her as hard as Mama was on me, maybe even harder. And since Ruby and I were sneaking to make love in my mother's house after school, two, three, maybe even four times a week, Ruby got extra static at home for being late so often. I had often wondered what Ruby's mother did for a living that allowed her to be home everyday, and it wasn't until much later that I found out she ran a small gambling operation. But in any case, her being home every day gave Ruby and me the blues, even though her being home gave Ruby and me the freedom we needed to be together. After all, Ruby's mother kept Gwen all day.

Around the end of July-- about the same time I saw the Air Force sign-- even Ruby started pressuring me. She wanted to get married and live with me, and I'll admit, the idea sounded good. I loved that girl. Or maybe I was just pussy-whipped. In any case, I wanted her near me all the time. But still, I waited.

Tank called me once or twice during that summer. The first time he called, which was shortly after he got busted in Hyde Park, we talked for about an hour. I explained to him what had happened that day and that I got back to warn him too late. He assured me it was cool, because he left about five minutes after I did. And even if I had come right back, I probably would have been too late. Then he invited me to a meeting with his group. I guess he wanted me to join it. I turned him down, though.

"I can't, man," I said. "I just don't have the time."

"I can dig it, cool," he answered. "That school trip is rough."

And the truth is, school and work and all were the *real* reasons I turned him down, not Mama. That and the fact that what Tank was into, though interesting, didn't fit in with what I was about. I was about leaving home and going to school and loving Ruby. Tank and his organization would only have gotten in the way, and I knew it.

As for Mama, I didn't care too much about what she thought anymore. I still loved her. It's just that I considered myself independent.

Of course, I wasn't, even though I gave her about half the money I made each week. But I thought and acted as if I were. So that, had I had the time to deal with Tank, I would have. I would have sneaked it. But, again, I didn't. So I turned him down.

The next couple of times he called, we just chit-chatted about nothing. Oh, he tried to tell me how fouled-up the country was and all that, but I wasn't interested. I responded with, "Uh-huh," to his hottest points. And after a while, he said he had a meeting or something to go to, and hung up. He didn't call anymore.

Finally, the last week of school rolled around. That week was especially busy, because I had to write papers for two classes and study for exams in all of them. I even stopped seeing Ruby for that week. But I got a lot done, and things were looking up. By that Friday morning, I had both papers done. And on my way to school that day I felt good. I got off the bus and walked to school proud, my head held high. I had my papers with me, papers that I truly thought were well written. The sun shone bright, and the sky was clear. It was windy though and that helped keep it a little cooler than normal. It had rained that night and morning, so the air smelled fresher than usual. And I just felt good. I even broke into a whistle. I still remember the song. It was "Stormy Weather." Don't ask me why I sang such a gloomy song on such a great day. I just did. And I guess I got so wrapped up in the song and the sunshine and the good feeling and all that I didn't watch where I was walking, because I tripped. I rounded the corner to the front of the school building, and tripped over a crack in the sidewalk. I must have sprawled ten feet trying to catch my balance. And just as I was about to fall right dead on my face, I crashed into somebody, and my papers and books and notes and everything soared. Naturally, a gust of wind came up at that exact moment, and before I could recover, a whole summer's worth of work curled down the street with the breeze. And as if that weren't bad enough, I looked down at who I had pulled to the ground with me. It was Maurice Martin, the boy I had had the run in with in the gymnasium on registration day.

I had seen Maurice only once all summer after our run in. That was in the drug store on Hyde Park Boulevard and Blackstone where I had stopped the day I met Tank. But as fate would have it, he didn't see me. He was sitting at the counter with his slick-head partner drinking coke or something, and his back was to the window as I passed by. When I recognized who it was, I hurried by before the urge hit him to turn around. That was the only time I saw him. And that once from that distance scared me.

Naturally, when I saw who it was right there beside me, I panicked. I scrambled up and took off back around the corner towards the bus stop. Slickhead took off after me.

I didn't know it at the time, but I knocked Maurice out. I had hit him in the chest with the crown of my head hard enough to crack two ribs, and he had to go to the hospital again. I know that boy was sick of me! But like I said, I didn't know it at the time. So I ran for dear life.

I had no trouble outrunning Slickhead-- the boy's real name was Roscoe Ward-- because he wore those same shiny black wing tips he had on registration day, and I wore gym shoes. He simply gave up after about a block. I ran for an additional three blocks, though just to make sure I was safe. Then I caught the bus home.

That was the last day I went to school. I didn't want to take any chances on running into those two again. In fact, I enlisted in the Air Force that afternoon. The following Wednesday, I shipped out.

VI

I did my basic training at Lackland Air force Base in San Antonio, Texas. The thing that stands out most in my mind about that eight-week period is the heat. The training itself wasn't all that hard. The food was bearable. But the heat was agony. We had an Indian summer that year, and it was hot through October. I never sweated so much in my life, before or since.

From Lackland, I got sent to Chanute, A.F.B. in Rantoul, Illinois. They taught me how to type, and made me a supply clerk. Big deal. I stayed there three months.

Within the first week of that tour of duty, Ruby and I got married. I made so little money, though, even with the dependent allotment, that she still had to live with her mother. But she dropped out of school again and got a job typing at Aldens mail order house, and we saved all our money so we could set up housekeeping. The little money we got in gifts from relatives just wasn't enough to do it. By the time we had what we thought was enough money to get an apartment and all, it was time for me to ship out again.

I found out about my orders to go overseas during lunch on a Tuesday in the chow hall. A tall brother named Moe from Detroit gave me the news.

"So are you taking your leave in the states or overseas?" he asked.

"What leave?" I asked back.

"I guess you know you got orders to ship out to Germany next month, don't you?" he said.

"*I've* got orders?"

"That's right."

"Germany?!"

"Right again."

"Oh," I said.

I was apprehensive at first. I guess it was because these new orders seemed to be a block in our plans. But when I told Ruby about them she said, "Oh, that's perfect. You can find an apartment *there* for us. Thank God! We'll be thousands of miles away from Chicago!"

We decided not to wait until I got settled and found a place for us to stay, though. Instead, I applied for and got a thirty-day leave. And because we didn't want to spend those days in Chicago, Ruby applied for a passport. When she got it and all the shots she and the baby needed, I took a MATS flight to Rhein Mein A.F.B. in Frankfurt, Germany. Two days later, she and Gwen got stand-by MATS flights. Within four days, we were all in Germany and, for the time, settled.

We stayed in a little hotel near the Frankfurt train station for about a week before going on down to Darmstadt where I was to be stationed. During that week, we took in a lot of sights. In fact, that week stands out in my mind as one of the happiest times of our stay in Europe. Ruby had studied a little German in school, so she knew a few words. And the little pocket dictionary we picked up helped a lot. But some of the situations we got into were so funny, I have to smile even now when I think about them.

Like, for example, the time when Ruby decided to try to explain in German that we weren't directly from Africa to a young student we met who thought that we were. You see, Ruby and I had gotten into the habit of speaking Pig Latin to each other much of the time. We started it right after we got married because her mother did *not* speak Pig Latin. So when the young man heard us talking, he simply asked, in German, what part of Africa we were from. He said that he thought he recognized me, but he didn't know from where. He stared at me keenly trying to remember, I suppose, the faces of African students he had known in the past. But rather than coming right out and saying that we were from the United States, Ruby began explaining what she believed to be the series of events from the West African slave trade to the Black Migration that made us who we were and where we were. I should point out, too, that we had had a couple of those heavy German beers, and that she was in a very talkative mood. The point is, though, that Ruby's German was so poor that the young man never quite figured out where we were from. So finally he just leaned back in his chair blinking his beady blue eyes and scratching his head. He hesitated a moment as if contemplating a deep philosophical question, then asked, "Do you speak English?"

I almost rolled off my chair laughing. We were in a little *Gasthaus* taking a break before going on an afternoon bus tour. The little old gray-haired waitress looked at me as if I were crazy. Her starched white apron looked stiff as she stuck her little veined hands on her hips. The young student looked surprised until I explained, in English, where we were from. Then he laughed as hard as I did. By now, the waitress didn't know what to think. So she just smiled and shrugged her little pixie shoulders and started wiping off a table some customer had just left. I don't think I'll ever forget the look on that student's face.

In Darmstadt, we were able to stay at a Youth Hostel. At first, it seemed as if they weren't going to let us stay, I guess, because we had the baby and I was in the military. But the old lady behind the sliding glass window talked in over with the old man in the office, and they decided to let us stay for a few days. She told us they had plenty of room. We only slept there one night, though, because we found an apartment the next day.

Some students at the University of Darmstadt had the place before us. And for some reason, all three of them were leaving town at the same time. The landlady, a stout, red-haired woman who looked to be in her late forties-- I later learned she was in her middle sixties-- with steel capped canines, told us the whole story, in German naturally, with a lot of hand waving and eyeball rolling and *ach-du-meine-Güte*s. The lady talked so fast, though, that Ruby hardly understood a word. So we never did find out what really happened. It must have been a juicy story, though, because she made gestures with her hips to simulate vehement love making about every fifteen seconds. And at intervals of about every minute or so, she formed the outline of an imaginary pregnant stomach with her hands. I sure wish I knew what she had said.

Anyway, we got settled in. Our place was on the second floor of a little stucco looking house with wooden shutters and exposed, wooden beam supports. It was very quaint, very European in the old style. We must have taken about a thousand pictures of the place. The best thing about the place, though, was that it was cheap. Most places charged American military personnel more than the normal rent rates, because they knew that the Americans could afford to pay the inflated prices. But Mighty Red-- that's what we nicknamed our landlady because her hair was mighty red from a poor dye job-- wasn't like that. She explained in waving gestures something about all of us being the same, and something about she wouldn't be able to sleep and she needed her rest, and something about God, and good and evil, and heaven and hell, and God knows what else.

Mighty Red was not stout in the same way that Grandma Daughter was stout. Mighty Red was big-boned and muscular. She looked like an athlete. She had short but heavy legs, and she walked with a short but heavy stride. We had no problem telling whether or not she was at home, because each step she took thumped aloud. She had huge breasts. And when she walked, she led with her breasts like a ram leading with its horns. Her walk reminded me of women I had seen in films on Prohibition leading teams of people into taverns and breaking open kegs of liquor with an ax. Her face was gentle, though. It was square and had more angles at the jaw than would normally be found in a woman's face. But her thin lips turned easily into a soft smile, and her smooth skin, upturned little nose and soft, friendly eyes that squinted when she smiled made me think of her more than once as Mrs. Santa Claus. Anyway, she charged us fair German rates. And as a result, we stayed in that one apartment all the while we were in Germany.

It didn't take us long to get accustomed to our new way of life. I worked from eight-thirty to five during the week as a supply clerk, and every night, I came home to great meals and a loving wife.

It was beautiful. Ruby bought a cookbook downtown, and every week we would have something strange and new to eat, and during dinner, she would relate the experiences she had had during the day.

Naturally, we had PX and commissary privileges, but Ruby bought a lot of things on the German economy so she could mingle more with the local people and improve her German. Mighty Red helped her a lot, too. In fact, they became pretty close in a mother-daughter kind of way, and from time to time Mighty Red would come up for dinner or to baby-sit while Ruby and I went out or whenever we just wanted to be alone.

Ruby's German got good before long, and she and Mighty Red talked together more and more the better her German got. They even went to movies together. And during the summer they went to the park often.

I didn't know it at the time, but Mighty Red put a lot of things on Ruby's mind during their little outings or, for that matter, whenever they talked together. It was to the point within a few months that they would spend most of the day talking, and usually in German. You see, I didn't get the exposure or practice that Ruby did, so they could sit up and talk right in my own living room, and I wouldn't know what was going on. But I could tell that the conversations became more and more serious. And it seemed as if Mighty Red began doing more and more of the talking. Ruby asked questions from time to time, but mostly she just listened and gave an occasional, "*ja*," or "*nein*."

I wasn't put off by Mighty Red's visits though. In fact, I rather appreciated them, because they afforded me the opportunity to muse over some of the unanswered questions with which I was still faced and which forced themselves onto my conscious mind with ever increasing frequency. Granted, I was not still studying subjects that bored me nearly to tears-- in all honesty, poetry ranked at the top of the list-- but I still longed to know the meaning of life. I felt certain that my new life was better than my old one. Yet, I also felt that the new one was only temporary. It seemed complete enough in that I was away from Chicago, supporting myself, married. Yet, I knew that there was more to life than I had. I didn't know what that 'more' was, but I knew I was going to find it.

I often wondered as I listened what Ruby and Mighty Red talked about, but I never asked. I suppose because I wanted to appear to be unconcerned with the trivial gossip of a house wife and her downstairs neighbor. Then one night as we were lying in bed, Ruby asked, "Noel, what do you think of the idea of life after death?"

The question piqued my interest, but because we had just made love, all I wanted to do was sleep. So I gave her the old line about we could talk about it in the morning, and I dozed on off. I faintly remember hearing her say something about she wanted to talk about it right then.

Naturally, we didn't talk about it the next morning either. In fact, I forgot about it altogether or rather, I remembered having dreamt something about the question of life and death, and so I merely dismissed it as simply a dream. It never crossed my mind that Ruby had some genuine interest in life after death, or that her interest was even remotely related to my quest for life's meaning.

That night, Mighty Red came up. The baby was asleep, and I was working on a model airplane kit I had bought that day. It seemed like any other night that Mighty Red came up to visit and talk, but it wasn't. Mighty Red asked Ruby something in German, and Ruby answered back, "*nein.*" Then they both sat silently looking at me. In fact, I was engrossed in my work until I noticed them not talking. When I looked over to see what was wrong, it was as if I had caught them spying. They almost instantly started fidgeting around with the buttons on their clothes and making small talk in German. So small that even I understood what they were saying.

"*Wie geht's?*" Mighty Red asked.

"*Ach, gut,*" Ruby answered. "*Und Dir?*"

"*Besser und besser,*" Mighty Red answered. "*Immer besser und besser.*"

One minute later, almost to the second, Mighty Red left. She yawned on her way out and said she was tired. That was it, she was gone.

"That was certainly a short visit," I said.

Ruby didn't answer. She looked as if she were deep in thought standing there with her hand still on the doorknob.

Then she said, "I'll be right back," and she left. I could hear the heel of her slippers clomping on the stairs as she went down to Mighty Red's place, and knocked on the door.

That must have been around nine o'clock. I went to bed around ten-thirty because I had to work the next morning, and she hadn't come back up, yet.

From that night on, their visiting patterns were changed. At first, Mighty Red visited us all the time. Now, she never visited. Instead, Ruby visited her all the time. Sometimes earlier, sometimes later. But she never missed a night. I guess I didn't really mind it until Mighty Red's time began cutting into my time. The great dinners we used to have every night dwindled in time down to cold cuts and Kool-Aid twice a week with canned vegetables and franks or hamburgers thrown in on the nights in between. Even that wasn't too bad. But when she began lying down at night like a dead fish so I could get off between her legs before I went to sleep, that was too much. Because after I would get through, she would hop straight up and go downstairs to talk to Mighty Red.

I mean, this is the girl who used to love to make love, who used to sneak over to my house after school to make love. For her to be hopping up out of bed after a two minute quickie was truly out of character. I intended to find out why.

I decided to try to be cool about it at first because I didn't want Ruby to think that I was becoming suspicious of anything. I simply accepted our drab meals and lifeless sex as if it were part of our normal routine, as if it weren't out of the ordinary in any way. I did this for about three weeks.

There's a second reason why I waited that long before making a move. I had to find a translator. I mean, what was I going to do, barge in on Ruby and Mighty Red while they were spitting German back and forth, and demand that she come home? Actually, I could have done just that. But I wanted more. I wanted to know what was going on. I didn't want to just come right out and ask Ruby about it, because I wanted to eliminate any possibility of her lying. After all, she had changed. This whole venture was an attempt to discover the extent of that change. I mean, she might no longer have been trustworthy, and that's exactly what I was going to find out. In order to find out for sure, I had to know for sure what they were talking about.

So I asked my N.C.O.I.C., Staff Sergeant Hankins, if he knew of anyone who might help me.

"What I need," I told him, "is someone who would be willing to listen at a keyhole."

"I know just the person," Hankins answered. He was average height, but better than average build, and he wore silver sunglasses like the ones Steve Canyon used to wear. He smiled a toothy grin as he said, "Frieda Mann."

He explained that Frieda was his ole lady's cousin or something, and that she welcomed any opportunity to improve her English.

"And the girl is a first class sneak," he added. "Whenever she comes over, she makes these blatant passes at me when her cousin's back is turned. And then tries to come on as the sweet little angel everyone thinks she is." Hankins paused a moment. "She even flashed that pussy on me! She sat where she knew I could see under her dress, and gapped her legs so wide, my heart leaped. And my ole lady was right there in the room!"

"So when can I meet her?" I asked.

"Anytime," he answered. "Just come by the house, and we'll call her over."

So then I schemed up on the idea of leaving my house one night after dinner under the pretense of going to one of the barracks on base to play cards with some of the boys. You see, if I had told Ruby that I was going to visit a friend who lived on the economy, she might have wanted to come, too. I wanted to eliminate that possibility. It was on a Friday, so I told her that I would be late and not to wait up. She smiled as I left, and said, "Have a good time."

Once by Hankins' place, I was surprised to find that Frieda was already there. I mean, Hankins had told me that she came by often, but I simply hadn't expected her to be there when I got there.

"Hey, man," he said, "come on in. This is Frieda."

"Pleased to meet you," she said.

What was an even greater surprise was the fact that the girl was fine. I mean, she looked as if she had just stepped off the cover of *Zeit* or one of those other German magazines. She had blonde hair, blue eyes, high cheek bones, clean white teeth, the works. You know, kind of like Elka Sommer or somebody.

We sat around and talked small talk and listened to records and drank Rummel beer for about an hour before I got around to asking Hankins whether or not he had told Frieda what I wanted her to do.

"Yeah," he answered, "but she said . . ."

"I will help you," Frieda cut him off.

Hankins looked at her.

"But I thought you said no," he said.

"I changed my mind," she countered.

Hankins shrugged his shoulders in disbelief.

"When can you do it," I asked her.

"Any time you want," she answered. "Here is my address." She scribbled it onto a little scrap of paper. "Come and get me whenever you are ready."

I took the address and tucked it away in my wallet and told her that I would be over within a week.

Shortly after that, she left. She said she had to meet somebody at the Frankfurt Airport in the morning, and wanted to get an early start.

As soon as Frieda was gone, Hankins' woman, a plump, dark-haired woman named Gretchen with two stainless steel-capped teeth at the bottom of her mouth and thick hair covering her heavy legs, smiled at me and said, "She like you."

"Is that why she changed her mind all of a sudden?" Hankins asked.

"*Ja*," she said. "She'll do anything for you."

"Aw, c'mon, baby," Hankins said. "*No*body would do *any*thing."

"She like that," she said. "I know her. She do anything for somebody she like."

Naturally, I didn't believe her. But I shook my head in agreement and pretended to be interested. Actually, I was interested to the degree that she would help me, but the do-anything part was too much to swallow at one sitting.

So, we sat up and drank beer and talked and listened to records until about twelve-thirty, and I went home.

Needless to say, Ruby was downstairs when I got in, so I went to bed alone.

I guess it was Tuesday of the following week that I went by Frieda's place. She lived in a two-room apartment out in Griesheim, a village just outside of Darmstadt, and as I knocked on the heavy wooden door, I felt uncertain about being there. First of all, she didn't know I was coming. Secondly, I didn't know what I was going to say when she opened the door. And thirdly, I kept asking myself, what if she really did like me? What would I do? How would I handle it? To tell the truth, I was half hoping she would not be home.

I knocked a second time so that when I saw her again at Hankins' house I would be able to say that I knocked twice. Sure enough she was there.

"Hello," she said as she opened the door. She wore a green and yellow cotton house dress and no shoes. Her head was wrapped in a thick white towel. "I almost didn't hear you. I had the water pouring on my hair."

"I can come back another time," I said apologetically.

"No," she said, "come in. You can help me dry my hair."

She sat in a straight back wooden chair and waited for me to proceed. I hesitated.

"Well, come on," she said. "I won't bite you."

So I unwrapped the towel and started drying her hair. I worked fast, because I found that I enjoyed it, and I guess I felt ashamed. Her hair smelled so good, or maybe it was a cologne she wore. I'm not sure. But as she sat there with one leg resting laterally on part of the seat of the chair and her other knee pulled up close to her chest, I began getting sexually aroused. I even caught myself trying to peek down into her bosom. So I hurried up, and got finished as fast as I could.

Afterwards, I sat on the blue stripped couch by the window and crossed my legs. Frieda hung the towel on the back of the chair, and sat on the floor next to me.

"Now, when would be a good night for you to help me," I asked. I guess I asked as much to hide my uneasiness as to get information.

"Gretchen told you about me, didn't she," Frieda countered.

I hesitated. "Well," I said, "she did say that . . ."

"That I like you?" Frieda cut me off.

"Yes," I answered.

"Don't be ashamed," she said. "Because I'm not. I do like you."

"You don't even know me," I told her.

She shrugged her shoulders. "So that? When I get to know you, maybe I won't like you. But for the time being, I do. That's all that counts."

"But that's not all that counts," I argued. "Suppose I beat you or something?"

"But you *haven't* beat me."

"But suppose I did?"

"Then I wouldn't like you. And I wouldn't see you again."

"Well, shouldn't you try to learn about me to see whether or not I might beat you up?"

"No," she said. "I should love you now, and head off the beating with kindness."

I didn't know what to say. I guess she could tell that I wasn't comfortable, because she stood up and smiled and said, "I'll be free this Friday evening."

"Good," I said, "I'll pick you up around nine o'clock."

The rest of the week went pretty fast. I had linen exchange duty Thursday, and that was a little bit tiring. But over all, it was an easy week.

During dinner on Friday, Ruby seemed in really high spirits. She laughed and talked about people we knew at home and played with the baby. For a short while, I thought the old Ruby was back. But eight o'clock rolled around and she changed on me. She got real serious, almost solemn.

"What's the matter," I asked.

"Nothing."

"People don't muse that deeply over nothing."

"You wouldn't understand," she said.

"Try me," I countered.

She looked at me a moment. Then she asked, "What do you want more than anything else in the whole universe?"

I chuckled, because the question sounded like one a child might ask.

"I'm serious," she said. "What do you want?"

I thought for a moment. I thought about Grandma Daughter and how she had died without knowing what her life had been for or about. I thought about how much I yearned to know of life and the universe, and I was going to answer just that. I was going to say, "Above all else, I want wisdom." But then I thought again. I thought about how my life had been when I was at home. I thought about how it had changed since meeting Ruby and joining the Air Force. I thought about the fact that my life was more comfortable now than it had ever been. The only thing wrong was that I didn't make enough money. So I looked at Ruby and answered, "I want to make Staff Sergeant inside of four years."

Ruby looked at me for a long minute, her face revealing no sign of emotion. "If you stay in, you'll make Tech Sergeant in five," she said.

"What makes you think that?"

"I've got to go downstairs," she said. "I'm already late."

She hopped up and grabbed Gwen into her arms.

"Wait a minute," I said as she headed for the door. I grabbed her by the arm. "I said wait a minute."

Now I'll admit that I grabbed her arm hard, but not hard enough to warrant her reaction. She snatched away, then swung at me with such force that she almost dropped Gwen. I barely avoided being hit in the eye.

"What is wrong with you?" I shouted recoiling. Her eyes looked wild like those of a cornered animal. "Answer me," I shouted again. She hissed at me like a snake and backed out of the room.

My plan was set. I was going to find out about the goings on between her and Mighty Red, and I was going to find out tonight.

I slipped into my trench coat, and caught the next street car out to Griesheim.

Frieda greeted me with a warm smile as she let me in. "How are you?" she asked. "You look worried."

"Are you about ready to go?" I asked back.

"Yes," she said. "As soon as I finish my tea."

I tossed my coat on the couch and plopped down beside it. I felt uncertain again. I wanted to hurry up and get started. I wanted to know what was happening at Mighty Red's. And at the same time, I feared knowing. What was she doing to Ruby to cause her to act that way? And what would I do about it? I didn't know, and I guess I was just about to work myself up about it when Frieda interrupted my train of thought.

"How do you take your tea?" she asked.

"Huh?" I said.

"I hope you like it with milk and sugar, because that's what I put in it."

She passed me a fragile, translucent white teacup, filled with warm fragrant tea. It tasted like sweet mint tea with cream, and the first sip seemed to soothe me, relax me a little. I liked it.

"Now, what are we going to do?" She asked as she sat gingerly on the other end of the couch.

"Just sneak up and listen at the window, I guess," I said.

"What do you expect to find out?"

"I don't know."

"What if we can't hear anything?"

"I don't know that, either."

We sat there silent for a couple of minutes. Then she gulped down her tea.

"I think I better wear some pants and walking shoes," she said. She stood up and walked across to the bathroom where she changed into a pair of tight blue jeans and a blue, hooded pullover.

"I'm ready," she announced warmly, and we left.

By now, it was cold out. I guess a combination of my wanting to get some place warm and also to get on with this little project influenced my action, but as we stood waiting for a streetcar, I hailed a taxi. It was more of an impulse than anything else. Because it was as if I saw the taxi one minute, and saw myself waving for it the next.

It cost me nine Deutsch Marks to get within a block of my house. We walked to rest of the way.

Our building was laid out so that we could find at least one window to any room in Mighty Red's apartment simply by walking around the yard. The only problem was that the shutters were closed on all the windows except those to the kitchen. By listening, we could tell that they were in the living room, clear at the other end of the house. We couldn't hear them clearly, though. The fact that they were inside and the noise of the traffic coupled to make hearing very difficult.

"I wish they would talk louder," Frieda whispered.

Finally, after listening for fifteen minutes or so and catching only a few words, I decided that maybe we should try slipping into the front hallway and listening at the door. So we tipped in and leaned down to

Larry Redmond   100   The Last and Final King the keyhole. Everything sounded clear now. Mighty Red did most of the talking, as usual. Ruby asked one or two short questions. The only problem was that Frieda couldn't translate what they were saying for me, because we didn't want to take a chance on making any noise. I signaled her to follow me back outside.

"What were they talking about?" I asked.

"Wow," she said. "It was weird, but it was interesting."

"What did she say?"

"She talked about the moon."

"The moon?!"

"Yes," she answered. "And about water."

"Water?! On the moon?!"

"No, she didn't say that. But they're connected, in a way."

"Well, how?" I asked.

"I don't know," she answered. "But she wasn't talking science."

"Well, what did she say?!" I was excited now, and wanted to shout even thought I had to whisper.

"To tell you the truth," she answered, "I don't know. It was mystical, and that's all I can say about it." She paused. "What she said didn't make very much sense."

"Well, tell me what she said even though it sounds stupid."

Frieda paused again, then continued, "She said that the water elemental's wisdom deals with the wisdom of the moon. And that the greatest wisdom that has reached the earth came from a remote moon period. The sphinx is the symbol of the wisdom of that period."

"The sphinx?!"

"That's what she said, word for word almost."

I couldn't help but think about that book of Grandma Daughter's of which I had read a part. I was intrigued. What did Mighty Red know about the sphinx? And why was this knowledge affecting Ruby so adversely?

I must have appeared dazed or something, because Frieda shook me hard by the arm.

"Are you all right?" she asked.

"Did she say anything else about the sphinx?" I asked back.

But before she could answer, we heard Ruby open the door to Mighty Red's place to leave. We had to get from in front of the house fast. We hopped over the short fence that surrounded the yard, and darted in between buildings like two convicts on the lam. And soon, we were on the streetcar to Griesheim.

We didn't talk much on the way back. In fact, we didn't talk at all. I was too wrapped up in thoughts about the sphinx and its meaning to talk small talk, and I guess Frieda could sense that. But once we got in front of her door, she broke the silence by inviting me in for more tea. I accepted.

"Was I much help?" she asked as she sat spooning sugar into our cups.

I told her that she was. I explained to her that I was fascinated by the sphinx and wanted to know more about it.

"Maybe I can help," she said. She fetched an English dictionary from behind a stack of boxes in her closet.

We looked up sphinx, but it didn't give us what we were looking for. It said something about a character in Greek mythology that was the combination of a lion and an eagle and a woman that went around asking of every man it met the answer to a riddle, and killing everyone who didn't know the answer. But since what I was looking for was Egyptian fact, not Greek myth, I discounted the definition all together.

Still I pondered. Frieda poured me some more tea, sugared it, creamed it and set it back in front of me. I hardly looked up. When I did finally look up, she was staring at me hard.

"What's the matter?" I asked.

"I'm just wondering if tonight is the night."

"The night for what?" I asked.

"For you and me to make love."

I paused for a moment, then asked, "Well, when do you think you'll have your answer?"

"You just gave it to me," she said. She came around the table and kissed me hard in the mouth as I slowly unzipped her fly and slid my hand inside.

VII

That night of snooping marked a definite turning point in the quality of my European stay. After that night, whenever Ruby went downstairs to rap with Mighty Red, I would simply go out to Griesheim and visit with Frieda. I didn't even care any more that Ruby fixed lunch meat dinners for me to come home to. I usually ate at Frieda's anyway. So it didn't really matter whether or not Ruby fixed anything at all.

And, too, my curiosity about the sphinx waned somewhat. It was not that I didn't want to know anything about it, it's just that I couldn't find anything about it. All the books I looked in had plenty on pyramids, but nothing on the sphinx. Naturally, I didn't dare ask Ruby or Mighty Red what they knew.

Before long, my new routine took on a quality of the expected norm. I mean, not only was I going out to Griesheim nearly every day to see Frieda, but I began to feel as if I was suppose to go out every day. It began to seem as if having a wife and girlfriend were a normal part of male existence in western culture. So much a part, in fact, that I became less cautious about what I was doing. I began going to Frieda's place straight from work. I stopped preparing excuses to give Ruby in the event she asked me where I'd been. And worst of all, I began going out in public with Frieda. I mean, it's one thing to have a girlfriend, and to visit with her regularly. But it's another thing all together to take her shopping and to a movie and apartment hunting, especially in a small town like Darmstadt. When the inevitable happened, I really shouldn't have been the least bit surprised. And yet, I was more than surprised; I was shocked.

"What do you mean, where have I been?" I asked, a genuine tone of indignation in my voice.

"I mean it's eight o'clock and you're just getting home. I know you didn't work late, and the people you usually visit all came by here looking for you," she answered.

"And?" I snapped.

"And I want to know where you've been." Her voice had an affected tone of sweetness.

Naturally, I had nothing to say. I mean, the girl had me dead to rights, and I knew it. But something in me kept trying to weasel out.

"I went for a walk," I said.

"A walk?!"

"A walk."

"Where?"

"Downtown."

"Downtown where?"

"By the statue." I never found out who the statue was of, but it always reminded me of the statue of Melvin Douglas near Pershing Road and the lake in Chicago.

She paused for a moment. Then she looked me straight in the eye and said, "You a damn lie."

The words seemed to hiss from her lips like steam. I was stunned. Then I laughed at her. Not so much because what she had said was funny, but because I wanted to undermine the effect her confrontation had had on me. She wouldn't be mollified.

"Don't laugh," she snarled, "'cause ain't nothing funny."

Just then, my whole approach to the situation changed. It simply didn't matter any more whether or not she knew where I had been. So I shrugged and said, "You've caught me in a lie. So now what?"

"So now tell me the truth," she said. And I'll be damned if she didn't sound genuinely concerned. I mean, her voice was low and controlled, and she looked as if she truly cared about what I was doing. The irony was that it wasn't a jealous concern. It was a compassionate concern, almost like the concern a mother might feel for a wayward son.

"I was visiting a lady friend," I said.

"Uh-huh," she said, and she said it like a doctor or journalist might say it, with the intent of making the other person keep talking. I did. I told her everything. Well, almost everything. I did not tell her that Frieda's house turned into a passion pit not less than three times a week, where we fucked like dogs in a fit of uncontrolled abandon. No, instead I told her that we talked and held hands from time to time. And I made it a special point to tell her about my interest in the sphinx, although I made it sound as if I had overheard them talking about it through Mighty Red's door while going out one night.

Then she asked the inevitable.

"Are you going to stop seeing her?"

I breathed in deeply and mustered up all the strength of character I could muster, and said, "I'm not sure."

Again, the inevitable, "Do you love her?"

And again the decisive, "I don't think so."

She paused a moment slowly blinking her now watery eyes. I couldn't help thinking these were crocodile tears. What did she expect? She spent more time with Mighty Red than she did with me. And we never did resolve why she tried to hit me.

"I'm not going to give you up," she said. "I love you, and I'll fight for you if I have to."

"You don't have to fight for me," I said. "I'm got going anywhere."

"You won't have any choice," she said. "Or rather, you'll choose not to exercise what little choice you *do* have."

"I'm not sure I understand you."

"It's simple," she said. "You're floating aimlessly in life. Your actions are whimsical. But her actions in this situation are directioned. She's out to get you from me. You can't resist her, because you don't know what she's doing. So I have to resist her. She's putting her vibration on you, and I have to get it off by putting mine on you."

"What are you talking about?" I asked. I was reminded of dogs cutting out their territories by pissing on fireplugs.

"I'm talking about women and the games they play that men don't even know about."

"What kind of games," I asked.

She didn't answer me. She just sat there staring out the window.

"What kind of games?" I asked again. She paused a moment, then went through another one of the strangest changes I've ever seen in my life. She breathed slowly and deeply a few times, blew her nose, wiped her eyes, and smiled. And that was it. The woman radiated such a genuine warmth and contented glow that it was hard to believe she had been sad and depressed not two minutes earlier. And I guess I must have really looked surprised or something, because she began to mimic a magician who had just pulled a rabbit out of a hat. She stood up and rolled her imaginary sleeves up with mock showmanship, and said, "And now ladies and gentlemen, the Great Rubini will perform the most awesome, breathtaking, spine tingling disappearing act ever witnessed on the face of the earth."

The irony was, I was truly enthralled. She looked as if she had been practicing this act for years. As a girl, she must have watched magicians with a keen interest, because she had all the moves down pat. Even her tone and cadence as she talked were perfect.

"This trick requires the help of someone from the audience," she said looking among the "people" behind me. "Do I have any volunteers?" she asked, then grabbed my hand and pulled me up on stage with her. "Well, thank you, sir," she said. "You're a very brave man." She affected a toothy show business smile, and blinked her eyes several times slowly like an owl. "And now," she said still mimicking the arm waving moves of a two-bit magician, "I want you to hold the tail of my dress and close your eyes."

"Huh?"

"Please, do as I ask," she said, "and keep them closed for ten whole seconds. Are you ready?"

"I'm ready," I said.

"Good," she said twisting the tail of her dress one or two turns and handing it to me.

"Now let's count to ten. One, two, three . . ."

I closed my eyes and counted with her. "Four, five . . ."

I tried to detect her movements by the movements of her dress tail, but it simply hung limp in my hand.

I was tempted to peek, but by the time I made up my mind, she shouted, ten, and I opened my eyes anyway.

And the look on my face must have been hilarious. And rightly so. I mean, some kind of way, she had slipped out of her dress and under clothes, and she stood there buck naked holding the other end of the dress with one hand. I literally felt my mouth drop open. And seeing me so shocked, Ruby broke into hysterical laughter.

"How . . . how did you do that?" I asked.

"Don't ask questions," she said, "the best part of this trick is yet to come." I wondered if the puns were intended. Then with the grace of a ballet dancer, she spun around and fell into my arms.

"But I want to know how you did that," I protested.

"Like this," she said, and began unbuttoning my shirt real fast. But now she was mimicking Charlie Chaplin or one of the Keystone Cops. All of her movements were quick and jerky and everything she did was wrong. I mean, one of the buttons got stuck, then it broke. Then the sleeve wouldn't come off. And when we finally got the damn thing off, she couldn't put it down. It was "stuck" to her hand. Then it got "stuck" to her other hand. I don't think I've laughed harder at anything in my life. And after we got all my clothes off, the woman changed again. I mean with zero transition time, she shifted from a brilliant showman into a sensuous and aggressive, yet tender, mistress. She used her hands and mouth and behind and even her feet to do things to me that I didn't know could be done, let alone that *she* could do. Was this what Mighty Red had been teaching her! And when she got though, I was drained, exhausted. All I wanted to do was sleep. And I did sleep, like a baby.

When I woke up, it was morning. And judging by how bright it was outside, it was late.

I was in bed alone. The baby's bed was empty, too, so I assumed that Ruby got up early and went down to visit with Might Red.

It was Saturday, and I knew I didn't have to work. But I felt an urgency to get cleaned up and dressed, because I wanted to see Frieda. Not so much just to see her as to explain why I didn't come by last night. I mean, she probably had fixed dinner and everything. The notion crossed my mind that I didn't have to explain anything to her. But I quickly forced that idea from my head. After all, I owed her an explanation. I mean, I really felt guilty.

I hurried into the bathroom and brushed my teeth. As I was washing my face, someone knocked on the door. I thought it might have been Ruby burdened down with the baby or something. So I ran to the door and opened it as I was. It turned out to be Mighty Red.

"*Tag*," she said, walking straight into the front room. "*Wo ist Ruby?*"

"Ruby isn't here," I said. "No is here." I tried to cover myself with my hands.

"*Sie ist nicht hier?*" she asked.

"No," I said, "*Nicht hier*. Gone. *Nicht* home."

Mighty Red smiled a knowing kind of smile as she looked me over from top to bottom. Then she looked me squarely in the eye and said, "*Ich komme wieder.*"

It pissed me off that I was the one who felt embarrassed. My glance shifted from the brown, hard wood floor to the white lamp shade in the corner to the woodwork around the door. I tried once to look Red in the eye, but her gaze was so powerful I had to look away.

"Yeah," I said as she left, "come back later." As I spoke, I resolved not to be there.

I dressed hurriedly in order to make sure I was gone before she came back. On my way to the streetcar stop, I felt small for having evaded her. I didn't dwell on it though. Instead, I tried to imagine how I would explain to Frieda the reason I didn't come by yesterday.

It was warm outside, one of the few warm days we had that spring, and I felt a warm glow in my stomach as I walked along the red cobble stone street pass wine shops displaying huge green bottles of *Schwarze Katze* wine and aromatic bakeries with two and three feet long loaves of bread in the window and cheese shops that smelled so strong at times, I nearly got sick.

As I walked, I found that my mind tended to wander. I couldn't hold it on the imaginary conversation I was having with Frieda, so I stopped trying. I simply let my attention wander as it may. I guess I must have been daydreaming aimlessly for several minutes before I noticed a dark green Mercedes Benz with a badly dented grill and broken left head light zigzagging down the bumpy street in my direction. It's ironic, but I remember thinking that the owner of that car must have been a rotten driver. After all, his car was already dented, and there he was now zigzagging down the street. I remember thinking that it must have been a teenager, like those who hot rod up and down the streets in Chicago.

It's funny sometimes how we tend to look at events in the world, and make them whatever we want them to be. The irony is that we believe that the way we see things is the way they really are. A case in point was the green Mercedes zigzagging in my direction. I was so convinced that that car posed no threat to me that I resumed window shopping, and was actually smiling gleefully at the antics of a downy-looking Cocker Spaniel puppy in a pet shop window when the vehicle crashed into a parked Volkswagen less than a car length away from me with enough force to nearly turn the VW over on its side, and hence, on me. The notion that I had nearly been hit sent a series of emotions through me. At first, I was annoyed, then angry. At the realization of how close death was, *my* death, I became fearful to the point that my knees quivered. In fact, they buckled once or twice, and my stomach churned for five solid minutes after it was over.

The driver of the car didn't appear to be hurt any more than having knocked his front teeth out. As he stepped from the car with rubbery legs, holding on to the roof and door of the car to maintain his balance, his cursing and angry gestures were punctuated with periodic pauses to spit blood and tooth fragments into the gutter.

The idea crossed my mind to scream at the man for having nearly killed me. But then I looked at him. I'll be damned if he wasn't more scared that I was. He was actually cursing to hide his fear. He wasn't young either. I judged him to be around fifty. He was short and stocky with legs that looked as if they were too short for his body. His head was big and oval shaped and bald on top and the thick crop of curly gray hair around his ears and in back was streaked with white. His face looked young though. A couple of crow's feet at the corners of his eyes were the only wrinkles I could see from where I stood.

By now, the man had stopped cursing, and was holding tightly onto the car. It looked at first as if he were holding the car up. I mean, his neck and shoulder muscles were pulled tight, and looked like tension wires under his skin. As he squeezed his eyes tightly shut, he tightened his jaw and set his lips as if he were trying to keep an immense pressure built up in his head, and began breathing heavily through his blood crusted mouth.

I walked around the cars and put my hand on his back.

"Are you all right?" I asked.

I hadn't expected him to understand me. It's just that I felt the need to be concerned. I was surprised, though pleasantly, when he looked at me and said, "Yes, thank you." He blinked several times to keep the tears welling up in his eyes from spilling out. He spoke with a heavy British accent. "The bloody brakes failed," he said. He looked at me with his eyes still blinking. After a moment, his gaze became fixed on mine, and he became wide-eyed with wonder. "It's you," he said.

I took him by the arm and led him gingerly over to the curb. "Sit down here," I said, "and I'll see if I can round up an ambulance."

He shouted for me to wait as I ran off towards the phone booth on the corner just north of us. I had no idea what I was going to say. The truth is, I was hoping the operator spoke English. It turned out that I didn't need her after all. Apparently, someone in a nearby shop or apartment had seen the accident, and called an ambulance right away. By the time I got in the phone booth and finished fumbling around in my pockets for coins, I could hear its caustic traffic warning signal in the distance. I paused a moment as the signal grew louder. Within two minutes, a dark gray van with a flashing blue dome light pulled up to the front of the pet store where I had been standing.

A feeling of relief swept over my body as I watched the attendants helping the man onto a stretcher. I hadn't noticed it until then, but apparently, the man had fainted, because they had to lift his limp, slumped-over body. For a moment, I thought maybe the man had died. But at the last moment before they had him completely in the van, he raised up and looked around wildly. One of the attendants, the young dark-haired one with the thick brown sideburns, eased him back down, and they whisked him into the van and closed it up. The van didn't pull right off, though. In fact, it stayed there for a good five minutes. And all that while, I just stood there in the phone booth waiting. It occurred to me that maybe the old dude was hurt kind of bad. If he was, maybe I could help.

Finally, though, the young attendant with the sideburns climbed into the driver's seat, put the vehicle into first gear, and pulled off slowly. He didn't shift into second, though. He revved the engine way up while in first gear until he was almost to the phone booth where I was standing. And just as I was beginning to wonder what in the world was wrong, he eased off the gas and came to a stop right in front of me. The young man sat there a minute still staring out the front window at the street. Then he rolled the side window down and spoke without turning his head to look at me.

"*Der Mann sagt, daß Du bist Gott, und er Dich liebt.*"

"What?" I said. "The man what?"

"*Er ist tot.*"

"I . . . I don't understand."

"*Du bist Gott, sagt er. Du bist Gott.*"

"*Tot?*" I asked, "You mean dead?"

"Dead," he said. "*Er ist* dead."

My heart leaped when he said 'dead' in English, almost as if saying it in English made it so.

The young attendant rolled his window back up, and drove off leaving the air around the phone booth thick with exhaust fumes.

That whole episode shook me. But I didn't realize just how much until I got to Frieda's place. I mean, almost as soon as she opened the door, she looked at me, blinked a couple of times, then squinted and asked, "What's wrong?"

"Nothing," I answered.

"Yes, there is," she said. "Come in and sit. I'll make tea."

I eased myself down on the sofa while she went into the kitchen. The next thing I remember, she was shaking me by the arm and telling me that my tea was ready. Apparently, I was daydreaming about the incident that deeply. I took a sip. It tasted warm and sweet and good. It smelled like warm flowers.

"It's Chamomile," she said. "Imported."

I took another sip, then went right into explaining what had just happened to me. When I finished, she said, "I knew something had happened to you, because you looked so bloodless."

"What does '*Du bist Gott*' mean?" I asked.

"It means, you are God," she answered. "That's the slogan of a religious group that calls itself *Seine Kinder*, His Children."

"That's the message he gave me before he died. Man," I said, "I really got an eery feeling when I heard it."

"Probably because the man had just died."

"Maybe," I said. "But whatever the reason, it was weird."

We finished our tea in silence, both musing, I suppose, over the accident. Then Frieda inhaled deeply and said in an overly sweet voice, "I missed you yesterday."

"I missed you, too," I said. "But I couldn't get away."

"I figured that's what it was," she said. "You've spent too much time over here for your wife not to notice."

"It'll be all right," I said.

"I hope so," she said, "because I don't want you to stop coming."

That pun again.

"I still can't get over the way that man died," I said. "I mean, he didn't look like he was even hurt."

"Maybe his heart was weak," she said. "Maybe he was hurt inside."

"And his telling me that I was God," I said. "I wonder what he meant by that."

"I think you're good, too," she said sticking her tongue in my ear. "Now ask me what *I* mean."

With a lead in like that, there was no way I could avoid making love to her. I didn't have much energy to put into it, though. Ruby had pretty much done me in last night. But I mustered up what little energy I had left, and it was enough.

All the while, though, I was curious about this movement and their notion that I was God. So, after we finished, I asked Frieda to show me where their temple was.

"I'll do better than that," she said. "I'll introduce you to a member of the group. Her name is Lillian Doss."

She put the telephone receiver to her ear, and before dialing the number, she cleaned the dust from the telephone cradle with her little finger. She waited a moment until someone answered. Then she talked in German for a few minutes with short pauses to listen. I tried to determine from her facial expressions and tone of voice what she was talking about. Needless to say, my efforts were for naught. At one moment, she smiled, all wide-eyed and toothy; at the next, she frowned forming deep creases in her forehead and little cracks around her eyes. After that, her expression was simply dead-pan. All the while her tone changed as well to match the expressions. I never did find out what all they talked about. When she hung up, all she said was, "She said to meet her at the temple in twenty minutes."

Their temple was on the other side of Darmstadt from Griesheim. They weren't a large enough organization to own a building of their own, so they held their meetings in the game room of the youth hostel, the same one Ruby and I had stayed in when we first got to Darmstadt. The balcony of the hostel overlooked a small lagoon where an occasional pair of wild ducks swam and bobbed for food. They looked care-free and content swimming and cleaning their feathers and eating.

We got there five minutes early. At Frieda's suggestion, we waited on the steps in front. The fact is, Frieda had seen Lillian walking-- or rather, limping-- up the street in our direction and wanted to wait and go in with her. As she came nearer, I could see that she limped because she was deformed. Her right leg was shorter than the left one causing her to have to wear an elevator shoe on that foot. Also, her right foot turned out at about fifty degrees. She walked with the aid of a heavy, gnarled stick that had been stained to make the wood grain stand out. She looked like a modern-day female Moses. I wondered if she were a leader of *Seine Kinder.*

By now, I could see the features of her face. I could see that she wore an expression of wide-eyed wonder as she approached me. It was the same expression the driver of the Mercedes Benz had had. She was a woman in her sixties. She wore an expensive looking gray tweed walking suit with a pale grey crepe blouse and a cameo broach at the collar. Her hair was white and set in crisp looking waves and curls. She looked as if she made it a point of looking reserved, unshocked and almost unshockable. It seemed so incongruous to see her limping slowly up to me with her steel gray eyes forced as wide open as she could get them, and her thin chiseled lips, red with immaculately applied lipstick, quivering as if from fear.

"*Ach, du liebe . . .,*" she said standing close enough to me so that I could smell the evenly patted make-up on her wrinkling skin. "*Du bist Gott!*"

Frieda looked as surprised at Lillian's behavior as I imagined I did. "*Lillian,*" she said, "*was gibt's?!*"

Lillian ignored her. Instead, she composed herself and looked directly to my left. "You are in grave danger," she said. "We must leave here at once."

Lillian's mouth was so tightly set that I could barely see her lips. "You must not go into the temple," she said grabbing me by the arm and leading me down the street.

"I've already been in there," I said, but she didn't hear me.

Frieda flitted from one side of the sidewalk to the other trying to get Lillian's attention.

"Lillian," she said, "what is the matter?"

"Don't look back," Lillian warned as she pulled me along. "No one there must see your face."

"Lillian, please, *was ist mit Dir los?*"

"Quiet, child," Lillian said. "This is neither the time nor the place to explain."

We walked fast in the direction that Lillian had come. As she spoke, she raised her cane high in the air and waved it. Her limp became more pronounced without her support, and the rhythmic tug on my arm became stronger with each unsupported step.

In response to Lillian's upraised cane, a large, blue and silver BMW with a rounded trunk and shiny silver wheels glided slowly from just around the corner. The driver, fat and red-faced with a heavy mole on one nostril of his veined nose, stopped in front of us less than six inches from the curb.

I opened the rear door and gestured for Lillian and Frieda to get in.

"This is no time for ceremony," Lillian said sternly. "Get in. *Frieda, steig bei Hans ein.*"

Frieda ran around the car and sat by the driver.

"*Frankfurt, Hans und schnell,*" Lillian said.

"*Sofort.*"

The inside of the car was as spotless as the outside, and the gray leather seats felt as if they were contoured to fit my body. It was a pleasure to just sit quietly as Hans raced through town and onto the *Autobahn.* We must have been nearly half way to Frankfurt before Frieda turned around with her arm resting on the back of the seat and asked, "Will you please tell us what is wrong?"

"How long have you been in this country?" Lillian asked without even looking at Frieda.

"A few months, I guess," I answered. "I don't know off hand."

Frieda turned back around and folded her arms like a sulking child. I couldn't see her face, but I knew she was pouting.

"Has anyone recognized you before today?" Lillian asked.

I told her about the student Ruby and I had met in Frankfurt who thought he recognized me.

"In Frankfurt?" Lillian exclaimed.

"Yes," I answered.

"*Hans*," Lillian said, "*Wir fahren nicht nach Frankfurt. Fahr uns nach Österreich.*"

"Why are we going to Austria?" Frieda asked.

"Austria?!" I said, "I can't go to Austria."

"You must go to Austria," Lillian said. "You are no longer safe in Germany."

I was about to protest further, but I was stopped by the startled look on Lillian's face. Apparently Hans didn't understand what she had told him, because he drove by the first exit where he could have gotten off the *Autobahn* in order to turn around and head for Austria. And he was on his way past the second one.

"*Hans!*" Lillian shouted. "*Anhalten!*"

Hans speeded past the second exit. It felt as if we were accelerating.

"He knows who you are," she said. Her voice was almost a whisper. She wasn't talking to me though. Rather, she was making a realization that manifest itself aloud. And the realization had her near panic judging from the way she looked wildly around the car. There was genuine fear in her eyes. She looked like a trapped animal, and I began to fear being in the car with her.

Up until this point, I was taking this whole thing rather lightly. Lillian appeared to be pretty excited, but so what if she wanted to take me for a ride to Frankfurt or Austria? It was the weekend. I had two whole days to ride this joke out.

But now things were getting serious. And when she lunged forward and grabbed Hans around the neck and began choking him as we sped along at about seventy miles per hour, things got more serious yet. Hans tried to pull free from Lillian's grip, but she had her forearm pressing hard on his Adam's apple, a trick I imagine she learned during the war. She bore back with so much force that Hans was raised up out of his seat, and the car began to swerve back and forth along the highway.

Frieda and I were both amazed. Frieda sat with her back pressed against the door, and she had a funny kind of forced smile on her face as if she were anticipating the punch line to a poor joke. I suppose I was hoping it was still some kind of joke, too. But when Hans let go of the steering wheel and clutched at Lillian's grip and began kicking in order to get out of the front seat, we both knew it was no joke.

"Lillian, don't," I said as I reached over to try to loosen her hold around Hans's neck. Her grip was like iron.

At the same time that I made my move, Frieda reached for the steering wheel. She couldn't control the car though because one of Hans's legs was wedged against the wheel. With his other foot he repeatedly kicked her off balance or out of the way. One of his kicks knocked the car out of gear. We were not slowing down as rapidly.

While Frieda wrestled with Hans kicking and the steering wheel, I wrestled with Lillian's grip. I could feel Hans go limp as he became unconscious, but Lillian squeezed even harder. She must have spent years in a wheel chair judging by the strength she had in her arms. Her arms were as powerful as those of a man. I closed my eyes as I pried, and I could hear gravel rattling in the right wheel wells. I could hear Frieda begin to whine as she wrestled to control the car. Her whine graduated into a scream, and I could hear gravel rattling under the whole car as we left the road.

"My God, Lillian," I shouted. "You are getting us killed."

The car dipped to the right as we ran off into the ditch beside the road, then jolted sharply and rolled as the front wheel burrowed into the soft soil. I felt the seat and floor fall away below me, and I remember we looked like wet clothes in a dryer as the car rolled over around us. My right foot got caught on one of the seats, and twisted my ankle. I heard glass breaking all around me along with the thumping and bending of steel and Frieda screaming. I felt myself being catapulted through the opening that was the back window and hurled into the air. I felt a sharp pain in my left arm just above the elbow as I landed and rolled under a bush.

I woke up still lying under the bush. I couldn't have been out for more than a few seconds, because when I crawled out and saw the car, a light cloud of dust was still settling around it. Apparently, it had hit a tree with enough force to cave in the roof, bounced back and landed in an upright position. Cradling my broken left arm, I limped over to inspect the damage. The area smelled of gasoline and wet leaves. Frieda lay across the back of the front seats, pinned there by the crushed roof. Her chest was crushed when the car hit the tree. Blood laced foam oozed from her mouth and nose. Hans lay heaped on the floor under the dashboard. He was covered with broken glass and dirt. Lillian sat in about the same position she had been in for most of the trip. Her face as covered with blood that ran from a gash in her scalp. Her hair was black with dirt and sticky with blood. I don't understand how she could see me coming with all that blood in her face, but she seemed to know when I got to the side of the car. She rested her head on the back of the seat as she spoke. "Don't stay here," she said. "The others are dead, and you can't help me." She paused a moment. "Leave the country," she said. "Go south." Then she stopped. I thought she had died, so I turned to make my way back to the road. "Wait," she said. "Take this." She handed her cane out the window.

"I don't need it," I said. "I can make it Ok."

"Take it," she said. There was a note of urgency in her voice.

I leaned down and clutched it under the good arm while still cradling the broken one. Then I turned and walked back towards the road.

Incongruent is the best way to describe the feeling I had as I limped back. Nothing matched. Everything was out of place. The sun looked like the perfect sun for a picnic. And the smell of fir trees would normally stimulate an appetite. Yet in that same sun and sweet pine smell the one person I would probably be picnicking with had just been killed. It seemed unreal like a scene out of a story by Poe. Everything seemed unnatural. Limping on my sore ankle, I stepped on what appeared to be solid ground. But as soon as I put my weight on it, it slipped away like sand, and I fell. I fell to the left. And since I didn't want to fall again on my arm, I tried to break my fall by throwing my weight on my shoulder. I thought that landing in a bush on my shoulder would prevent me from hurting my arm any worse than it already was. I couldn't have been more wrong. I managed to land on my shoulder Ok, but the shock of the fall was enough to send stabs of pain through my whole arm, and I immediately lost consciousness.

Time and space seemed warped when I became cognizant again. I could hear a ringing sound in my ears like a gospel choir singing amen and holding the last note of '-men.' It seemed to have a relaxing effect on me, and I wanted to slump down and sleep. But my position was too uncomfortable to sleep. The ache in my arm still gnawed in the back of my consciousness, and a broken branch of the bush I had fallen into poked me in the back just hard enough so that I couldn't recline fully.

I squirmed around trying to get comfortable, but I couldn't. Then I heard Grandma Daughter's voice. "Get up, son," she said. The choir music grew louder behind her.

"Grandma Daughter," I called out. "Is that you?"

"You can't lie there, son," she said. The music now sounded as if it were composed exclusively of nonverbal tones held for as long as the breath of the singers lasted.

"Where are you, Grandma Daughter?" I called out again. I opened my eyes and pulled myself up out of the bush. "Where are you?"

"I'm on the road, Noel," she said.

I fought the pain in my arm and ankle so that I could see if this was really Grandma Daughter talking to me. But when I got to the roadside, she wasn't there. I turned around in a full circle looking for her. There were only the trees and the road and cars speeding by and the sun beating down. "Where are you?" I shouted.

"Walk," she said. "Walk along the roadway."

"Where are you?!"

I hobbled along the road following the voice that always seemed to be just ahead of me, but behind a tree or rock. I could see little yellow lights blinking in my field of vision as I walked. I squeezed my eyes shut to clear the lights away, but when I opened them again the lights were popping like little bubbles. The bubbles and popping grew until they filled my field of vision. The popping noise grew, too, until it became a droning buzz that blended right in with the choir music to fill my head and consciousness with sound. My knees buckled, and I slumped by the side of the road.

". . . was he doing out on the road to Frankfurt?"

"I don't know, miss. You'd have to talk to the ambulance driver."

"How long has be been here?"

"Three days."

I opened my eyes just long enough to confirm that it was Ruby asking all those questions. She and a man in a white jacket stood at the foot of my bed.

"Three days?!" Ruby said, "He's been missing for six days. Where was he the rest of the time."

"I don't know, Ma'm. You'll have to ask him." The man motioned in my direction with his thumb. He then turned both his palms up and shrugged as he backed out of the room. I closed my eyes.

I had been unconscious for six days. It certainly didn't seem that long. All I remembered was Grandma Daughter's voice. I kept trying to remember her face the way it looked when I was young. I tried to recall the sound of her voice, the lyrical yet rough edged sound it had those days she told me about her life as a little girl. And I tried to compare that remembrance with the voice I heard on the road. I felt as if I had been making that one comparison from the time I fell on the road until now. Yet I still wasn't sure. That is to say, in my mind I wasn't sure. In my heart, I knew. It was her. But, the heart is illogical. So is hearing the voice of one's dead grandmother.

I opened my eyes. I looked to my right and saw Ruby sitting by my bedside. She smiled.

"Hi," she said.

She wasn't wearing the same clothes she wore when she talked to the man in the white jacket.

"Hi," I said.

"Think you might stay with us a while this time?" she asked.

"Have I been gone?" I asked back.

"Yes," she nodded, "for eight days. And I was afraid you might be gone for good."

I looked around my room. There were five other beds in addition to mine. The patients in them as I panned from bed to bed all had expressions on their faces that seemed to be a mixture of joy and amazement. They seemed to be pleasantly surprised that I had awakened. None of them spoke, though. At first, judging from their assorted bandages and casts, I thought it might have been difficult for them to speak, too painful. Then I looked down at my own body, or rather at the white mound of bandages that formed what looked like a giant cocoon around me. I realized then that I was the one who was in the worst shape of all, and that they were indeed surprised whether pleasantly or not to see me awaken at all. To them, I probably looked like a mummy who had been dead for a long time already.

"What happened to me?" I asked.

"We don't know," Ruby answered. "We were hoping you could tell us."

I wondered who she referred to when she said 'us.' The people in the room right now? The doctors and her, the cooks at the chow hall, the base and squadron commanders, the world at large? Mighty Red?!

"I don't know," I said.

"All we know about are your injuries."

I looked back down at the cocoon.

"What's wrong with me?" I asked. I had to stifle the impulse to limit my meaning to physically wrong.

"Your arm is broken, your ankle is cracked, you've got a concussion, most of you ribs are cracked, your pelvis is fractured, and you've been burned."

"Well," I heard myself saying, "I've been burned before." My voice sounded aloof and airy and . . . detached.

"Not like this you haven't," she retorted. "You've got first and second degree burns over nearly half your body. Your whole front except parts of your face has been scorched. Can't you feel it?"

"I don't feel a thing," I said. And I didn't. In fact, I was surprised at how little I felt. I had the sensation that I was two people, one that felt the pain, and one that didn't. More precisely, there were two places where I could center my consciousness. One was in this body in the area of the head where it always had seemed to be. The other was outside this body in a 'place' that just kind of hovered nearby.

My consciousness was in that other 'place' now, and I could not feel the pain in my body. It was as if the sensation of pleasure and pain were tied to the physical plain. The other 'place' was non-physical, and experienced no sensations. The burns truly didn't hurt. They couldn't hurt, because my consciousness was not where the pain was.

"I guess they must have you pretty doped up," Ruby said.

"I guess they do," I answered.

Ruby began talking about the quality of health care in the military. At about the same time, I began to see the little blinking lights and bubbles that I had seen the day of the accident. I heard voices again in my ears, too, like a crowd humming.

The accident! I hadn't thought a single thing about the accident since it happened. I tried to open my mouth to ask Ruby about Lillian. But my face felt stiff and immobile as if I were pushing the button on an appliance, and the electric current were shut off. I tried, but nothing happened.

The shifting of my consciousness back and forth between my body and the other place began for no apparent rhyme or reason that day in the hospital. But in time I became able to control the shifts. I became able to shift to the other place at will though I never knew for sure before hand where the other place was. For instance, sometimes it was above me, sometimes it was behind or beside me. Whenever my consciousness was in this body, the other place seemed nonexistent. But whenever I willed myself, I could slip into the other place instantly. And I would always be surprised when I found out where it was. The other place became like another person, and I began to talk to it. "Oh, there you are," I would say. Or, "What are you doing down here?" After a while, I began identifying more closely with it. I would say things like, "Why are *we* here?" until I realized that the other place did not exist until my consciousness got there. That's when the questions became, "What am I doing here?" I began to be the other 'place.' And whenever I was the other 'place,' sensations of the body disappeared.

"Shhh, he's waking up." It was the man in the white jacket again talking to Ruby. I wondered what they were talking about that I wasn't supposed to hear.

"Where's Lillian," I asked, "and what happened to my cane and the car?"

"Is that her name?" Ruby asked.

"She's the old woman who was still sitting in the car," I answered.

"What car?" the man in the white jacket asked.

"The car that we crashed in!"

"Is that what happened to you?" the doctor asked, "Were you in an automobile accident?"

The doctor was a tall heavy man with pock marks, blackheads and pimples covering his fleshy jowls and nose and forehead. The expression on his face was mock concern. I could hear Lillian's words clearly again, "You are in grave danger."

"When can I leave here?" I asked.

The doctor's voice was deep. "Oh, not for a while," he said.

'A while' turned out to be three months. But they passed without incident. At least there were none out of the ordinary in the hospital. But according to Ruby, there had been a couple of out-of-the-ordinary incidents at home. The first one happened on the seventh day I was missing. Ruby got home from the dispensary just in time to see a bald-headed dwarf wearing a cape leaving our building. The strange part is that our apartment had been broken into. Nothing was stolen. Indeed, nothing appeared to even be displaced. But the lock was broken and the door was ajar.

I asked her where Mighty Red was during that time, and she told me that Red had taken Gwen to a carnival of some sort.

Since the police could find no evidence aside from the broken lock, they didn't bother to make anything more than a perfunctory investigation.

The second incident was a little more disturbing. It happened about five days before I was released. Two men, both Americans dressed in business suits, came by the apartment and asked for me. Ruby told them that I was in the base dispensary. She explained to them that all the people to whom I normally reported had been notified. She told them that I was not AWOL. But they didn't seem to be satisfied. One of them, the tall man with the face of a fifteen-year-old, said that they had to talk to me, even if I was still banged up from the accident. The irony is, they never showed up again, neither one of them.

It was hot the day I left the dispensary, over ninety degrees Fahrenheit. And though my arm and ankle and ribs felt fine, the whole front of my body where I had been burned ached, and my pelvis injury felt uncomfortable.

Ruby picked me up in a taxi. Gwendolyn jumped into my lap as soon as I sat down and gave me a warm rousing, "Dad-dy, Dad-dy, Dad-dy, Dad-dy!" She stood in my lap and marched in place to her singing. She had a cold, and I could hear the rattling in her chest with each of her little steps. Ruby tried to take her so that I could get some relief, but Gwen kicked up such a fuss that I kept her in my lap. I sat her down, though, to stop the marching and ease the pain.

Ruby gave the driver our address, and he eased the taxi away from the curb and down the road.

I thought about the accident and Lillian and my cane. I wondered why the ambulance driver hadn't seen the wrecked car when he found me. I took a deep breath and exhaled slowly.

"Ruby," I said, "tell the driver to take us along the road to Frankfurt."

"Why?" she asked looking at me.

"Please," I answered, "just do as I ask."

"*Nach Frankfurt, bitte*," she said to the driver.

He turned the cab around and headed for the *Autobahn*.

"What's wrong?" Ruby asked, "Why are we going to Frankfurt?"

"We're not going to Frankfurt," I said. "We're looking for some answers."

I told her about the accident, and I told her that I wanted to find the area where it happened. I did not tell her about Lillian's warning to me or the cane. They both seemed too far-fetched to be believable.

As we drove, I scanned the scenery for familiar landmarks. I didn't see a single familiar object. And before long, we were within the Frankfurt city limits. Had I imagined all of this? I knew I had had an accident. Why didn't any of the scenery look familiar to me?

I had Ruby direct the driver back to Darmstadt. Once again I combed the road side for landmarks. It was more difficult now, though, because I had to look beyond the oncoming traffic. And it seemed as if a truck blocked my view every time I thought I saw something familiar. But then as we made a gradual turn to the right, I saw what I was looking for. The road banked slightly as we turned and the oncoming road and traffic dipped just enough to allow me to see the tree that the car had crashed into. The bark as we passed didn't appear to have been badly rutted enough to have been hit by a car. But I knew that that was the tree.

Ruby curled her lip with impatience when I told her that we had to go back again, but she instructed the driver to once again drive north towards Frankfurt. We came to the curve again which this time banked left. But once again, nothing looked familiar. I couldn't find an opening in the bushes large enough for a large car to have gone through. So I had the driver stop by the road side.

I examined the ground along that curve for nearly an hour before I saw the hint of tire marks leading from the road into a clump of bushes. I didn't remember going through any bushes as we left the road. But sure enough, as I lifted some of the branches, I could see where most of the branches had been broken or badly bent or scrapped. Apparently, the bush filled back out during the time I was in the hospital. I stepped into the bracken and paced slowly towards the tree where Lillian's car had crashed. I wasn't sure what I expected to find, but I waded through the fronds feeling the ground with my feet as I went.

The tree was an oak, and it was huge. It looked out of place as well, because the rest of the trees in that part of the forest were fir trees. It looked stronger than the others owing to its massive trunk. Yet it looked gentler because if had leaves whereas the others had needles. It looked eerie standing there creating a vast protected area below it. I rubbed my fingers along the scars in its bark, the ones caused by Lillian's car. They felt shallow. I wondered why I had even considered the notion that the tree might have been hurt. I walked around its trunk while dragging my feet in its fallen leaves. The rustling sound reminded me of walks I used to take in the park on autumn afternoons with Grandma Daughter. God, I missed that woman! I remembered seeing her in the kitchen stirring a bowl of gingerbread batter when I was about eight. As she beat the mix with a circular rhythm, the fatty flesh on her upper arm rotated around the bone as if it were floating freely under the skin. I looked up at the tree as I reached the far side, and I realized that the tree reminded me of Grandma Daughter. They were both strong yet gentle. I looked down the trunk at all the nicks and scars and gnarls. As my gaze neared the ground, I saw a stick with a shiny brass cap. Lillian's cane! What was it doing here? And who had placed it so meticulously against the tree? I wheeled around half expecting to find whoever it was still lurking in the bushes behind me. I turned slowly back around, and Ruby was standing beside the tree. She looked small.

"Honey," she said, "we've got to go. This taxi is costing us a fortune."

Damn! I had forgotten all about the taxi. I picked up the cane and headed back towards the road.

"Is this what you were after?" she asked.

"I'm not sure," I answered, "but I believe it is."

By the time we got back home, I was exhausted. To have just gotten out of the hospital, that trip to the woods was a lot of activity, and it took its toll on me in energy. As soon as we got in the apartment, I lay down across the bed. Ruby and Gwen went into the kitchen to fix some lunch. I didn't really sleep though. I just hovered in that zone between being awake and being asleep, that state where it feels as if you are awake, but where it is impossible for you to sit up or talk, that state where it feels as if you can hear things around you, but where you are unable to affect those things. I wondered if Rod Sterling got the name for his show after experiencing that kind of sleep. It truly felt like a twilight zone.

Then I remembered how Lillian's cane got placed by the tree so deliberately. I had placed it there. *I* had placed it there?! The sudden remembrance and the fact that I had totally forgotten until now gave me an uneasy feeling. I began to squirm in my sleep, but I could not wake up. I wanted to tell Ruby. I wanted to tell the doctor Ruby had questioned in the hospital. I wondered why Ruby had not asked me where I had been for three days before being found by the side of the road as the doctor had suggested she do. I had the nagging feeling that she knew, that she asked the doctor where I had been so that it would not appear that she was not concerned about her husband. But how could she know? I did not know where I had been.

Suddenly, I could smell the gasoline and leaves again. I could feel again the sharp pebbles vibrating against my face as I lay listening to the trucks roaring by on the Autobahn. My arm and ankle and ribs began to ache.

I could hear footfalls approaching. I opened one eye and saw Hans limping in the gravel towards me. He favored the leg with the wet blood stain at the knee of his gray uniform trousers. His nostrils flared as he fought off the pain. His hazel eyes in his round red face looked like poker points. As he neared me, he bared his teeth in anticipation. He did not know that I had regained consciousness, so that he was completely off guard when he got within range of my good leg. I kicked him in his injured knee as hard as I could with my left foot. He cried out once, and dropped down on his good knee. He cradled the injured leg with both arms.

I scrambled to my feet as fast as I could, but despite my hustle, I was slow getting up. I used the cane as much as I could. My right ankle burned with pain. Hans scrambled up, too. Once up, he carried all of his weight on his left leg just as I did. He lunged at me, but fell. I wanted to hit him while he was down, but I could not take a chance on falling, too. Both his arms were strong. If he got me on the ground, I would be finished. I half hopped, half ran back in the direction of the car. I used just the toe of my right foot.

"*Komm her, Schwarzer!*" Hans shouted. He strained to get back up again, but apparently my kick and his fall took a substantial added toll on his knee. He crawled after me dragging his right leg gingerly.

I stumbled against the car still clutching the cane in one hand. Apparently, the gas tank had ruptured and spilled gasoline all around the car. My shoes were soaked with it, and I began to feel dizzy from the smell. Lillian was still in the car, but she looked unconscious. Her head rested limply on her chest. I tugged at the door. It was stuck. Hans was dragging his leg less gingerly now, and was crawling more quickly. He groaned each time he pulled that leg. I did not want him to catch me, but I also did not want him to kill Lillian. When he left the car, he probably thought she was already dead. I was sure that my tugging at the car door tipped him off that she was not.

Then I noticed that the caved-in roof had jammed all the doors. Hans must have gotten out through a window. "Lillian," I shouted. "You've got to wake up!"

Hans rested at the perimeter of the gasoline spill, about six feet away. He fished around in his pockets.

"Lillian," I called again.

"*Lillian kannst Dir nicht helfen, Schwarzer,*" Hans said pulling a Zippo lighter from his pocket. "*Sie ist tot, wie Du auch sein wirst.*" He flicked it once. The spark did not catch.

"Lillian!" I shouted. "Wake up!"

Hans flicked the lighter again and it caught. I lunged at him with the cane, and knocked the lighter out of his hand. It sounded like a thrown rock making contact with the side of a tree. He crawled into the bushes to get it. His right pant leg was soaked with blood.

"Lillian!" I tugged wildly at the door. Then I dropped the cane, and reached into the window with my good arm. The pain in my left arm as I released it was like being hit with a bat. I grabbed her around the waist. I used my hip against the door for leverage, and pulled her as hard as I could. She was a small woman, and I managed to pull her high enough to get her out, but the angle was wrong. I had her horizontally against the window, her neck jammed against the doorpost, her hip against the rear portion of the car roof. I dropped her, and slumped against the door resting on one knee.

Hans was back again flicking the lighter. It caught on the first try, and Hans stuck the flame to the edge of the gasoline spill. In a panic, I reached into the car and pulled Lillian by the back of her suit coat. I pulled her like a sack of dirty laundry right through the window, and dragged her away from the gasoline stained area. Apparently, it did not matter, though, because Hans could not get the fire started. The gasoline had soaked into the soil enough that the vapors coming from the ground were too faint to burn. Or maybe he just did not get the flame close enough to the ground to ignite the fumes. I dragged Lillian about ten feet beyond the stained area on the far side of the oak tree, and dropped her. Upon hitting the ground, she groaned like a dead body releasing trapped gas through the voice box. I looked around at Hans still fussing with the lighter. I hobbled back over to the car to get the cane. That was when the fire started. I was not sure the ground was even burning at first, because I could not see the flames, they were so faint. But I could smell it, and the grass was being scorched away from the place where Hans had dropped the lighter. Before long, the fire was at my feet, and my clothes were beginning to burn. I hopped on my good leg out of the burning circle clutching the cane and my injured arm. My clothes must have gotten spattered with gasoline, because the front of my pants and shirt began to burn out of control. Figuring that there was no need in it getting burned up too, I placed the cane by the tree. Then I covered my face with my arms feeling the flesh on the front of my body being burned away. I belly-flopped on the ground at Lillian's feet. I was weary and injured and powerless to struggle further. I was content to die knowing I had done the best I could.

I felt myself lapse back into normal sleep.

Then I remembered that Ruby and Gwen were supposed to be fixing lunch. When I didn't get called for lunch after what seemed to be a reasonable length of time, I woke up. I listened for a minute to the quiet, and pondered the incident in the woods. Then I noticed that Ruby and Gwen were gone. I wondered how long I had been lying there. I sat up and looked in the corner where I had placed the cane. It was gone, too. Mighty Red! I got up and slipped down the stairs and listened at Mighty Red's door. Ruby was down there, and they were speaking in English. English?! I had thought Mighty Red spoke only German. I wondered why she concealed the fact that she spoke fluent English.

An image of Frieda pinned under the crushed roof of the BMW flashed into my mind. I could see the blood still wet in her nose and on her lips and teeth, her eyes half closed and focused on nothing. "Does he know?" Red asked.

"I don't think so," Ruby answered.

"Then we must see to it that he never knows," Red said.

Ruby hesitated before she began, "You don't mean . .." Then she stopped.

"It might come to that," Mighty Red answered, and Ruby began to cry.

I had heard enough. I slipped back upstairs. I remembered Lillian's command to leave the country. Just as I closed the door behind me, I heard Ruby leaving Mighty Red's.

"You must not fail," Mighty Red said.

They were still speaking in English, so apparently, they thought I was still asleep.

"I won't," Ruby said softly.

I lay back down across the bed so Ruby wouldn't suspect that I had heard them. I listened to her measured steps as she opened the door and tip-toed in. I knew she was alone, because I couldn't hear the cold rattling in Gwen's chest. Why had she left Gwen downstairs? She stepped on a squeaky floorboard that I recognized as being about half way between the door and the bed. I became nervous in my stomach. Why was she trying to be so quiet? I turned over and looked up at her, and she blinked her eyes as if I had caught her off guard. Then in one wide arcing swing, she lunged at me with Lillian's brass capped cane.

"Ruby!" I called out as I rolled away from the blow. "What is wrong with you?"

The cane thudded on the bed.

"What is wrong with you?" I called out again. I felt my body cringing against the headboard.

Ruby cocked the cane over her shoulder like a baseball bat, and swung again. I lunged to the floor on the far side of the bed, and the cane crashed into the oak headboard. The cane's brass head popped open on a hinge releasing a sepia-colored photograph which had been concealed inside. It fluttered down into the rumpled blankets like a wounded butterfly. Ruby made a lunge to grab it. But since it had landed right within my reach, I scooped it up before she could reach it. Before I could look at it though, Ruby was on me. She clutched my hand with both of hers.

"Anna-ah!!!" she screamed as loudly as she could. She reminded me of a woman I had heard in the alley when I was a little boy crying out that she was being cut with a razor by her boyfriend. "Anna, he knows," she cried out again. Then she bit into my thumb.

I screamed in pain. The blood from my thumb flowed freely down my wrist. I flung Ruby to the floor and hit her several times in the face with my free hand before she let go. It looked as if her nose was broken, but she didn't seem to care. She swallowed the blood that had gathered in her mouth. Then she licked her lips like a dog and smiled up at me.

"What has that woman *done* to you?!" I asked.

"I've freed her soul," Mighty Red said from the door.

I hadn't heard her come in, so hearing her speak startled me. I turned sharply around. Mighty Red stood in front of the door like a soldier. Her flaming red hair was gathered in a ball on the top of her head, and she pinched her lips tight with determination. She looked like a boarding school disciplinarian preparing to deal with an especially unruly pupil.

"What have you done to my wife?" I shouted. I remembered that Ruby had tried to hit me once before.

"Give me the picture," she said. Her voice was calm and deliberate. When I didn't respond, she extended her left hand and began pacing towards me. She held her right hand behind her back as if concealing a weapon. The image of a butcher knife flashed into my mind. I grew tight as I realized for the first time that I was truly in serious danger. Mighty Red was no small woman. I knew that it was her intent to hurt me badly, maybe even kill me. I felt the urge to have a bowel movement. From the corner of my eye, I could see Ruby getting up off the floor. Then I noticed Lillian's cane on the bed where Ruby had dropped it. Ruby noticed it, too, and we both leaped to get it. I got to it first. I rolled over the bed with it, and landed on my feet on the floor prepared to swing at Mighty Red. I was surprised to see Mighty Red landing on the bed apparently where she had thought I was going to be. Pulling my knees up and rolling had saved my life, because Mighty Red moved from my field of vision when I leaped for the cane, and she took that opportunity to lunge at me with the knife she had had concealed behind her back. She missed me, and stabbed Ruby deep in the chest. Ruby squealed once, then went limp. Her eyes rolled up into her head.

"Ruby!" I shouted, "Oh, my God!"

I was petrified. My legs and arms grew numb as my inability to help Ruby, to revive and save her, became more acute.

I remembered the graceful way she had run across the street to talk to me when we were in college. I remembered the party at her house and all the love-making we did at my house. I remembered the hiss of the snake the night she swung at me. What the hell was going on?! This whole ordeal seemed as unreal as a Dali painting. But I slowly realized that it wasn't, and my realization was like an awakening. Life was brutal at times, and at times it was tender. And it shifted back and forth between the two with as much capriciousness as the wind.

Mighty Red struggled to free the knife from Ruby's chest, but apparently it was caught on a bone. Her entire attention was occupied. I raised Lillian's cane high over my head, then hit Mighty Red as hard as I could. She slumped over unconscious.

The room was quiet now. I looked at the blood-smeared picture lying crumpled in my hand. It was so old, I could barely make out any details. It resembled the head of a deceased Egyptian pharaoh, but it was different somehow. The headdress wasn't the same, wasn't quite Egyptian. Or maybe it was very early Egyptian. I wasn't sure. I squinted my eyes to try to recognize a clue. Then I saw that it wasn't the headdress I was recognizing at all. I was recognizing the face. The person in the picture looked like me. Older, much older. And drawn. But this person looked almost exactly like I imagined I would look in fifty years and having just died. I had the eerie feeling of being in the past and in the future at the same time. I literally felt dizzy as if someone had flicked a finger and thumped one of my inner ears. I dropped the picture and sat on the side of the bed. Suddenly, I heard a man's voice in Mighty Red's apartment. "Anna," the voice boomed. "Anna!" I could hear the man opening and closing doors in his search. I remembered Lillian warning me that I was in grave danger. When I heard him rummaging around in Mighty Red's kitchen, I ran quietly down the stairs, and out of the house.

IX

I ran like a man possessed. All the while I ran, I cried. I could barely see where I was going because of the tears in my eyes, and several times I bumped into people on the street and darted out into moving traffic. I couldn't get Ruby out of my mind. My sweet Ruby. What had Might Red done to her?! Why had she turned on me that way? I ran all the way over to the *Autobahn* where I hitch-hiked a ride south.

The car that stopped, an old round-backed Volvo, was painted red, blood red. The young and gaunt Swedish driver marveled at my brown skin and light brown eyes all the way to Bern, Switzerland. "I wish I had your color," he said more than once. He had business there with a manufacturer of fine chocolates, and he fully intended, he said, to suggest that they introduce a new line called Swiss-Africa and Swiss-Africa Light that were the same shades as my skin and eyes. From there he was going on holiday to Italy. I thanked him, and took the road that led into France.

I wound up a week or so later near Algeciras, Spain. It was raining. I spotted an abandoned farm house not far from the road as I was walking towards the dock. My intention had been to take a ferry across the Straits of Gibraltar to North Africa, then head south as Lillian had said I should do. But I stopped because I was tired and soaked, and my body ached for Ruby.

The house was a simple, one-room structure made of weather-beaten, crumbling stone with a roof that had fallen in at one corner. The north end of the roof did keep the rain out. The house was surrounded by low hanging trees and bushes, and the view from the front door reminded me of a scene one might expect to find in a geography book. The plain below the hill spread away to the west like a green and yellow argyle sweater beneath a gray, rolling sky. And in the evening as the light faded leaving the plain in shadow for several full minutes before finally surrendering the hill and my house to the night, I remembered the poster of Spain in the window of the travel agency on 53rd Street. I remembered the Flamenco dancer and the castles. But there were no castles here. No castles, no music, no joy. I lived in that house for nearly a month.

During that month, I left the house only at night to wander the town and scrounge from tourists. Once in a while, I would find newspapers printed in English. I read one small article in the Armed Forces newspaper, *Stars and Stripes*, detailing the murder of Ruby Bodie in a small apartment in Darmstadt, Germany. According to the article, there was one eyewitness to the killing, the victim's landlady, Anna Müller. The victim and her child were being flown back to Chanute Air Force Base via MATS, the funeral to be held in Chicago. The suspected killer, Noel Bodie, was still at large and believed to be heading north.

That article, however, wasn't nearly as interesting as the one I read that same week in *Time* magazine. The *Time* article was short, comprising about half a column in the religion section. It said that members of a religious sect in Germany known as *Seine Kinder* claim to have witnessed the second coming of the Messiah. It went on to say that *Seine Kinder* were in something of a holy war with "a rival religious sect known as . . ." That part of the article was missing owing to the fact that the pages were stuck together, and when I forced them apart, a small piece of the article was torn away. The article ended with a comment on how baffled the German police were.

I remembered the man who had crashed his green Mercedes into the parked car the day I was heading for Frieda's place, and who told the ambulance driver that I was God. Could it be that they believed that

I was the Messiah? The thought was so ludicrous I laughed aloud. Then I remembered Lillian's warning and the peculiar way Ruby and Mighty Red began reacting to me after my accident. I began wondering who that was in the picture in the cane handle as well as where and when it was taken. Clearly, the person in the picture could have had no connection with anyone in my family, but why the striking resemblances. Remembering the picture reminded me of registration day at school and the similarities between Grandma Daughter and me. I wondered if she had ever seen a copy of that picture.

I called Mama collect from a public phone in town to find out what she knew. The connection crackled and clicked all the while we talked. "Hello? Mama?"

"Noel!" she said. "Don't talk 'cause folks be listenin' in on this line. Folks been here looking for you, too. One of 'em was a midget with a funny accent. So be careful, son. Please, be careful." She hung up.

"Damn," I said aloud. "Damn!"

I had no idea of what to do next. I was down to my last five dollars, and I had sold my watch and rings on the way down here. I couldn't get back to Chicago even if I wanted to, and going back to Germany was out of the question. I missed Ruby and Gwen. I felt my eyes beginning to water. I didn't want to cry in public, but I couldn't help it. I was so alone.

For the first time since leaving Darmstadt, I took stock of my situation. I suppose I simply hadn't realized before now that I might have to make do for a long time with the few things I had with me.

I had enough money when I left Darmstadt to buy two pairs of underwear, a field jacket, a blanket, some socks, and a laundry bag from some soldiers on maneuvers in the south of France. Apparently, these guys sold lots of government supplies on the black market. I bought a small camping knife in Switzerland with the money I got for my gold class ring, and I still had Lillian's cane. Aside from the clothes I was wearing, that was all I had. I kept the spare clothes rolled up in the laundry bag, and tied the bag to the cane. I carried them over one shoulder like a hobo.

I headed for the dock. I suspected that five dollars wasn't enough to get a ferry ticket to North Africa, but I headed toward the dock anyway hoping something might turn up. The fact is, I more than hoped, I *knew* something would turn up. The feeling that something would happen was so strong as I left my house on the hill for the last time that I was only mildly surprised to see Lillian climbing slowly out of a cab in front of the wharf ticket office.

"Lillian," I called, "what are you doing here?"

"Looking for you," she answered matter-of-factly. She wore a tan cotton dress with a simple string of cream colored pearls around her neck, and a green shawl around her shoulders. She walked with a new mahogany cane, and carried a blue airline bag. Her white hair was pulled straight back from her face and gathered into a ball at the back of her head. "How did you know I'd be here?" I asked.

"How did *you* know that *I'd* be here?" she asked back.

I stopped for a long moment to think.

"There is no point in pondering the imponderable," Lillian said. "Besides, we've got to consider what we should do next?"

"About what?"

She looked at me incredulously. "Sage to simpleton," she said. "A man for all seasons."

I followed her into the ticket office where she purchased two round-trip tickets to Tangier.

She did most of the talking for the next two hours or so. She talked at length about the condition of the ferry. It smelled of oil; it needed painting; it rode too low in the water; it didn't have enough lifeboats; it had too many life jackets. She talked about the water. It was too choppy, yet the white caps were too small to be really beautiful. She talked about Gibraltar, its monkeys and its other assorted and sundry primates. When we arrived in Tangier, she talked about the Casbah and its dank and haunting streets. They were too narrow, too dirty, too cryptic. The bazaar was too congested, too disorganized. She did, however, manage to buy two gold bracelets for what she appeared to believe was next to nothing.

All this while, I tried with no success to get her to talk about my predicament and what she thought I ought to do about it. But she totally ignored my efforts. Then, with no prompting from me and no preamble, she said, "You must leave that house you've been living in."

"How do you know about my house?" My voice sounded indignant.

"Everyone in this town knows about you and that house," she said. "You've become a legend in your own time."

"How so?"

"There aren't many men of your race in this part of the world, and these are a backward and ignorant people. They think you are a Moor, and they fear you. The news of a Moor living in an abandoned house can travel a long way very quickly in this area."

"Who else knows I'm here?"

"I won't bore you with some of the wild stories I've heard about you."

"Who else knows I'm here?" I asked again.

"We'll talk about that on the train."

"Train?! What train?"

"The train to Stockholm."

I remembered the *Stars and Stripes* article. "We can't go to Stockholm," I protested. "They'll be looking for me up there."

"They-- whoever 'they' are-- are looking for you down here."

"But the newspaper said they-- the police-- were looking in northern Europe."

"The person who gave the police that bit of misinformation would like nothing more than to have the authorities looking north while they pursue you themselves south."

"Who else is looking for me?"

"Lots of people."

"Lots of people like who?!" My voice was getting loud. "And what do they want with me?"

We were on one of the few wide streets in the Casbah in front of Cafe Central. Whitewashed adobe houses loomed around us like cliffs with such simplicity and similarity that I never knew where we were from one turn to the next. Even the green shutters and dark doorways all looked the same. Lillian directed the way. I walked with my bag and cane resting on my shoulder. Lillian hobbled a few paces behind me.

"Don't walk so fast," she said. "I am an old, crippled woman."

"What do they want with me?" I asked again.

"They want your life, and you know it," she answered glibly.

The street narrowed again and sloped down towards the beach, the cobblestones slick and uneven. An old man, a beggar, sat chanting, "alms, alms," with his wrinkled, brown hand out-stretched waiting and with his coarse, sagging, tattered jellaba damp and stinking, his face hidden in the shadow of his hood.

"They can't seriously believe I'm God." I stepped over the beggar's gnarled, crusted feet. "Or can they?" I asked. I turned to see how well Lillian was faring on this part of the street. She was stopped by the beggar and fishing in her bag for some change. She gave him a dirhem.

"They probably know more about you than you do," she said stepping over the beggar. "But we can't discuss it now. Not here."

"Why not here and now?" I asked. I had wanted to sound self-righteous. Instead, I only whined. "It's my life they're after."

"True," she answered, "but knowledge, especially knowledge of this sort, might hinder rather than help you save it."

"I don't care," I said, "I want to know."

"On the train," she said. "On the train."

The ferry ride back was the exact antithesis of the ride over. Going, Lillian talked almost non-stop; coming back, she barely spoke a word. Going, I took comfort in the fact that I had found someone who might be able to at least help me understand what was happening to me. Coming back, I felt as though that someone might be contributing to the confusion. Why would she not tell me what I wanted to know? What could she have to say that could possibly be so dangerous? I could not even imagine any words that when properly juxtaposed could pose any more danger than I was in already.

The bus ride from Algeciras to Madrid was much like the ferry ride from North Africa to Spain. Lillian was as laconic as a stone, so I spent most of the ride looking out at the rows and rows of twisted, squat looking olive trees like an army of bent and frail and naked old men standing in a field.

Once we had boarded the train in Madrid, I asked Lillian how she knew to come to Algeciras.

"I have a house in Algeciras," she answered. "I came down to recover from the accident."

The accident! How could I have forgotten again! "How did I get . . .? Who put out the fire? What happened to Hans?" She ignored my questions.

"You are God," she said. "Or rather, you *look* like God. More precisely, you look like the person who shortly after World War I formed a movement, a cult, who set himself up as the cult's one and only prophet, and who prophesied shortly before his death that he would return and lead his children, *Seine Kinder*, to heaven."

"Wait!" I said. I remembered a picture I had seen years earlier in Jet magazine of Daddy Grace being carried down a street in Harlem. More than anything else, I remembered the man's foot-long fingernails, and I imagined that Lillian's prophet had foot-long fingernails as well. "You can't be serious," I said.

She didn't hear me. Or maybe she just ignored me again, she was so deep in the telling of her story.

"He called himself the last and final king, the son of no man, the father of all. He was tall and black, and he walked like the king he claimed to be. He looked great in a doughboy uniform, and he looked even better in the red silk robes I made for him.

"I met him in Paris in the winter of 1918. I was young then, and impressionable. I had never met a black man before, and I was fascinated.

"It happened in a bar. The war was over and people were dancing in the streets. I sat at a table drinking beer and people were kissing each other and the world was good again. They did not know that I was German because I spoke perfect French. I also had Swedish papers, but I rarely had occasion to use them. I'll tell that part later.

"Anyway, women were hanging on the black soldiers by the dozen. After all, they were heroes. For six months, they kept the Germans out of Paris. They had been awarded the *Croix de Guerre*. The Battle of the Marne! They were living legends, and every woman there wanted to be with one of them. And I suppose I was no exception.

"Buddy was among the people at my table. He was face down on the table drunk. The wine flowed like water! Suddenly, he stood up and forced his way out into the street. He left his hat, though, so I picked it up and followed him. By the time I got outside, he was in an alley vomiting, but nothing was coming up. He had the dry heaves. He was blind drunk, and about to pass out. So I helped him up to my room. I felt so ashamed having a drunk soldier in my room! But I undressed him, washed him, and put him to bed. His naked body was so thin and yet so well defined. It took me a while to work up the nerve, but I crawled into bed beside him. I was so afraid that he would hate my deformed leg. And since we shared no common language, I would be unable to explain to him. Not that there were any words that I could use even if we did share a language. I was ugly and I knew it. I just hoped that he would not kill me in the morning. After all, he was a soldier. He was accustomed to killing. And in Paris in those days, it was as if he could do no wrong.

"The following morning, I awoke before he did. I got up and put on a long gown to hide my body. I fixed breakfast and waited beside the bed for him to wake up. He slept for another three hours before he raised his head and looked around. He said something in English which, naturally, I did not understand. I offered him coffee. I knew that Americans liked coffee in the morning. He ate the bread and marmalade and cheese, and he drank the coffee. He sat there a moment musing, staring out the window. Then he gestured for more coffee. He sort of pointed to the cup while looking at me with those big brown, cow eyes. I looked away from him. He must have sensed that something was wrong, because he asked me something. All I could tell, though, was that his voice was deep and gravelly and-- tender. That is the word. His voice was tender.

"He gestured for me to come over to him, but I sat still as a deer in the woods. I didn't want him to see me walk. By now, he could sense that there was something wrong with my legs. I felt so ashamed.

"He pulled his covers off. His body was dark and lean as he crossed the gulf between us and sat naked on the floor directly in front of me. I could feel myself getting tense. I could feel the self-hatred welling up inside me, pulsing in my face. I stood to leave, but he gripped my ankles with hands that were like vices. Men at war quickly become very, very strong. I sat down, and allowed him to put his hands under my gown. Hands that were like those of a robot a minute earlier were now like those of a priest. As he compared my legs, explored the gnarled and twisted flesh, I wept. I wept out of shame and gratitude that he didn't laugh out loud, and out of hope. He made me feel hope. Do you know what hope is to one who has felt no hope for most of her childhood and all of her adult life? The power of hope is as strong as the power of love. Especially to one who had no medium through which to express love. In time, he gave me that medium, and I did love. I loved him. I adored him.

I taught him German in about six months, and he began telling me about some of the visions he had had in the trenches when he thought he was going to die. I remember one in particular. He said that he was in the middle of a shower of machine gun bullets when he saw a light envelop his body, a clear white light that protected him from the gunfire. All around him, his friends were being shot, but he slipped away unnoticed. It was as if the enemy could not see him. They simply didn't shoot his way. Or if they did, the bullets were unable to penetrate the orb of light."

"Did they bounce off," I asked.

"No," she answered, "the globe was like a time-space warp. As the bullets entered, they became slow-moving spots of light that he simply avoided. As they left, they returned to being bullets. And all of this was apparently unseen by everyone except him. To this day, I believe his experience was a modern day miracle.

"I believed everything he told me after that. It was easy for me to believe that he was the messenger from God that he said he was, and it was I who recommended that he spread the Word. His message was simple. He believed that God singled him out when He enveloped him in the globe. He also believed that God could single anyone out. He believed every man had a direct connection to God. We simply had to open it. Once it was open, we were free; we were no longer a part of this world even though we might still be in it. His favorite quote from the bible was, 'Greater is He that is in thee than he that is in the world.' He believed that one ought to act in accordance with that knowledge.

"And spread the Word he did. He would hold meetings and have people giving him money by the fistful, a neat trick in Germany after the war. But that's the kind of influence he had on people. He also had an influence on women. He had more women in public than most men ever have in private. He had three of us with him around the clock, and we used to vie for his favors. Our names were Laura, Louise, and Lillian. We were the three Ls of his life. And we each had a physical deformity. I had the club foot. Laura was cross-eyed, and Louise had a small hump in her back.

"He used to say that deformed people were special. They were God's chosen few. He taught us of an old African tradition in which the masses revered the likes of us because of our special powers. He told us that we were gifted in the spiritual realm because we were short-changed in the physical.

"God, I loved that man! And those times were good for us, very good. But when Hitler began to acquire power, his followers used to beat up the people who came to our meetings, and terrorize our members. I sometimes think the second war was waged to wipe *us* out, not the Jews. In any case, we went underground, and stayed there until about three years ago. Then we came out, bought a temple, and began waiting for the return of the prophet."

"And then I showed up," I said.

"There's more," she said. "When we reemerged, so did our opposition. There are people out there who want to nip our growth in the bud. They don't want us to regain the influence we once had. I think that they think that any influence you gain would be influence lost to them. And eventually, they want to regain national if not continental influence. Your presence would spark an unparalleled resurgence of the popularity of *Seine Kinder*, and turn the attention of the people away from them. Therefore, your presence must be eliminated-- forever."

"That ain't news," I said.

"Maybe this will be," she retorted. "Anna Müller is one of their leaders."

"Mighty Red?!" I shouted. "I lived in that woman's house for months!"

"I know," Lillian's voice became soft, almost insidious. "And all that time she was studying you, learning about you."

"Why didn't she kill me a long time ago?"

"Because she didn't want you to become a martyr. If she had killed you, we would have found out, and our enthusiasm would have doubled. If your wife, however, had killed you, no one would have been the wiser."

My pulse quickened remembering how Ruby had tried to club me. I could not believe what I was hearing. "Do you mean . . .?"

"Exactly," Lillian cut in. "Anna Müller indoctrinated your wife . . ." She looked at me and gestured for a name.

"Ruby," I said.

". . .Ruby, with the laws and edicts of *Das Innerste Feuer.* She then persuaded your wife to-- remove you."

"But Ruby loved me. What could she, a total stranger, have possibly told Ruby that would make Ruby want to kill me?" I became irritated and impatient with Lillian and this whole incredible story.

Lillian apparently sensed my irritation, because she began mitigating the force of her words with a more soothing tone. "I don't know," she said. "Besides, what words she used aren't important. The fact that she drugged your wife is."

"With what?"

"Among other things, Lysergic Acid Diethylamide. LSD."

"Damn," I said.

"And there were others, many others. Anna Müller is a master at concocting hallucinogenic drugs. She was a doctor in the Third Reich, and she studied for years in out-of-the-way places in the Caribbean and Africa.

"Anna Müller and I were children together. We were both born in a little town called Kolberg. At least, it *was* called Kolberg. Now it is a part of Poland, and is called Kolobrzeg. It is on the Baltic Sea by the Parseta River and has probably changed greatly since last I was there.

"We were very different, Anna and I. She came from a family with four brothers and three sisters. She was the youngest. I had one brother. I was the eldest. She was strong, loved sports and was popular with the boys. I . . ." her voice cracked, "was a cripple who was forced to read a lot."

Her father was a sausage maker who owned his own shop. He was a robust man with an appetite for life. His name was Adolphus. Adolphus Müller. They called him the Wolf because of his love of sausages. The rumor was that he ate as much as he sold. As you can imagine, he was a big man. Anna gets her build from him, and her walk. Admittedly, his sausages were the best in all the land. When holidays rolled around, people would make special trips from neighboring farms and towns to get Herr Müller's sausages. They were very popular.

"Naturally, the Müller's prospered. Hildegarde, his wife, was a frail woman who devoted her life to Adolphus and the children. She didn't talk much, but she smiled a lot with squinting eyes. Whenever Anna smiled, she always reminded me of Hildegarde. The boys-- Erik, Frederick, Otto and Conrad-- all followed in their father's profession. The girls-- Audrey, Adeline and Ronalda-- all married and raised families.

"*My* father was a blacksmith. He was nothing special around the town. He made horseshoes and fixed wagons. That was it. The local regulars came to our shop because we were close. My brother, Clinton, was two years younger than I. Clinton worked with Daddy until he was fourteen. The year was 1911. He went ice-skating on the river before the ice was thick enough. He drowned."

"I'm sorry," I said.

"My father was crushed. His whole life was rapped up in Clinton. He took special care to teach Clinton everything, and Clinton was a fast learner. He was tall and rangy just like Daddy. And he had a face like Errol Flynn. You know Errol Flynn, the big movie star."

I remembered seeing Captain Blood on television when I was about ten years old. Was *that* the way her brother looked?

"Daddy resented me even more after Clinton died. After all, I was a girl and I was crippled. A deadly combination. I was an extra mouth to feed, and by age sixteen I knew that I would never marry. Daddy knew it, too. The following year, my mother died of diphtheria. The town lost a lot of people that year. Anna lost her brother Frederick. I thought Daddy would appreciate me more because I could cook for him. He resented me even more because I could not be a wife to him. At least not for the first year or so after her death. After he used me for his wife, he resented me because of the guilt he felt.

"I met Anna personally for the first time in 1913. I had traveled to Berlin with the hopes of learning French. It was early summer. Daddy had died that spring from loneliness and remorse, and so I sold all the shop and left hoping to find a better life. I had always wanted to travel, so I went to Berlin hoping to become a secretary to a diplomat.

"Anna was on her way to Heidelberg to study medicine. She was going to be a doctor. I envied her so much! She was in Berlin visiting one of her brothers for the summer. Erik, I believe. He had opened up his own sausage shop there two years earlier. He married a woman there, too, and already had three children. I had just arrived at the train station that morning, and was wandering around like any country girl in the big city. Naturally, I stumbled over something. It was she who helped me up. She recognized me as being from Kolberg-- she recognized my walk-- and invited me to her brother's house. They had a big house because his wife's father was a merchant or something, and they had plenty of rooms to let.

"We talked a lot before she left for Heidelberg, and I was sorry for some of the mean things I had thought about her while we were in Kolberg. What impressed me most about her was her idealism and the concern she had for other people. She told me that I was one of the reasons she wanted to become a doctor. She had seen me around Kolberg, and had always wanted to fix my foot. The other reason she wanted to be a doctor was so she could find a cure for diphtheria, the disease that had killed Frederick. "I told her what I wanted to do, and she was completely supportive. I was shy and tentative. I was not altogether sure I was doing the right thing. She assured me that I was and even found a French instructor for me. She also helped me find a job as a chamber maid. I was sorry when she left for Heidelberg. I considered her the only friend I had ever had.

"I learned French quickly. I spoke it as well as my instructor by the year's end. I studied hard because I wanted to impress him. He was young and arrogant and married, and I thought I loved him. He never gave me a second look, though, so I left for Paris in December of 1913, just after Christmas.

"I got lucky in Paris and got a job in early 1914 translating papers from French to German and from German to French. The man I worked for was Italian, a merchant who dealt in textiles, cottons from America. He spoke fair French, but no German at all. And most of his non-French customers were German. He told me that not many people in France spoke German, so it was hard to find the kind of help he wanted. The truth was he didn't get the help he wanted because he was cheap. I didn't mind, though, because I was glad to be in a job where I could use my French.

"Then the war broke out, and Germans left Paris in waves. I stayed, though. I had no family in Germany; I had no home in Germany. I felt like a woman without a country, and I liked it. I lived in a little room over the warehouse where the stock was stored, and Giuseppe simply told anyone who asked that I was from Sweden. My hair was blonde in those days."

"Seems like a dangerous way to make a living," I said.

"It was, but I liked it. I stayed out of sight as much as I could, and Giuseppe got some papers for me. It was harmless enough. He became like a father to me, the father I never had. He was kind and supportive. I think he thought of me as the daughter he never had. He loved and protected me as if I were his daughter. And all the while, I worked on my French. By the middle of the war, I spoke French like a native. By 1918, I could pass for French.

"It was the Christmas of 1918 that I met Buddy."

"But what about Anna?" I asked.

"I'm coming to that," she said. "Anna studied at the University of Heidelberg for two years. She got good grades. Around 1916, she became an army nurse. She served on the Western Front, a good deal of the time in France. In fact, she and Buddy both served in the Champagne area though on opposite sides. And she was as idealistic when she joined as she had been in Berlin. She wanted to help the wounded and the sick. The war changed her, though, and changed her permanently. It was the carnage. I guess she thought the world wanted peace. But it didn't. It wanted war. It wanted death. Her change sounds simplistic, but you must bear in mind that she was a very impressionable young woman, much as I was. And during the war, she thought she saw the true character of man. Man was not good and noble and humane. He was a savage. He was a killer. It was man's true nature to kill. Raw bones and flesh didn't bother her the way they bother most people. But remember, she was a butcher's daughter. She was accustomed to seeing animals die at her father's hand. She was accustomed to seeing their bodies disgorged, their members ground up and eaten. In her mind, the lives of these animals were given for the benefit of a higher good, the lives of men.

"Apparently, it was a short step for her from the death of animals to the death of men. A lot of men died as she worked to save them, in her arms if you will. She saw the eyes of countless young boys go out of focus as she stared into them, and I guess it became like watching the eyes of sheep or pigs or goats. Some people can't even watch an animal die, listen to its bleats for mercy. Other people have no trouble at all. *She* could listen to *men* die. She was able to keep the greater good-- the good of the cause-- foremost in her mind as she watched men's bodies shot and bombed and gassed. Professional soldiers have that ability. They have to in order to do their jobs. I suppose clergyman have to have that ability as well. Certainly, Anna had it. She told me once that she had to have it in order to be in the war and not go insane. I suppose she was right.

"After the war, she went back to Kolberg to discover that all of her brothers had been killed on the Eastern Front. Erik was killed in late 1916 on the north bank of the Bug River in Russia. A piece of shrapnel from an artillery shell crushed his head like a peach. Otto's lungs were burned out by Mustard Gas in 1916 because a strap on his gas mask was cut by a dying Russian soldier near the town of Luck in Poland, and Conrad was shot in the heart as the German army approached the Tagliamento River in Italy on October 31, 1917. Her sister Adeline, who also helped in the war as a nurse, was crushed by a British tank in Belgium. Audrey was widowed, but otherwise fine. Ronalda's family got through the war untouched.

"The effect on Anna of all this death in her family was profound. Religious conviction had formed the basis of her sensitivity as a young woman. The death she had seen as a nurse was one thing, and she was able to handle it. The death of her family was quite another. She began to question her faith, and she was plagued with bouts of depression for months. It was depression that caused her to abandon a short-lived medical practice in Kolberg.

"She left Kolberg in 1920 bound again for Berlin. Erik's wife, Sophia, now ran a brothel in the house where Erik used to live. Anna worked in that house for over five years. During that time, she became deeply involved with hallucinogenic drugs. She experimented on herself as well as on the other women there.

"One of her patrons was a Duke from Prussia who had gotten a substantial amount of money out of Germany before the war was over. They married, and traveled to West Africa where they bought a rubber plantation. Anna studied the plants used by the natives in the area, and cataloged them along with the effects they had on the mind. The Duke also financed her trips to Cuba where she did pretty much the same thing. In the islands around Cuba, she learned that drugs could be used to control people, and her avocation took a new twist. She studied the drugs used to turn people into zombies.

"In 1935, the Duke died. There was a rumor that Anna killed him while conducting an experiment on herself. In any case, Anna sold the farm and moved back to Europe. She had become known in Europe as an authority on hallucinogenic drugs, a subject in which the Nazis had a keen interest. They offered her a laboratory filled with equipment and young research assistants eager to expand upon the work she had already done. She said that she had no interest in the Nazis, but she accepted anyway, and began experimenting in earnest. Many of the drugs she created were used on prisoners in the concentration camps across Germany. Many, many people died."

My mind reeled as I recounted the strange way Ruby acted after she met Red, the compulsion to visit her, the absence of lust.

"Why hasn't she been arrested," I asked.

"She has been, but she has never been convicted of any crime during the war or since. At Nuerenberg, for example, it was successfully argued that she was not aware of the fact that her drugs were being used on human beings, so she was acquitted. And the authorities have never been able to prove that she has been directly responsible for anyone's injury or death, indeed that she has even possessed illegally any dangerous controlled drugs."

"What about *Das Innerste Feuer?*" I asked.

"She joined them after the second war," she said. "They're a very closed circle. About them, I have already told you all that I know except that Anna is truly one of them. She is not being used against her will or without her full knowledge."

A lump began to form in my stomach. I was getting madder by the minute. "I have been tricked and used," I said. "And I'm not even the person they think I am."

"Well," Lillian said, "maybe you are and maybe you aren't."

"And what does that mean?"

"Even if you are not the returned king, you look enough like him to cause the kind of resurgence in *Seine Kinder* that *Das Innerste Feuer* is afraid of and wants to prevent. And if you are him . . ."

She didn't finish the sentence. We both knew she didn't have to.

After a few moments' pause, she continued.

"Now comes the dangerous part," she said. "*Seine Kinder* knows you have returned." She paused again.

"And?" I said.

"And whether you are the true last and final king or not, they are waiting for you. They are waiting for your orders."

"Orders?" I said.

"*Seine Kinder* number nearly ten thousand in Germany alone. In the rest of Europe, Africa, the East, the Americas, indeed in the rest of the world, no one knows how many we number."

"And they're all waiting for me?"

"Well," she answered, "not all. Not all of us know you've returned. But most of us in Germany probably know by now. A handful of us in Germany are waiting for your orders. And within weeks, most of us throughout the world will know of your return and edicts."

I was confused, and I wanted some time alone to think. But I also wanted some more questions answered.

"Don't you care whether or not I'm the real thing?" I asked.

"No," she answered. "Do you?"

"Yes."

Lillian opened her purse and withdrew a faded, yellowed envelope. It looked, as she handed it to me, as if it had been stored in an attic for years. The paper had long since lost its crispness, and was in fact brittle. The envelope smelled of cedar.

"That is the only article of his that I own. Read it and tell me if you recognize anything in it."

The letter was hand-written in pencil, and barely legible. It looked like something a third-grader might have done. The letters were of uneven size, and the parts of each character were irregular. The lines were crooked and not parallel; the circles wavered and were out of round. The note was dated simply 1920, and read:

Dere Buddy,
   Ant Minie Bell died to day.
               Lou

I strained to see the name on the envelope.

"His name was Buddy King," Lillian said reaching for the letter. "This grand missive was from his sister."

"Means nothing to me," I said, and it didn't. Grandma Daughter and Paw-paw were the only family I knew of besides my mother on my mother's side. Their names were Paul and Betty Adams. My mother had no siblings.

My father was also an only child, and his parents were both killed during the depression. I had never heard their names mentioned even in passing at any time in my life.

"You know of no one in your family by those names?"

"Nope."

Lillian sat back in her seat. "Then you aren't him," she said. She looked disappointed. She slumped visibly.

I looked out the window at the rows of trees flashing by, orange trees with thick green leaves dotted with pale green fruit. The mountains in the background reminded me of the view I had had from my little house in Algeciras, and I tried to imagine how this train would look from the mountains as it snaked its way through the citrus groves. The clatter of the wheels, however, and the vibrations, and swaying of the coach thwarted my efforts. My mind was pulled time and again back to the little green upholstered train compartment I shared with a crippled old woman who hoped, for whatever reason, that I was a returned messiah.

"What about the accident," I said.

"There's nothing to tell," she said.

"Who put out the fire?"

"I did."

"You were knocked out."

"Only until someone dropped me on the ground by the tree," she said. "I smothered the flames with my coat."

"And Hans?"

"Hans died in the crash."

"My ass!" I said, "Hans set the fire!"

"The German police report reads that Hans died of a crushed skull obtained in a car crash."

"You killed him," I said.

"He died in an automobile accident," she countered.

It was pointless to pursue that line any further. "Where was I up until the ambulance picked me up?" I asked.

"In the temple," she replied. "We smuggled you in. We dressed your wounds, but the burns became infected. So we carried you back out to the road and called the American ambulance."

"We?" I asked, "We who?"

"Some others of *Seine Kinder*."

"How did they find us?"

"I called them."

"There was a phone in the tree," I said.

"I hailed a truck with a radio," she answered.

"After you killed Hans?"

"After I pulled you out of the burning wreckage in which Hans died."

Lillian's gaze was fixed on me. She looked me straight in the eye, her stare unwavering. I closed my eyes and slipped into an uneasy sleep.

I dreamed that I was a child again playing hide-and-seek with Grandma Daughter as a little girl. The rules were different, though. Instead of one of us hiding and the other one searching, Grandma Daughter hid the book with the description of the sphinx, the one I had seen once, but was unable to find after she died. And she gave me clues as to where it might be. The clues were concealed in a song:

King of the sky,
King of the sea,
You can see my shadow,
But you can't see me.

Throughout the dream in a little girl's voice, Grandma Daughter sang this song over and over again.

"I'm not getting the clue," I would say to her. "I'm not getting the clue!"

But she would keep on singing, "King of the sky, King of the sea, . . ."

"Stop singing and tell me the clue!"

". . . You can see my shadow, . . ."

"Stop singing, Lou!"

". . . But you can't see me."

I bolted up in my seat. It was dark out except for the pale light cast by the half-moon which filled our compartment at irregular intervals as clouds drifted by like schooners out on the open sea. Lillian was stretched out along the three seats opposite me with her shawl over her chest and arms like a blanket. She looked like a corpse in the milky light.

"Lillian," I said. "Wake up. I remember the connection."

"What connection?" she asked still half asleep.

"I remember seeing it written on the inside cover of the book on sphinxes."

"What?" she muttered.

"Betty King!"

Lillian turned her head toward the wall and snored aloud.

"My grandmother's maiden name was King."

X

Our train pulled into Paris the following morning. I was sure Lillian had not heard me tell her Grandma Daughter's last name the previous night, but I decided to not tell her again that morning until after I had confirmed my suspicion with Mama. I genuinely did not want to have to call Mama again, because I would be increasing the risk of revealing my whereabouts. I had to call, though. I had to be certain. After Lillian explained to me that the train would be delayed in Paris for about an hour, I decided to call from here rather than waiting until we reached Stockholm. That way, even if someone were listening in, they would think I was living in Paris. I liked the idea.

I explained to Lillian my plan to call home from Paris rather than Sweden, and she liked it, too. In fact, she placed the call for me. I did not, however, tell her the real reason why I wanted to call home. I simply told her that I had not talked with my mother in weeks and that I was homesick. She smiled as she handed me the phone, then headed off to buy something at one of the station's shops.

"Listen, Mama," I said trying to keep my voice as low as I could, "I'm going to make this quick, because I don't want to give whoever is listening any time to trace this call. What was Grandma Daughter's full name?"

"Betty Lou Adams," she said. "Why?"

"I'll explain later," I answered. Half of my hunch had been right; Grandma Daughter's middle name was Lou. "Did she have a brother?" I asked. My pulse quickened as the question formed in my mouth.

"Yes," she answered. "But why you ask that?!"

"What was his name?"

"I don't know. He died when I was a girl. I didn't know him to speak of."

"What about a nickname? Can you remember Grandma Daughter ever mentioning anybody by the name of Buddy?"

"Yeah!" she cried out. "Uncle Buddy! But how do you know 'bout him? He died before you was even born. I know Mo'Dear didn't tell you 'bout him, 'cause she couldn't bear thinking 'bout his death."

"How did he die?"

"Mo'Dear told me once that you were his spitting image. But-- Lord!-- how you find out 'bout him?"

"I met a woman who knew him during World War I."

"Who, pray tell?"

"I'll tell you later," I answered. "But right now, I've got to know how he died."

Just then, the phone made a funny sounding click. "Bye, Mama," I said. I heard Mama screaming my name into the phone as I hung up. I hated hanging up on her that way, but I knew that her fears and anxieties would soon be assuaged. I knew what I had to do, and I wondered why I hadn't thought of doing it before now.

Lillian was back near the phone booth again, back from browsing around at the stands and racks of books, magazines, and food. She held a copy of *Paris Match* under her arm as she nibbled on a chocolate bar.

"I'm going home," I said.

She stopped chewing.

"Don't be a fool," she said. "If you go back home now, you'll be dead within thirty days."

"Why?" I said, "I'm a threat only if I try to lead *Seine Kinder*."

"You are a threat for as long as you breathe, especially now that you know who you are."

"Meaning what?"

"The reason you called home is obvious. And if the expression on your face as you hung up was any indication, . . ." She hesitated. "Need I say more?" The look on her face was imperious and condescending like that of a teacher who had just caught the class clown cheating on the final examination. I didn't like the idea of being so transparent.

"Give me some money for a plane ticket," I said.

"No."

"You can't stop me," I said. "There's nothing you can do to get me back on that train, and I intend to stay in Paris and steal money if I have to."

"You *must* come to Sweden with me," she said.

"I just told you I'm not going."

"You'll die if you don't."

"I might die even if I do. Or do you have the power to guarantee life?"

We stood silent for a moment before tears began welling up in her eyes.

"You have an army of people in Europe who are willing to lay down their lives for you."

"I don't care," I said.

"Don't be a fool!" she said.

"I am going home, and that is final."

She sniffed and wiped her eyes. "The man who would not be king," she said. She opened the airline bag, removed the train tickets and the gold she had bought in Tangier, and gave the bag to me. "Take this," she said. "There is enough money there to get you home and back if necessary."

I hefted the bag onto my shoulder.

"The bag also contains a gun. Use it if you have to."

"A gun!" I said, "Honey, how am I going to get a gun by customs?"

I pulled the pistol from the bag and handed it to her. I made no effort to try to hide it, because I didn't know how volatile a situation could become when a gun is introduced into it.

As Lillian took the pistol, a woman passer-by who appeared to be in her thirties and who wore a floor-length sable colored gown saw the gun and let out an affected gasp. Lillian heard the gasp and wheeled around on her good foot to see why the woman started. The woman, overly made up as if for a stage production, saw the barrel pointed in her direction. Her scream resounded throughout the train station, and could probably have been heard outside the station for half a block in all directions. After she screamed, she settled to the floor like a dropped lace handkerchief, her best profile up.

The scream, however, was genuinely harrowing. People throughout the station cringed and whirled to see. An old man by the front exit fell to the floor clutching his chest and gasping for air. Another man, tall with the face of a child, ran in our direction from the news stand where Lillian had just bought her magazine. Lillian saw him coming and raised her pistol with both hands, her cane clattering to the floor.

"Lillian, no!"

I then noticed that he had a pistol of his own, and it dawned on me that he was one of the men who had come looking at the apartment for me while I was in the hospital. Lillian fired once, but hit nothing. The people around us began fanning out towards the exits or any available cover. I dove to the floor. I remembered the shooting incident in Hyde Park, and half expected to see Tank, head shaven, black and arms hard as engine parts, diving to the floor beside me. I imagined the warmth of having a friend near me. Lillian fired again and missed. The man wasn't aiming back at her, though. He was aiming at me. I tried to get up and run, but my feet slipped from under me. I had dived into someone's vomit. It smelled of sour salami and schnapps, and my scrambling smeared it like paste all over my hands and clothes and shoes.

There were only a few people still left in the station by this time besides the baby-faced man, Lillian and me, and all of them were huddled along the sides of the walls like bundles of old discarded clothes. The man fired once. But because I was able to sense his movements, I began rolling just as he fired, and the bullet missed me. Lillian fired a third time. Her bullet struck him in the throat. I tried to sense his movements again, but with no success. I could not anticipate his actions, so I closed my eyes and began rolling across the floor as if that would somehow render me less visible. I rolled as fast as I could waiting for his shot to burn into my body. I felt as if my whole being twitched and quivered as I rolled and when I finally hit the wall, I knew I was an easy target. Instantly, I became visible, corporal, and I feared the pain of my impending death. I was just about to slip into my other 'place' so I couldn't feel the pain when I opened my eyes and saw the man heaped on the floor. He was settled on his knees and chest with his buttocks sticking in the air, his arms flung out at right angles, his toes pointing in towards each other, his head resting in a pool of blood.

It wasn't until I had watched the police lead Lillian out of the station-- gingerly because she was an old woman-- and help her into a waiting car that I noticed that I was already in my other 'place.' My consciousness was centered in a point just above my head. I remembered then that I had shifted into it right in the middle of my dive to the floor. I remembered feeling myself seeping up through a pin hole at the top of my head. I must have willed the shift from someplace other than my conscious mind. Sitting upright with my back resting against the wall and shifting my consciousness slowly back into my body, sifting slowly back through the pores of my skull, I began to wonder where that someplace might be.

My rational self was in complete control again. I realized that this was the first time I had changed states of consciousness in that manner since leaving the hospital. All the while I was in the hospital, I believed my consciousness shifts were a function, at least in part, of my having been injured and in pain and on medications. But today, the pain was gone, the injuries healed, the medications flushed from my body. Then it hit me. Could Ruby have slipped some of Mighty Red's drugs into my food back then? Was my experience today some sort of psychedelic flash? I had no answers. I pondered as I cleaned myself in the Paris train station lavatory, during the taxi ride to the airport, indeed, during the whole flight to Chicago. But no answers came.

Once back in Chicago, I decided that I couldn't go home. Mighty Red's people wouldn't hurt Mama as long as I wasn't visible, as long as they needed her to find me. So, I wandered the streets until I found an abandoned apartment building on Seventy-seventh and Lakeshore Drive by Rainbow Park. It was a three-flat in which a fire had gutted the first floor. The back porch was still in tact, though, and the third floor was surprisingly clean. All of it, that is, except the kitchen. The kitchens on all three floors were destroyed. I slept in the master bedroom huddled against the closed door so that no one would walk in on me undetected.

I left and reentered the house only after dark like I had done in Spain. I didn't want anyone to know that the house was being used. I even rearranged the rubble at both entrances to discourage anyone from exploring. It was perfect! I felt like Ellison's invisible man. No one knew I was there, and yet I had all the comforts of a paid-for apartment. One outlet in the building still worked. It was located in the basement behind the furnace, but it didn't appear to draw juice from the building's circuits. I used a series of extension cords to provide power to my room on the top floor. A space heater and hot plate provided me with heat and warm beverages throughout the winter.

I called Mama just once, at Christmas, from a subway phone. I told her I was in New York and not to worry. I didn't call her again, because I thought it might be too risky. The following spring, she died. I had called her just to let her know I was still doing fine. The woman who answered the phone told me she had had a heart attack the week before, and had died in Cook County Hospital. She knew of no next of kin. I hated not attending her funeral, but I knew Anna's people would be there, too.

With Mama's death, I finally felt safe. I knew there was no way that Anna could track me down. A tramp leaves no trail, and I was prepared to be a tramp forever.

BOOK II

That which is born of the flesh is flesh;
and that which is born of the Spirit is spirit.

The Holy Bible
St. John 3:6

I

Sitting in Rainbow Park, I watch and I ponder. Being born is an incredible phenomenon. Most of us think of birth as a beginning. We always hear phrases like "The birth of a nation," or "The birth of a song." But being born is an end rather than a beginning. It is the consummation of long hours of arduous work. It is much like the building of a ship. The idea for the ship is the seed; the launching is its birth. In between are hours, days, months of drawing, fabricating and welding. And surely no one would claim that a baby *begins* its life upon emerging from the womb. Rather, it ends its gestation.

Our changing personalities are much like fetuses. We plant in our subconscious minds seeds of character that are reflections of the quality-- and sometimes the content-- of the thoughts that we think. We nurture these seeds with emotions, love, fear, even hatred. And the seeds grow. But when they finally mature and unfold before us, we are often surprised. We are surprised because we are just as often unaware of the seeds we are growing until those traits or character nuances are born. We unwittingly suckle personality "children" for years. Then one day they are born, and we realize on that day that we are no longer the same. We metamorphose without having been aware of the cocoon. And while some of us come out butterflies with beautifully designed wings, others of us come out vermin.

II

It was in June that I noticed mail being left in the mail boxes. I knew of all the routine things that happened around this building and the neighborhood. From my bedroom window, I watched the boys delivering papers in the mornings, the phone men installing and repairing lines, the gas men fixing pipes. I also watched the postman delivering the afternoon mail. He never stopped at my building. The regular postman, however, had been replaced by a student who, at first blush, didn't want to have to deal with mail for the tenants who failed to send change of address cards to the post office. I, on the other hand, didn't want the mail to pile up. So, I collected it. I later learned that the new young student postman was using this address for applications he and his friend were writing for credit cards. In fact, I overheard him and his friend talking one afternoon.

"It is so easy to make these assholes believe these names are real."

"Pick a name, any name."

Before long, though, they abandoned the scheme. For the balance of the summer, new students would have this route for one or two weeks, then be replaced by other students. The mail for the fictitious people kept coming, though, and the regular postman never returned.

By the time the weather began to turn cold again, I began to see a pattern-- a character, if you will-- developing for these names from the mail coming for them, offers to subscribe to various magazines, catalogs from various stores and discount houses. Then one day, a credit card came from Carson Pirie Scott with the name Al Pearsons. This name was new, apparently, one of the last applications submitted. I began to wonder what kind of character I could create using that name. Then it hit me! Not only could I *create* a new character; I could *be* a new character. I began to imagine myself living a completely new life devoid of any distinguishing characteristics. The name Al Pearsons was perfect. Using it, I would become every man, the quintessential John Doe. I would melt into American society like a rabbit melts into the thicket. Mighty Red would never find me!

I wrote to the credit bureau for the information they had on Al Pearsons. They sent it without question, one canary yellow sheet with the name Al Pearsons and the address of this house. Carson's was the only credit reference listed, and the rating was good. I wrote to Carson's for a photocopy of the application I, Al Pearsons, had completed. They were sorry, but that information now resided only on their computer. My account, however, was in good standing, and I could charge anything I wanted.

It was obvious that someone at Carson's had screwed up until it dawned on me that the student postman could have known someone at Carson's who approved the application. I was the beneficiary of a credit card scam that provided for the paper existence of a previously unknown character. I decided to provide that character with substance. I decided to become Al Pearsons, to ease back into society, to live the life of a normal person, and hope Anna's people wouldn't find the new me.

Over the months, I began to realize that becoming a new character was not the same as becoming a new person. Anna's people had not yet found me, but try as I may, I couldn't shake the feeling that Al Pearsons was vulnerable because he was Noel Bodie in new clothes. And in fact, he *was* vulnerable. I had become a new character by simply deciding. But I needed to become a new person. Becoming a new person required a new birth.

New births, however, are not always easy to come by. In the course of becoming a new character, I got a job selling for the American Biscuit Company, rented an apartment and bought furniture, and met a woman and got married. And all the while, I was Noel Bodie under cover. I felt like a fake, a fraud, a spy. I wasn't building this kind of life because it was the kind of life I wanted to live. I was building it in order to hide. I was literally hiding from my past.

And it was hard. I thought about Ruby and Gwen constantly. I thought about Lillian and my bolt from Paris. I even went back to Fifty-third Street a couple of times looking, I suppose, for some hook to reality, some measure by which to gauge the substance of my life. I found only a tavern where the travel agency had been. I walked inside. I sat at the bar and ordered a beer. I looked at myself in the mirror behind the bar as I sipped the foam head. Then I saw it. The model ocean liner that had been in the window of the travel agency was now behind the bar next to the mirror. Two ships both sailing north between the two mees, one staring east, the other staring west. I paid the bartender and left.

Once, I even ran into Ruby's mother. I had forgotten that the woman looked just like her. Short and fat, but with the same light brown eyes mixed with gray, the same rounded jaw, the same wide forehead. She even walked like Ruby. I saw her, and a sadness came over me that lasted for two days. She didn't see me, though, because I was in a bakery buying cupcakes, the ones with the chocolate icing. I was standing by the door getting ready to leave. She was on the other side of the door getting ready to come in. She didn't see me because she was lost in thought. And whatever she was pondering caused her to change her mind about coming in. She looked in her purse, pat herself down, then turned abruptly, and retraced her steps back down the street. I stepped out behind her, and watched her from behind for a full half block. I couldn't call out to her, because I knew that she knew that I was wanted for her daughter's murder. I turned and crossed the street, sick with sadness and questioning again the meaning of life, wondering again where it all led.

Then one day, almost without realizing that I was doing it, I planted a seed, the seed of my conception. The date isn't important, but as it happens, it the same day that the second moon shot was launched, November 14, 1969. And it began as many of the mornings around that time in my life began, with an argument.

"I still don't see why we can't afford a new El Dorado," my new wife, Ida, said.

"Because I don't make enough money," I answered.

"Well, ask for a raise!"

"I just got a raise last month."

"Well, ask for another one," she shouted.

My head throbbed as I sat in front of my breakfast of hard fried eggs, burnt toast and bacon, and weak coffee. I wondered where I had gone wrong. In becoming Al Pearsons, I had had the perfect opportunity to create the perfect life. Yet, my life was an open sore, and I wasn't sure of how it got that way or what I was going to do about it. I felt trapped. Married life was supposed to be a pleasure. I remembered Ruby and Gwendolyn and the first few months we spent together in our apartment above Mighty Red. Whatever happened to sweet, smiling wives who cooked fluffy eggs and golden toast and crisp bacon? I felt betrayed. My wife was supposed to be my mate, not my bane. But, no. Instead, there she sat across the table from me with her permanent-straightened hair rolled up on pink rollers and talking over a cup of rich black coffee. Where did she ever get the knack of burning my breakfast and giving me weak coffee whenever things weren't going her way?

"You've been with the American Biscuit Company for a long time now," she continued. "Tell them you want to be a district manager."

"Ida, it doesn't work that way. I can't just go up and ask to be a district manager. I have to wait."

"Wait for what?" she shouted. "For Lady Luck to hit you over the head with her wand? Ha!"

She rocked her head from one side to the other to emphasize each word. Her voice had a sing-song tone. She made me feel small.

"I just have to wait, that's all," I said. I felt low and inept, and I tried to hide my feelings by reading the morning paper.

She made another remark in the same tone and with the same head movement, but I forced myself to read.

The headline read that all systems were go for that day. I visualized the rocket poised on the launching pad with men and trucks all around making last minute checks and rechecks. It gave me a strange feeling to realize that I was alive when man was making his first couple of trips to another heavenly body. I knew I could never do anything that great, but still it gave me a good feeling to know that greatness was achievable, even if only by daring men. I remembered my musings of almost ten years ago. Was this the answer to the big what-is-life-all-about question? Achieve all that you can while you can? Then another feeling came over me, slowly at first like a sunrise, then faster until the thought behind the feeling filled my whole consciousness. I wanted to be more than ordinary; I wanted to be daring! Oh, I could call Lillian and be 'god' again. But that was a passive kind of daring akin to putting oneself in a position to be acted upon, in this case, being killed. But I wanted active daring, the ability to go out and take charge. All of my life, I had merely reacted to things around me. But I wanted to be the master of my own destiny. Wasn't daring one of the mandates of the Magi? Then the feeling faded. How was I going to be the master of my life? The character I had become was too fragile to do great and daring things. He had to be careful. There were people out to destroy him, like Mighty Red and the Inner Fire. Or mold him into some fantastic image they carried in their heads of some returned messiah. Worst of all, he was wanted by the U.S. government for desertion and murder. A demonstrative life was out of the question. Better he should experience vicarious greatness through the lives of other men. Better that he should be just an ordinary man with an ordinary job, a job that he had to go to while other men went to the moon. I smiled at the unintended pun. I felt miserable. I wanted to settle back and wallow in my self-pity, but I couldn't. It was Friday, and I had work to do.

Fridays were heavy days for me. All of my customers wanted to place orders for their next week's stock of cookies and crackers on Fridays, so I had to go.

I pushed the hard eggs and black toast away. I pulled myself up and headed out of the kitchen.

"Don't you walk out of here when I'm talking to you," Ida said.

I turned around, and she hopped up and stuck her hands on her hips. She was wearing the white, rose-print bathrobe I had given her for Christmas, and her cocoa brown hands looked like weeds in a rose garden as she stood clutching her sides.

"What were you saying?" I asked.

"You mean you weren't even listening to me?" she spit the words through clenched teeth, her eyes drawing into narrow brown slits. She hated it when I didn't pay strict attention to her ranting. "I'm sorry," I said. "I must have been reading."

With that, she grabbed the hard eggs from my plate and threw them at me. I ducked, and they splattered a greasy spot on the yellow wall. She grabbed something else off the table and threw it, too, but I was gone before it landed. I don't know what it was. Luckily, I had set my attache case by the front door the night before, and I could just grab it and my coat on my way out.

I wondered what had happened between Ida and me. When we had first gotten married two years before, we were the perfect couple. We laughed together, sang together, made sweet love together. We were great. She was a lot like Ruby, and yet a lot different. So what the hell happened?! What happened to the songs and the sweet smell of love? What happened to the trips to Riverview Amusement Park in the middle of a work day; the cakes we baked that never turned out quite the same from one baking to the next, but that always tasted good anyway; the walks by the beach where we heard drummers playing congas and bongos in the distance? How had I gotten trapped in a dead-end job, an apartment that cost way more than it was worth, and a wife who wanted only more, more, more? I felt a sharp pain growing in my stomach, and to fight it, I squeezed the paper I was holding. I read the headline again. Again I saw the trucks and technicians and bright lights and video monitors. I pushed the button to summon the elevator so I could get to work.

I really envied those moon men. They were about to embark on a journey thousands of miles away from the tension on this planet. They were their own men, and they knew what living life was about. Were the Magi spacemen? I wished I were one of them. The elevator came, and I got on. I had the whole elevator to myself, and I imagined that I was an astronaut being taken down to the launch pad. I walked out of the building and into the parking lot. I climbed into my Galaxy 500, fastened my seat belt and started the engine. I checked my controls. Gas gauge, one-quarter full, enough for this mission. Oil light, off. Generator light, off. Ammeter, charging. Brake light, off. Count down, ten, nine, eight, seven, six, five, I put the car in reverse, four, three, two, one, blast off! I eased out of my stall.

When I got to the office, my boss, Joe Landowski, greeted me with a form to fill out. Joe was a short man of about thirty-five with stubby legs and a head that seemed to be too big for his body. His head was shiny on top where he was prematurely bald. And with his smooth, fleshy, young-looking face and pale blue eyes, he looked like a one hundred and fifty pound baby.

The form was to enroll me in the program to buy shares in the company. I didn't want to buy the shares because I didn't want to spend the money. I needed that money. But since Joe had been bugging me for the last three months about it, I decided to go on and sign up. He used to mail me one of these forms every month after I became eligible to buy shares, and every month I used to pretend that I had lost the form or forgotten to fill it out or filled it out but forgotten to turn it in. But this morning, I had no excuse, so I pretended to be glad he finally caught me when I had some time. "Thanks, Joe," I said, "I'd been meaning to fill this out, but kept forgetting."

Joe smiled a lot. And his smiles looked electric, as if he showed too many of his even white teeth or pulled his fleshy cheeks back just a little too tight. Even when he was sincere, his smile looked phony, his eyes lifeless. And he was smiling that smile now as he said, "That's all right, Al. I understand. Just try to get it back to me before you leave."

"Good deal," I said. Then, to show him how interested I was in the company's stock program, I asked, "Does this give our office 100% participation?"

"No," he said. The current to his smile shut off, "Felton Kirby is still holding out."

"Damn," I said, "That's too bad." I turned to walk away.

Joe stopped me. "Al," He said. "Look, you know Kirby. Why don't you see if you can get him to sign up?"

I looked at Joe, and for the first time since I'd known him, his dead blue eyes looked almost animated. I hadn't expected my patronizing act to work so well. "I don't know if I should, Joe."

"Ah, c'mon, Al! It won't hurt you to try."

I didn't want to do it. But I didn't know how to tell him no. "Well, Ok," I said, "I'll see what I can do." As I walked towards my desk, I was sorry I had committed myself to asking Felton to sign up. It was one thing to compromise myself, but another to try to drag Felton in, too.

I sat down at my desk and started filling out my customers' order forms. It was all mechanical, though, because all my customers' orders were usually the same. So my thoughts were elsewhere, namely, on Felton Kirby sitting at the desk next to mine. Felton looked over at me, and winked. "What's up, brotherman," he said. Then he went back to his writing.

Felton was a big man. He stood six feet six inches tall, and weighed two hundred and ten pounds. Every inch of him was solid owing to his avid interest in sports, and in particular, weight-lifting and boxing. The man had muscles that protruded like knots on trees, and he loved to fight. He was good at it, too. He was the golden glove champion of Illinois during his senior year in high school. But one would never guess it by looking at him. He was big, but he looked harmless. He looked like the proverbial gentle giant. He was light brown-colored like unfinished oak, and his rust-colored hair fluffed out from his head like a thick wool carpet. His eyes drooped at the outside corners, and they made him look as if he were soporific or lethargic. His mouth had subtle curves almost like a girl's. And when he smiled, his whole face seemed to light up.

Joe had been right. I did know Felton. I knew him well. Being the only two blacks in Joe's group when I started, we had lunch together often. It turns out that he and I had lived in the same neighborhood-- Garfield and LaSalle-- when we were kids. We never knew each other personally, but we had had some mutual friends.

He was worldlier that I was, more street wise. The reason is because his mother raised him by herself. And since he was an only child, he was responsible for himself during the day at an early age.

Felton never knew his father. Though his mother worked hard to provide for him, he was bitter. In fact, his own words best sum up his feelings about his father: "Fuck that dude!" I'm not sure, but I believe his father left his mother the day Felton was born. She never saw him again, and she never forgot or forgave. She never let Felton forget, either. She was filled with hatred for all men, and he was simply filled with hatred, maybe because he *was* a man.

Felton's bitterness was like a double-edged sword. It prevented him from having many friends-- I may have been the only one he had during this period of his life-- but it also provided him with ample opportunities to fight. He used his bitterness like a tool to create hostility in potential opponents, often chiding them into fights they had originally attempted to avoid. The man's immense love of fighting fed his bitterness and honed his ability to use it to his own end.

As a youngster of 12 or 13, the man was wild. While his mother worked, he ran the streets getting into more trouble than any other kid in the 'hood. They called him Pookie then, after Pookie Hudson of the Spaniels, because he liked to sing. He played hooky more than anybody else in our school, and as a result, he got the poorest grades. His grades were so bad, he would have flunked out of elementary school were it not for a law that kept kids in school until age 16. Eventually, he graduated and went on to Marshall High School where he again eventually graduated.

He was one of those in our school who fought in the gang wars in Garfield Park, the stories of which served to fuel countless rumors around school. More often than not, the rumors mutated into tales of him winning in grand style against heavy odds. Naturally, the rumors were rarely true. Nonetheless, they gave him a reputation that he defended like a gunfighter after school in the playground. I knew of his reputation even then. He recalled having seen me around from time to time, but he never knew my name. I never told him my real one, Noel. He only knew me as Al.

Yes, I knew Felton, certainly better than he knew me. He was my friend, my buddy, my ace boon coon. I knew him too well to be giving him any financial advice, especially advice that I myself was trying to avoid.

I hurried to finish my orders. I filled out the form for the shares, and stood up to leave. I wanted to get out of the office and away from Joe and away from the compromise I had just made. If Joe stopped me, I would tell him that I planned to talk to Felton over the weekend. But Felton stopped me before I could leave. "Wait up, Al," he said, "I'm almost through."

I could see that he was half finished with his last order, and rushing to get through it. In a few seconds he was done. Lately, Felton had started wearing his rust colored natural longer, too long to suit Joe, and as Felton and I left together, Joe gestured for me to talk to Felton about a hair cut, too. I nodded, gave him the form for the shares and closed the door. We walked in silence down the concrete and tile corridor towards the glass double doors at the front of the building. I swallowed hard and said, "Joe wanted me to talk to you about getting a hair cut."

"Man, Joe can go get laid." Felton's voice was high pitched and raspy from singing out of his range. "I got it cut this short for him and this penny ante job. I ain't cuttin' no more." He paused a moment. "He's been trying to get me to buy shares in the company, too. But I won't do it."

"He asked me to talk to you about that, too," I said.

"What are you, his flunky, or something?"

"No, man," I said in the best tone of resentment I could muster, "but he's striving for 100%, and . . ."

". . . and you thought you would help him," he cut in.

"I was only doing him a favor," I said. I sounded overly apologetic.

"It doesn't matter," he said, "I ain't getting no hair cut, and I ain't buying no shares."

"Why not?" I asked.

"Because they ain't worth a dime," he said. "Do you remember the Christmas party we had last year?"

I nodded, "Yes."

"Well," he said, "that was when I really got hip to their game. You know, when I first started here five years ago, employees needed five years with the company to be eligible for shares, and each share cost five dollars. The shares were worth something then because nobody ever said anything about them. We didn't have these 100% participation programs like we do now. It stayed like that for two years. Then, at my third Christmas party, they lowered the eligibility time to three years and the price to three dollars. I was two months short of three years, so I still wasn't eligible. The following summer, they initiated a program to push company shares. But by then, Lois was pregnant with Felton Junior, and I couldn't spare the money. At the next Christmas party, shares and eligibility time dropped to two years. I figured that that was as low as they would go. But because the pressure still wasn't on my to buy them, I didn't. Then last year, the shit hit the fan. Eligibility time and cost dropped to one year and one dollar. Right then, I figured that the company must be in trouble."

"And on the strength of that," I said, "you won't buy?"

"That's right," he confirmed, "I won't buy. And if he keeps hounding me, I'll bust him in his mouth."

"Try not to do anything rash," I warned.

"Don't worry," Felton said. "We're not in grade school anymore." He smiled.

By now, we were in the parking lot. I was about to say good-bye and head for my car. He stopped me. "You got a minute, Al?" His voice had changed to a more serious tone.

"Yeah," I answered, "What can I do for you?"

"Nothing," Felton said, "It's what I can do for you. A couple of friends of mine are coming by tonight for a little meeting, and I want you to come, too."

"What's the occasion?" I asked.

"No occasion," he answered. "Just a meeting."

"Ok," I said, "what time?"

"Ten o'clock," he said, "and bring Ida. She might dig it, too."

"Do I have to," I asked. I remembered this morning and the argument we had had.

"No," he answered, "but if you don't, you might wish later that you had."

I told him that I would be there.

I wondered later what in the world could be so important as to elicit that tone of concern from Felton. In fact, he seemed serious all the time here lately. His usual scowl of bitterness had mitigated into a scowl of concern and severity, and I wondered why.

III

On my first day at work with Ambisco, Felton got assigned the responsibility of showing me around my district. Joe was supposed to show me himself, but he was afraid to go into the all black west side district that I would be working. So he worked Felton's mixed north side district while Felton showed me around out west. Of course, this suited both of us just fine. It gave us plenty of time to talk about the old 'hood and some of the people we knew.

My company car wasn't ready yet, so we drove around in Felton's car, an olive green Plymouth. It looked like an Army staff car. Naturally, Felton did all the driving. The first time we rode together, I saw how the wild streak in him manifest itself. He drove with one foot on the gas and the other foot on the brakes. Both feet were heavy. Felton liked to work hard in the mornings and coast in the afternoon. Consequently, he drove like a demon. We hopped one second and stopped the next, and we darted in and out of traffic like a fly. On our first day out, we had close calls with accidents six times. Each time Felton swore the other guy was inattentive.

His parking was worse yet. No matter how tight the space was, Felton would back in peeling rubber, then stop with a jolt. I often wondered how he avoided hitting anyone by such a narrow margin with such consistency. But the truth is, Felton's driving record was spotless. He hadn't had as much as a single ticket or fender-bender in all the years he had worked for American. The man won a good driving plaque every year he was there. Moreover, he consistently finished a whole day's work in just under five hours. We worked during the morning. Then we ate lunch and talked all afternoon.

Felton told me about lots of things that happened to him after his family moved out of the old 'hood, but I was listening for one thing. I wanted to know what motivated him to give up the street life, the numbers running and gang banging. As might be expected, it was a woman. Her name was Lois.

He got very animated the day he told me about their first meeting. "I hit the broad in the mouth," he said.

"That must have been some meeting," I countered.

"It happened right in front of Hank's ole barber shop up on Fifty-ninth Street." He smiled at the remembrance. "You see," he continued, "me and ole football-head Charlie Coleman were squaring off because he accused me of holding back some cash he had won. Well, I never did like that chump nigger anyway, so I told him to go get fucked. Just like that. I said fuck you, chump! And he swung."

Felton stood up by the table in the restaurant where we were eating to demonstrate. "He lead with his right. I stepped back like this to slip the punch and then countered to his ribs." He pantomimed as he talked. "But I stepped into some dog shit and lost my balance. When I flung my arm out to catch myself, I caught her dead in the jibs. Pow!" He curled his hand back to where Lois' face had been that day. "Knocked her flat on her ass." He sat back down again. "Her mouth was puffed up for a week."

He went on to tell me that she was the one who had persuaded him to try his luck in the ring. His boxing career wasn't great, but it wasn't bad, either. He was the state golden glove champion in his senior year. He tried out for the Olympic boxing team and made it. But a pinched shoulder nerve that he sustained in a bicycle accident prompted him to hang up his gloves. The pain of holding his guard up round after round became more than he wanted to bear. Lois was influential in the making of that decision as well.

It wasn't until Ida and I gave our New Year's Eve party that I met Lois. I also got a chance to see another side of Felton. The man was a partier. And Lois complemented him perfectly. The Simmons, the Jeffersons and one or two other couples were already there when he and Lois came, but the party was dead. Nobody danced, and nobody had had more than two drinks. Then Felton came. He and Lois, a dark woman weighing about ninety pounds with no tits and short, greasy looking hair, had already had a couple of drinks before they got there. They had their own noise-makers, and were bubbling with the holiday spirit. As soon as they walked in, they started blowing their horns and dancing. They didn't even rest their coats. They just came in jamming. With the ice broken, everybody else that was there joined right in with the fun. Sometimes it takes a couple of real fools to get things going, and the Kirbys were the ones. They were the fools, and they made the party.

That spring, Lois told Ida that she and Felton had discovered some civil rights organization, and were pretty deeply involved with it. About that same time, I noticed a change in Felton. He was less bitter in the old way, but still deeply moved by something. I assumed it was the organization. He never told me anything about it, though. My feeling was that tonight was the night.

When I got to my district, I breezed through most of the stores with no trouble at all. They all wanted the same orders they always placed. Only three stores had pick-ups to be made. It took me about ten minutes each to package the outdated product for the delivery man, and fill out the pick-up slips so that the stores could get credit for the unsold boxes.

I didn't hear about the lightning striking the moonship until I got to the Blue Pigeon Super Market. The manager there was a short, bow-legged man with a shiny clean-shaven head. He and I usually had a little bull session for about fifteen or twenty minutes in his office every Friday. That was the only break he took on Fridays, so usually he was glad to see me. Today was no exception.

"Hey, American Cookies," he said. He always called me by my company brand name. "You're late today. I was beginning to think you weren't coming."

"Late?!" I said, "I'm early, BP." I called him BP for Blue Pigeon.

"Well, maybe the day is going slow for me," he said. He had been stacking some cans of green peas on the shelf, but he stopped, "Come on into my office." He led me back to the frosted glass enclosed area next to the produce section. I sat in the chair in front of his desk and watched him pull a half full pint bottle of VO from his middle drawer. He offered me a swig. I refused. Then he gulped the whiskey another inch lower. "Man, that's good stuff," he said, "I don't know if I could make it through the day without it."

"Why not," I asked. I had smelled liquor on his breath a few times before, but I didn't know it was a crutch.

"Nerves," he said. "Since I've become manager, the owner has cut the overhead allowance 25%. I don't have enough stock boys and I could use another cashier. Naturally, I have to pick up the slack and manage, too."

"Why do you stay?" I asked.

"It's a decent buck," he answered.

Then he told me about the lightning hitting the moonship, and we spent the rest of my stay talking about that.

I had only five more stops to make when I left the Blue Pigeon. I made them in near record time-- after all, Felton the speed king had been my teacher-- then I headed east on Lake Street towards the outer drive. I wanted to get home in time to see any special reports that might be broadcast from the ship. I didn't miss any scheduled broadcasts of the first moon shot, and I wanted to see as many of this one as I could.

Traffic was tight when I got downtown, tight and slow. I squeezed across State Street on the yellow, and had to weave around the outside of the pillars supporting the L-train to keep from blocking up the intersection.

At Wabash, a cop was directing the traffic. Because cars were stopped for the whole block on the other side of Wabash, he redirected some of the traffic from Lake Street left onto Wabash to keep his intersection clear. When I got to the intersection, though, the traffic on the other side started moving, so I proceeded straight across. Before I knew it, the cop jumped in front of me, and slammed his hand on my hood. I stopped the car, and he came around to my window. This dumb cop was going to make me late for my moonship progress report. I rolled the window down about an inch.

"Where do you think you're going, boy?" he said.

His thick face was red, probably from the cold, and his nose was flat and crooked which, I supposed, was the reason why his raspy tones sounded so nasal.

"I'm headed across the intersection," I said and I pointed to the clearing traffic ahead.

He didn't even look around. "Didn't I order you to turn left?"

It was obvious that he was looking for a confrontation, so I didn't answer him. By now, horns were blowing from behind me as well as from the Wabash sides of the intersection. To clear the street, he gestured for me to turn left. But, hell! I wasn't going fifteen minutes out of my way for nothing, so I started straight across again. After all, the way was clear. But he was determined to rein supreme. He tapped on the window of the car, and gestured for me to pull over by the curb. This fool was going to give me a ticket for no reason other than to appease his bruised ego. He came to my window again, and said, "You're one of those smart ones, ain't you?"

I didn't answer him.

"Give me your license," he said.

I gave it to him.

"Do you have an insurance card?" he asked.

I gave him that, too.

He walked to the front of the car and studied the license and insurance card for a good five minutes. What in the hell could he have been contemplating? He was making me late for my progress report. Just then, a police car drove by, and he hailed it. The other officer stopped about a half a block ahead of us, and the cop with my license ran, dodging traffic, to where the squad car was stopped. The other officer stepped out to meet him. I noticed that whereas the cop with my license wore a white service cap, the other officer wore a black one. Was the other officer of a higher rank? I had no way of telling. They talked for about a minute. Then the officer with the black service cap shook his head back and forth indicating, no. He got back into his blue and white Chevy, and drove off. The cop with my license stood there a moment as if perplexed. Then he proceeded back across the street towards me. But apparently he wasn't watching where he was going because he stepped right out in front of a mint green VW covered with blue, red and yellow centered love daisies. The VW screeched its brakes and swerved into a parked Lincoln Continental enough to swap some paint. The cop jumped out of the way, but wasn't hit. He fell as he was trying to catch his balance. The driver, a young woman with long stringy brown hair and wearing a grungy brown suede jacket, climbed slowly from the car to see what the damage was. I got out of my car, too, and walked over. The cop picked himself up off the ground.

When I got there, he was asking for her license and insurance card, too. She gave him her license. Then she said, "I don't have an insurance card."

Her voice was whispery and low.

"That's Ok," the cop answered.

I wondered why it was Ok for her, and not Ok for me, so I said, "Well, give me my card back."

"You shut up," he snorted flatly. Pulling his ticket book from his pocket, he said to the girl, "You ought to watch where you're going with that bug. You could have killed me." He started writing out a ticket.

The girl, who looked to be about twenty, stood for a moment with her thin white lips propped ajar and her blue eyes blinking. Her thin stringy hair waved in the cold evening wind. Then she said, "You're the one who should be more careful."

The cop didn't answer.

I could see that she was getting upset, so I said, "Don't pay him any mind. He's just trying to get you riled up. I saw the whole thing, and it wasn't your fault."

I don't think she had even noticed me up until that moment. But all of a sudden, I was the center of her undivided attention.

"You saw the whole thing?" She said, smiling a smile that pulled her lower lip tight across her bottom teeth. "Oh, groovy!!" She turned to the cop, "Hey, man, I've got a witness. This man saw the whole thing."

The cop kept writing.

"I've got a witness, man," she said again.

The cop stopped writing. I thought he was going to give her the ticket, then start on mine. But he didn't. Instead, he told us to wait there a minute, and he dashed into the building by the alley. The girl and I stood there for about three minutes waiting for him to return.

Now that the sun was beginning to set, the wind felt colder than before, and my feet were beginning to grow numb. I invited her to come sit in my car out of the cold. But when she suggested her car because it was closer, I accepted.

We must have sat there blocking traffic eastbound on Lake Street for another fifteen minutes before a blue and white Ford squad car roared up behind us with its blue dome light flashing, and stopped. The girl and I both turned around at the same time. When I saw the flat nosed cop with our licenses sitting next to the driver, I knew that something was up. The girl knew it, too.

The driver of the squad car signaled us to come and get into their car. We did, the girl behind the driver, and me behind the cop with the licenses. As soon as we got in, the driver said to the other one, "Try not to move that knee until the ambulance gets here." Then the driver looked around with his right elbow on the back of the seat. He looked at me, at the girl, then back at me. "Ok," he said, "which one of you hit him?"

For a second, I was so sure he was joking that I almost laughed. But when I saw that his beady black eyes were as steady and level as two rifle sights, I knew this was no joke. This man was dead serious. I glanced at the girl and she just sat with her eyes blinking again.

"You must be kidding," she told him. "Hit who?"

"Officer Angelo here," the driver replied gesturing to the cop with my license.

I had been trying to stay calm, but I couldn't hold it any longer. "There's nothing wrong with him," I said.

The sentence was barely out of my mouth when a red fire ambulance came squealing off of Michigan Avenue with what looked like half a dozen red and white lights flashing like fire crackers on top. Two firemen hopped out. I had almost expected to see the same two guys who picked up Maurice Martin the day I was trying to register for college. The image of slickhead popped into my mind. While the white fireman opened the back of the ambulance, the black one came over to the squad car. "We got a call to pick up a wounded cop," he said.

"Ok, buddy," the driver said to him. Then to Angelo, the one who still had my license, "Which one of them hit you, Lou?"

"He did," Lou Angelo said pointing his thumb straight back over his shoulder at me.

"Ok, buddy, take him away," the driver said to the fireman.

The two firemen eased Angelo out of the car, onto the stretcher and whisked him into the back of the ambulance. I noticed that Angelo looked mighty comfortable in that fire wagon. Then, just as fast as it had come, the ambulance was gone. I remembered again the day the ambulance came to Wilson Junior College to get Maurice Martin. I could feel that same sick feeling coming to my stomach.

"I didn't hit him," I protested to the driver.

"But he said you did, guy," the driver said.

"She saw him," I said, "He was running and jumping around like a wild man."

"Yeah," the girl said, "I'm his witness to that."

"Maybe he was in shock," he said while writing out a ticket.

The girl and I both sat back and kept quiet. I was totally disgusted, and I could tell that she was, too.

When he finished writing the ticket, he gave it to me along with my insurance card. He gave the girl the ticket Angelo had written out. Next he got out and went around to the trunk of the car where he had a camera. He took pictures of both cars then got back in. "That's it," he said. "You can go now."

He was right. There was nothing more the girl or I could do there. I got out of the squad car, and she followed. The cop drove off.

It was dark now, dark and cold. I was cold and disgusted. "Look," I said, "Here's my name and phone number." I wrote it out on the back of a yellow pick-up slip. "Call me when and if you need me." I gave her the paper. "What's your name?" I asked poised to take it down on another pick-up slip.

"Amelia," she said. "Amelia Walker."

I wrote it down. "And you number?" I asked.

She gave it to me. "You should be hearing from me soon," I said. I headed for my car. There were bound to be several moon progress reports all during the evening, so I wasn't worried about the ones I had missed.

"Wait a minute," Amelia Walker said behind me.

I turned around.

"That cop is obviously trying to build a personal injury case against us," she said, "and I think we ought to make a record of everything that has gone on here while it's still fresh and vivid in our minds."

I couldn't very well disagree, because I knew she was right. "What should we do?" I asked. "Write it out?"

"Exactly," she answered. "And the sooner the better. Like tonight! Now! I don't want that creep to sue me five years from now hoping that I will have forgotten the facts.

Damn it! She was right. We had to act now. "The Little Corporal Restaurant is right around the corner," I said. "Lets go there."

She agreed and we parked the cars at a city parking lot and went to the Little Corporal. Once inside, we found one of the round booths in the little room on the left. The whole place was done in an 18th or 19th century military decor with different color accents in each room. This one was red. The carpet, drapes and walls were all blood red. Amelia seemed to like the place. Our waitress, a young woman with false eye-lashed that seemed to weigh her eyelids half closed, asked if we wanted cocktails.

"Yes," Amelia said, "after that cop, I need a Martini."

I ordered V.O. and water and as soon as the drinks came, we started working.

I had thought it was going to take us a couple of hours to record all of the facts of the alleged accident, but in less than forty-five minutes, we were finished. Now we sat musing together over Lou Angelo.

"You have to give him credit," she said, "it took a lot of balls to pull a stunt like that."

"Balls hell," I answered. "He knew he would get away with it long before today. he was just waiting for the opportunity to do it."

"But he kept such a straight face," she said.

She looked at me and smiled faintly, then looked down into her drink.

We sat there silent for a few moments listening to the noise around us. In the booth next to ours, some woman was scolding her nine-year-old son for spilling his milk. At the bar, the bartender was shaking a drink with crushed ice in a metal container, and behind the bartender, a young man with curly yellow hair like wood shavings and red lips like a girl's played cocktail music on the piano. He sounded like Ahmad Jamal. I wondered if Ida had cooked tonight. Even if she had, it would be burned. I decided to eat there. "I'm going to order something to eat," I said to Amelia still staring into her drink. "Would you like something, too?"

"I guess I will order a tuna sandwich," she said.

I called the waitress. I ordered Amelia a tuna sandwich and a broiled steak for myself. Just as the silence between us was beginning to grow noticeable, she asked, "What do you do for a living?"

"I'm a salesman for the American Biscuit Company."

"Sounds exciting," she answered.

"And you?" I asked.

"Nothing."

"That sounds even more exciting," I said. "How do you get money?"

"My parents," she answered. "My father is president of Tak-Yor-Frate, Inc."

"And you do nothing?" I asked again.

"Oh, I work now and then typing or filing, and sometimes I go to school. But mainly I do nothing."

"Don't you get bored?"

"No," she said, "I never do. I'm their daughter. And they have enough money for me to live my life ten times over and they'll never spend it. Besides," she said, "*work* is a bore."

"But what about fulfilling your purpose in life?" I asked. "Everyone has some purpose, some meaning." I wondered as I asked the question what mine was.

"You're wrong," she said sipping her drink. "But even if you were right, woman's traditional quote purpose in life unquote is having babies. I'm not ready for mine."

"Expound on that," I said.

Just then the waitress brought our food and set it before us. Man, that steak smelled good! So did the baked potato cooked nice and hot with steam rising slowly from the deep gash in its brown hull. The lettuce salad with blue cheese dressing was fresh and crisp.

Amelia bit into her tuna sandwich, and spilled bits of tuna and lettuce back into her plate. She began talking around a mouthful of food. "My whole theory revolves around the notion of reality, and the question, Do I exist? Descartes showed relatively well that he could not be sure that his body existed. But he finally decided that he at least could be certain that he existed in the form of pure thought. 'I think; therefore, I am,' he reasoned. Some years later, Hume came along and noticed that when *he* introspected, he was aware of thoughts, but not of a thinker. He reasoned that he could never know the I, because there was no object from which the idea of I could arise. As far as I know, that question, Who am I? or, Do I exist? is still unanswered. If I could answer those questions, the notion of reality relative to the rest of the world would be simple. I would simply apply the rules or laws by which I exist to the rest of the world, and by those laws *it* would exist."

I wondered about the place from where I had willed my 'shift' in the Paris train station. Could *that* have been the source of her elusive I. "Just because you can't prove that there is an I," I said, "doesn't mean that an I doesn't exist."

"I know," she said. "but I'm not finished. Around 1930, Gödel proved his incompleteness theorem, which states that for any consistent system of logic adequate for recursive arithmetic there is a statement about the system which can neither be proven nor disproven within the system."

I wondered where in the world she was coming up with this tripe.

"Now as I see it," she continued, "the mind is a consistent system of logic adequate for recursive arithmetic. It is literally a Turing machine."

"A what?" I asked.

"A Turing machine. This means that there is a statement about the mind which can neither be proven nor disproven within the mind. I claim that that statement is quote the mind exists unquote. In other words, I'm saying that I have no absolute claim to knowledge since I have no absolute knowledge of the means by which knowledge is had, namely the mind. Therefore, I cannot in any absolute sense know that I-- or the rest of the world-- exist or don't exist."

I missed most of her argument, but I didn't let on to her that I missed it. Instead, I tried to focus on the last statement she made. "Well," I said, "how do you account for us sitting here with all these things around us?"

"Simple," she said, "we all learn to assume that our minds and everything else exists. Most of us live our whole lives on that premise."

"Most of us?" I asked.

"I don't," she said, "I assume that nothing exists. But since everything is in the same stage of non-existence, nothing is out of place."

"Like the negative of a photograph," I tossed in.

"Exactly," she averred.

I guess it made sense. She had no purpose in life, because if nothing existed, there was no purpose. But what about a negative purpose? So I asked, "Why not have a negative purpose to fit the negative world?"

"Why bother? My purpose is to know absolute truth, not truth relative to a positive or negative world. But since I can't know absolute truth, I have no purpose."

"Do you value nothing in this world?" I asked.

"Since I do assume that I and the world non-exist with equal validity, the non-I values non-things that keep non-me in non-existence. In other words, I value food, clothes and shelter to the extent that I need them, and I value social customs that don't make me uncomfortable. Morality is a different thing. Morality tends to imply knowledge of absolute good or bad. But I have no absolute knowledge. Therefore, I'm not moral or immoral; I'm amoral."

Yes, sir! She had all the answers. But now I had her trapped in her own little bag. I had the perfect way of testing her belief in this ridiculous theory. I was about to say, "Let's fuck!" but my pulse surged. I didn't have the nerve to do it. Jack Karoac I am not. Instead, I used a euphemism. "Suppose," I said, "I asked to make love to you?"

"Is this a supposition, or are you asking me for real?"

Damnit! Who was testing whom here, me or her? And she had the nerve to be looking me straight in the eye. I thought Ida had had nerve, but this chick beat all. My pulse beat steadily at a faster than normal rate. I had to put the pressure back on her. "I'm asking for real," I said.

Her white lips drew into a faint smile as she waited for the dramatic high point of the situation to give her answer. She looked almost indifferent. Then, just at the peak as I was just about to say that I was only joking, she asked, "Your place or mine?"

Obviously, she had been reading the same books I had. Still, the line sounded fresh and new. I pulled my Winstons from my coat pocket and offered her one as deliberately and slowly as I could. I was putting on a display of unruffled collectedness. However, my stomach felt as if it had been tied in a knot. That steak had been good, but now I was over full and had that stuffy feeling. I wondered what Ida would say if she found out I was cheating on her. After burning my dinner the way she had been, she deserved any hard time I could give her. "Your place," I said as I lighted her cigarette. "And we can leave right now."

She lived on the second floor of a brown brick, three-story building near Armitage and Dayton. West Town the area was called, the area where all the real hippies moved when Old Town became a tourist trap. All the while we were driving up there, she in her car and I in mine, I couldn't help wondering if maybe she wouldn't try to ditch me. But she didn't. She pulled up by the curb in front of her house, I pulled up behind her, and we went up together.

Judging from the dirty, worn steps and dingy, peeling walls in the hallway, I expected her apartment to be a real dump. It wasn't. But it sure was different. All three rooms were painted a medium shade of gray enamel like battleship gray from top to bottom including the ceilings and floors. There was nothing in the kitchen except the stove, refrigerator and sink, and all of them were painted the same shade of gray. A mattress on the floor was the only thing in the bedroom. It reminded me of the old apartment I had over on Seventy-seventh and Lake Shore Drive, and I became nostalgic. The living room was the only part of the house with any color. She had strewn about twenty-five blue, green and yellow pillows like daisies all over the gray carpet in that one room, and three of the four walls were covered with paintings and sketches. The fourth wall, the only one in the room that didn't have a doorway or window in it, was itself a massive painting. Black, green and orange splotches like bird drippings and wavy forms like rippling water covered the whole wall from corner to corner. Only occasional glimpses of the original gray background had been allowed to show through.

Compared to the rest of the apartment, this room with a mobile made of stained glass and varying shades of brown wood hanging from the gray ceiling looked like a visual circus. I noticed, though, that as soon as I had walked into this room, I felt a pleasant sense of relief, relief from the humdrum gray of the other two rooms. I almost felt glad to be there. Was that the purpose behind the design of this apartment, to make one feel relieved, even glad to enter the living room? "Who did this place?" I asked.

"I did," she answered. "This place is symbolic of my present psychiatric state."

I was about to have her elaborate, because I wasn't sure of the connection between the two. But before I could ask, she said, "Take your clothes off."

I had thought we would talk or cuddle or something before we made love, but she seemed to want to get right down to the real nitty-gritty right now. At least, that's what I had thought all the while we were getting undressed. But as soon as we were naked and my dick was so hard it hurt and my chest throbbed visibly with each heart beat, she said, "We have to do some breathing exercises first."

"Some what?"

"Breathing exercises," she said. "Sit down."

I sat down on a pillow, and she flipped the wall switch by the door. Sitar music from speakers concealed in each corner filled the room with soft eastern chords and rhythms as in an Indian restaurant, and a bulb concealed in the mobile shot about ten lines of multicolored light out symmetrically like spokes in a wheel along an area of the wall five feet above the floor. By the time she came and sat down in front of me, the heat from the bulb had started the mobile turning slowly, and the rays of light began refracting off of hundreds of bits of mirror embedded in the walls at various angles. It was like sitting in the middle of a shooting gallery watching all those short flashes of light around me. "Ok," she said pulling her legs under her into what she later told me was a half lotus position. "We're going to do some Kapalabhathi for about ten or fifteen minutes."

"Some Kapala-what?"

"Kapalabhathi," she said. "Just sit like this and breathe in and out slowly and evenly."

She closed her eyes and started breathing. I counted sixteen seconds for each inhalation and sixteen for each exhalation she made. Before long, she sat so still I thought she was in a daze. Then I tried it, but with no success. I had too much energy to just sit like that with my eyes closed and breathe. I kept thinking about other things and losing count. But she was into it. Her white breasts with little pink circles for nipples rose and fell with each breath, and her stomach moved in and out evenly.

I took this opportunity to get a good look at her. The girl was cute, but fragile. Her figure reminded me of statues I had seen in Europe. It was gaunt, almost anemic. Her ribs showed behind her breasts. In this light it was hard to tell for sure, but it looked as if she were almost devoid of color. She looked as white as the bottom side of a fish. She looked like a piece of stone with her yellowish-brown corn-silk hair hanging around her shoulders like moss. Her face had a statuesque quality as well. Her eyes had no hair around them; her nose was bony and angular; her mouth was thin with deep, pronounced corners. I wondered if she were healthy enough for the rigors of sex.

We sat with our knees nearly touching. After about ten minutes, she slowly opened her eyes and looked straight into mine. "Lean back," she said. I rested back on my elbows. She played with my dick, pulled the foreskin back off the head, caressed the split lightly with the tip of her thumbnail, then leaned forward and put the whole head of it into her mouth. I was surprised that her mouth was so small. It just barely fit in. Whenever Ida ate me during our back togetherness periods, I was disappointed. I couldn't feel anything. But Amelia ran it in and out of her mouth and sucked it hard and rubbed her teeth lightly over it and worked her tongue back and forth along the slit. It felt so good, my toes curled. I lay all the way back and caressed her ears and played in her hair and wanted this to last all night. Soon I reached a climax. I had expected her to move her mouth when I came, or at least if she didn't do that, to spit it out. But she did neither. She swallowed the semen straight down and kept sucking. Usually, my dick gets semi-soft after a climax. Not this time. It stayed hard, and she kept sucking. But not for long. It was so sensitive now that I cringed with each wave of her tongue, and I had to make her stop. I simply couldn't stand it any longer.

"Good grief, girl," I said, "you really . . ."

"Shhh," she said, "don't talk. Let's just do it and dig it."

She leaned back with two pillows propped under her behind. When she drew her knees up to her chest, her pussy was set high and fully exposed. I bent down over her and separated her pubic hairs with my fingers and opened her pussy, pink and moist. It smelled fresh and good. She had been calm up until then, but as soon as I ran my tongue up her clitoris, she tensed up and her breathing abated as I reached the top. Then I put the whole thing in my mouth and ran my tongue sometimes hard, sometimes soft around and around, up and down, and from side to side. I looked up once and saw her knees open spread eagle and her fingers digging into a pillow over her head and dots of red, blue and yellow lights blinking all over her bony, white body. Then I closed my eyes and worked my tongue up and down until my jaws ached, and all the while, I was savoring the soft, fresh aroma of her pussy. Finally, she reached a climax and made me stop sucking her over-sensitive clitoris. Still lying between her legs, I stretched out and rested my head on her stomach.

My first thought as I lay there was of Ida. I wondered if she would divorce me if she were to walk in and see me like this. She probably would. I remembered Ruby's reaction to discovering that I was spending time with Frieda. How did she get out of that dress?! I tried to recall the feel of her dress in my hand that day hoping to remember a jerk or tug that would reveal how she did it. Nothing came.

I wondered about the connection Amelia had made between her psychiatric state and this apartment. With such a sharp contrast between this room and the rest of the place, she was probably schizophrenic. This room represented her as she was now. The gray rooms represented another her, a side that she knew nothing about except for its existence. I was feeling proud for having diagnosed her case. I guess I wanted some slight recognition or praise, because I said, "Tell me if I'm right. You're schizophrenic, and you . . ."

"Wrong!" she cut in. She sure didn't waste any time setting me straight. My feelings were hurt. "I knew you wouldn't be able to forget that remark until we finished screwing."

Now I was really hurt. I didn't like her implying that I was trite, especially in the face of supporting evidence.

"But I'll tell you," she said. "I'm a manic-depressive."

"A manic-depressive?"

"Yes," she said, "but let's fuck. We can talk later."

Damn this chick! Who did she think I was, some ten-year-old. I put my hand between her legs, and slid my thumb into her already wet pussy. She cringed a little from the amount of force I used, but I didn't care. I felt as if my masculinity were a stake, as if I had to prove to her that I could dominate our young relationship. I worked my thumb around in her until she was sopping wet. Then I mounted her. One of the most penetrating positions I knew of was the cross-legged, side position, Ida's favorite. In fact, it was for the deep penetration which it afforded that Ida liked the position. I made Amelia cross her right leg behind my right leg, and I pushed into her until I could literally get no deeper. She moaned a little as I hesitated to ease the pressure inside her. I suppose hearing that little moan boosted my ego some. But when I started stroking in her and she hissed and moaned and groaned with each thrust, I felt like the king of the mountain. I had her where I wanted her. I was in control. But I had to make sure I stayed in control, so I forced my mind off the good feeling that I was getting. If I didn't think about it, I wouldn't reach a climax. I forced myself to think about the strange and colorful array of lights flashing around us. I thought about Angelo and his scheme to sue us. Then I wondered if she could tell that I wasn't what I appeared to be. Her moans grew louder, and I knew she was nearing an orgasm.

"Oh, Al," she moaned.

I am Noel Bodie, Noel Bodie, Noel Bodie.

She hadn't been moving her behind all this while, but now she pushed it forward and squeezed me as tight as she could. Now I would get her. I reached my hand around to her butt, and worked my finger right in the middle of her ass. She almost screamed when her orgasm came, and for nearly half a minute, she bucked as if she were wild. Then it was over. She lay there limp and panting like a work horse.

I had been so intent on out lasting her that I didn't reach a climax myself, so I started again. It didn't take long for me to come, and as I did, she flopped her arms around me and hugged me tenderly. Then we both went limp.

When I woke up, I still lay sprawled on her motionless, white body. She snored a little, and the lights still flashed. I got up and flipped the wall switch off. She woke up too as she felt me getting off of her, and now she sat yawning and rubbing her eyes.

"What time is it?" I asked. I wanted to be sure to get to Felton's place when the meeting started.

"Look at the clock in the store window on the corner," she answered.

I did. It was nine o'clock. Felton's meeting was at ten.

"I've got to go," I said pulling on my pants.

"So soon?"

"I'll be back tomorrow," I said.

"What time?"

"I don't know. I'll call first."

IV

Felton lived in a yellow brick courtway building on Essex near 75th Street on the southeast side of the city. In fact, he lived about a mile from the building where the character Al Pearsons came into being. I drove by just to see how the old building was. It was still there. The front was a stand of weeds, and a rusted old car was parked by the curb. I drove back to Felton's place. I rang his bell, and, shortly thereafter, the hall door buzzed open. A meeting, he had said. A civil rights meeting? I was surprised when he opened the door with the burglar chain still on. "Al," he said taking the chain off. "I thought maybe you weren't coming."

"Am I late?" I asked.

"No, man, it's ten o'clock straight up." He took my coat and hung it up. "Come on in, man, we were just getting started."

Six or seven other people besides Lois and Felton were gathered in the living room, and one of them, a young man who looked to be about nineteen years old and who was dressed in a long black silk dashiki and who wore a necklace of long, pointed teeth separated by little red beads, stood before the others with a notebook opened to the first page.

"This is Mike, my little cousin," Felton said.

"What's happenin', brother?" Mike said to me.

I sat on the couch next to Lois, who now wore her hair in a skimpy looking, too short natural. Mike started in on his lecture.

"I've come here tonight to show you one thing," he said, "that the honky is a mad dog."

So this was it. This was the meeting Felton wanted me to attend. My feelings had been right.

"I don't expect you to believe everything I've got to tell you," Mike continued. "But I hope that I'll be able to open your eyes a little to what is going on around you."

The smug expression on Mike's face piqued my interest as much as-- if not more than-- the stark words and prophetic tone with which he opened the lecture. I genuinely wondered what he had to show us.

Mike droned on in a matter-of-fact tone of voice, "The first thing I want to show you is a map of the distribution of black people in this country." He held the notebook open to a map. "As you can see, about fifty percent of the black population live in the major metropolitan areas in the northeast, north and far west. Most of the rest live in the southern states of Louisiana, Mississippi, Alabama, Georgia, South Carolina and Florida. This next map," he slipped a transparent page with little green dots on it over the first page, "shows the positions of military installations coast to coast. It's plain to see that an abnormal number of installations are centered near major metropolitan areas. What's not so plain," he said lowering the cloth-backed book, "is the reason why." He looked around at me, at Lois, at Felton. "I say," he continues, "that the reason is to control black people in these areas, and if necessary to be in a position to exterminate them."

I thought that that was at best far fetched. But I wanted to give him a chance to prove it. So I asked, "What makes you think that?"

"I'm coming to that part right now," he said. His mouth curled down into a sardonic smile. "The reason for this belief can be found in the conclusion of the McCarran Act, or HUAC's Original Internal Security Act." He read from his notebook. "Quote:

Once the ghetto is sealed off, and depending upon the violence being perpetrated by the guerrillas, the following actions could be taken by the authorities:

(1) A curfew would be imposed in the enclosed isolated area. No one would be allowed out of or into the area after sundown.

(2) During the night, the authorities would not only patrol the boundary lines, but would also attempt to control the streets and, if necessary, send out foot patrols through the entire area. If the guerrillas attempted to either break out of the area or to engage the authorities in open combat, they would be readily suppressed.

(3) During a guerrilla uprising, most civil liberties would have to be suspended, search and seizure operations would be instituted during the daylight hours, and anyone found armed or without proper identification would immediately be arrested. Most of the people of the ghetto would not be involved in the guerrilla operation and, under conditions of police and military control, some would help in ferreting out the guerrillas. Their help would be invaluable.

(4) If the guerrillas were able to hold out for a period of time then the population of the ghetto would be classified through an office for the 'control and organization of the inhabitants.' This office would distribute 'census cards' which would bear a photograph of the individual, the letter of the district in which he lives, his house and street number, and a letter designating his home city. This classification would aid the authorities in knowing the exact location of any suspect and who is in control of any given district. Under such a system, movement would be proscribed and the ability of the guerrilla to move freely from place to place seriously curtailed.

(5) The population within the ghetto would be exhorted to work with the authorities and to report both on guerrillas and any suspicious

activity they might note. The police agencies would be in a position to make immediate arrests, without warrants, under suspension of guarantees usually provided by the Constitution.

(6) Acts of overt violence by the guerrillas would mean that they had declared a "state of war" within the country and, therefore, would forfeit their rights as in wartime. The McCarran Act provides for various detention centers to be operated throughout the country and these might well be utilized for the temporary imprisonment of warring guerrillas.

(7) The very nature of the guerrilla operation as presently envisioned by certain Communists and black nationalists would be impossible to sustain. According to the most knowledgeable guerrilla war experts in this country, the revolutionaries could be isolated and destroyed in a short period of time.

Unquote."

Like everyone else there, I was shocked. "What's the source of this information?" I asked.

Mike looked at me. "The passage I just quoted as from a report by the committee on un-American activities."

"How did you get it?" I asked.

"I stole it," he answered.

"Well, do other people know about it, black people in government?" Surely he couldn't expect us to just believe something as ridiculous as that.

"Yes," he answered, "some of them know about it."

"Did they know about it when it was being voted on?" I asked.

"Yes."

"Well, why didn't they vote against it?"

"Maybe they did," he answered.

"Well, how did it get passed?"

"The honkies out number the brothers in congress, and out voted them."

"I don't believe it," I said. I began to get irritated. "I don't believe that that piece of material you read is law."

"That's Ok," Mike said, "You'll find out for sure soon enough."

"But even if it were law," I argued, "it goes into effect only if the national security is endangered. They wouldn't just go into any area and kill people with no reason. I simply don't believe anyone would stoop so low. In fact, the act said guerrillas only. Innocent people with identification cards would have no problems."

"How are they going to know the guerrillas when they see them?" Mike asked, "Do you think they'll be wearing guerrilla T-shirts, or something?"

"They'll know," I said. My voice must have been getting loud, because Felton asked me to be cool so as not to wake felton, Jr. I continued in a lower voice, "The CIA and the FBI know all about those groups."

Mike must have been getting a little mad, too. "Just what does the CIA know?" he asked. "You tell me and all those senate investigators who have been questioning CIA people and trying to find out with no success."

"I don't know exactly," I answered.

"Well, how do you know that they don't have a plan to kill all the niggers in this country?"

"How are they going to do it?" I asked back.

Mike smiled with his shiny forehead beading sweat.

"In case you didn't notice," he said, "the honkies have just recently shipped poison gas from Denver to New York to be dropped into the ocean."

"So what?" I asked.

"Just consider these questions," he said. "Why would they decide to transport lethal gas nearly two thousand miles through a densely populated area to drop it into the Atlantic Ocean which is not more than seven hundred feet deep for one hundred miles off shore? Why do that as opposed to transporting it one thousand miles through a sparsely populated area to the Pacific Ocean which is not less than six thousand five hundred feet deep one hundred miles off shore?" He looked around at his audience, and chortled. "Why did the train have to make twenty-five top secret safety stops between Denver and New York, stops that, again, a U.S. senator couldn't even learn the nature of." He looked straight at me. "Well, consider this answer. The honkies have distributed that gas throughout the major metropolitan areas of the north and northeast for the sole purpose of killing niggers. Light niggers, dark niggers, smart niggers, dumb niggers, *all* niggers."

I looked around at the other people there, and they all looked as if they were dazed. Lois' jaw hung limp, and her lower lip seemed to quiver lightly. It was obvious that she believed every word that Mike had said. "Sure," I said, "the evidence seems to point to the direction you indicate, but after what happened in Germany in the forties, it just couldn't happen here."

"Why couldn't it?" Mike asked.

I had him now, "The Germans are of a different basic mentality than the Americans."

"How so?" he asked.

"The Germans," I said, "are a military minded people who believe they are superior to the rest of the peoples of the world."

"But so are the Americans." Mike repeated each word slowly and distinctly for emphasis. "So are the Americans." Then he said, "Do you realize that close to ninety percent of the taxes collected on individual incomes goes to support the Pentagon?" He paused a moment. "If that's not military minded, what is?"

"How do you know it's ninety percent?" I asked.

"I heard it on the evening news." His voice sounded smug.

I didn't want to argue that point, because he might have been right. So I said, "Well, they still wouldn't just round us up and kill us."

"Didn't they round up the Japanese during World War Two," he asked.

"Yes," I said, "but they didn't kill them." I had him on that point. "and they wouldn't kill us either."

"Well, why the gas train," he asked.

"Maybe they wanted to drop it in the ocean just like they said," I snapped.

"Why the Atlantic?"

"Maybe the currents are better in the Atlantic."

"Better for what?"

"Goddammit," I said, "I don't know for what." What did he want, *the* answer? I didn't have *the* answer. "And you don't know what you're talking about, either," I continued. "All you're doing is conjecturing."

Then Felton jumped in, "Nobody can know anything, man. We don't really even know whether or not the world is round. All we can do is take somebody's word that it is."

That sounded like something Amelia would say.

"And I suppose we should take his word on this," I said.

"No," Felton said, "just consider the evidence."

"What evidence?" I snapped. "Who else knows about this besides him?"

"Everybody in the whole world is hip to this man's game," Mike said. "Do you know why the man is pulling troops out of the Nam?"

"Why?" I asked. This was going to be good.

"Because he knows he can't win over there. Do you know why?" he asked.

"Why?" This *was* good.

"Because the Cong won't kill no niggers unless they absolutely have to."

"What?" This was getting ridiculous.

"That's right," he said. "I got wounded once, and was lying in the middle of a huge field full of American bodies. I was shot in the stomach, and couldn't run. As I raised up, I saw the Cong walking through the bodies and killing everybody who was only wounded, everybody that is except brothers."

"Are you serious?" I asked.

"Sure I'm serious," he said. "I didn't believe it at first myself. But when I raised up again, they were walking right by me. I looked up and straight into the eyes of about three of them. And the white dude next to me who was wounded got his brains blown out." He paused a moment. "They won't kill us. They know that we're on their side against the honky even if we don't know it ourselves."

I wondered whether or not Mike was some kind of compulsive liar. "I don't believe you," I said.

He went on as if I hadn't said anything. "When I was sent back to the front, I even talked to them," he said. "They play Citizen Joe by day, and by night, they made weapons for the Cong. The honky can't win!

Even when we searched villages for the Cong and ended up camping there for the night, the niggers got all the young pussy. Those sisters would offer it to us. But not to Chuck. He would have to get drunk and take some from the old ladies. They are on our side, and together we can win!"

"It sounds good," I said, "But I don't believe a single word."

"That's Ok," he said "What you don't see and believe today, the honky will show you and make you believe tomorrow."

"But what reason could they give for killing us?" I asked.

"Reason?" he said, "They don't need no reason! But they got one anyway."

"What?" I asked.

Mike leaned back a little in his chair, and the necklace he wore shifted across his chest. "Because they don't need us," he said, "And we might cause trouble."

"But they would lose a lot of status in the world," I argued.

"The business, political and military leaders of this country don't care about status. They care about power and money."

"Do you mean to say," I asked, "that the man would kill all of us at a time when he's trying to win African confidence?"

"The man is not trying to win Africa," Mike said. "He's trying to take it. He wants to win their confidence enough to keep black Africa separated and struggling. That's why the U.S. backed Tshombe in the Congo even though most black Africans hated him. But at the same time, the U.S. sent and still sends big businesses for economic support to South Africa, a country that openly purports white supremacy."

"I suppose you think White people are trying to take over the whole world?" I asked.

"You damn right!" Mike asserted.

I had heard some stupid notions, but this beat all. "You can't be serious," I said.

"Why can't I?" Mike said, "Honkies have been killing and exploiting third world people for years, and they still are."

"But that seems like reason enough to not kill black people in this country," I argued.

"It would be reason enough to not kill us except for one thing," Mike said, "black people are getting hip. Too hip! We are demanding an equal share of the pie, and that's too much. The honkies know that in order for this economic structure to survive, there must be people in it who have nothing. Nothing! For years, niggers have been the ones with nothing, and we liked it. But now, black people want more, much more. And they would rather kill us than give us any power or money."

"I don't believe it," I said.

"You'll believe it when you're standing inside a concentration camp waiting to be gassed, won't you?" Mike said.

I knew he was being smart, but I ignored his remark. "But what about all the white people in this country who are protesting America's method?"

Mike lowered his voice slightly. "The only people who protest are those who are well-to-do enough to think about the issues. People who have to spend all their time trying to get food and shelter don't have time to protest. The big wheels know this. And right now, they are creating a depression. As soon as the depression comes, all protests will stop. And in a few years when they decide to end the depression, the people will love them, fight wars for them and back all their foreign policies, because they will be our saviors. And if they blame the depression on niggers, the honkies will gladly kill us all. In fact, that might be how they intend to do it. All the newspapers will read,

'Niggers Caused Depression' and all the honkies will say, 'Yep, the depression started when niggers started getting ahead.'"

"Do you realize how stupid you sound?" I asked.

"You don't believe me, eh? Well, why did the man replace all silver certificates with Federal Reserve notes?" He smiled at me. "You don't know, do you? Well, try this. There wasn't enough silver in this country to back up the paper certificates in circulation, and they didn't want any runs on the banks for silver. And do you know who has all the silver?"

"No," I answered.

"The syndicate," he said. "The syndicate controls the one-armed bandits in Las Vegas, and has a hold on most of the vending machines and pin-ball machines around the country. All they do is collect silver coins."

"I don't see the point you're trying to make." I said.

"The point is this," he said. "Prices and wages are becoming more and more unstable. Pretty soon, currency as we know it will be worthless. Only gold and silver will be stable enough to use as money. Now," he said, "the people can't get gold to trade. And without silver certificates, they won't be able to get silver, either. And that means that when you go to the bank and demand your savings, the man will give you a pile of worthless Federal Reserve notes, which are backed up by absolutely nothing."

Everyone in the room was quiet. And judging from the amount of attention they all gave him, Mike had done what he had set out to do, convinced them that the honky was a mad dog.

Then Mike went on talking about how the Minute Men would start the mass murder, and how the Jews and hippies would get killed, too. He showed pictures in his book of mutilated black bodies, bombed churches and white policemen enforcing 'Law and Order' in Selma,

Alabama. And at eleven-thirty, it was over. We all shook hands and congratulated him on his fine presentation. And as they began a question and answer session, I asked Felton for my coat. At the door, Felton said, "I'm glad you came, Al."

"So am I," I lied.

When I got home, Ida was already in bed asleep. I was glad. This had been a long day, and I wasn't in the mood to bicker with her about why she couldn't have an El Dorado or where I had been all day. Besides, I hadn't even thought up a lie to tell her, yet, and her being asleep gave me some extra time. I pulled off my clothes and crawled in next to her.

I remember wondering how in the world Mike could believe all the stuff he was telling us, and the next thing I knew, the sun was shining down hard on the top of my head as I walked down a street named *Berliner Strasse*. And as I passed a shop with three big African paintings in the window, paintings that I thought I had seen at Amelia's place, Mike stepped out from the doorway and said, "It's hot out here, isn't it, man?"

I wiped the sweat running down my face with the back of my hand. "No, man," I said, "it's just that I've been walking for so long."

His black dashiki waved loosely in the hot breeze.

"Do you know where you've been going?" he asked.

"Where?" I asked back.

The corners of his thick lips drew down into a sardonic smile. "Here," he said.

"Here?"

"Yes," he said. "We've been waiting for you."

He opened the heavy wooden door, and I walked into the shop, and he took my coat. I had expected to see more of Amelia's paintings, but the pale yellow walls were bare. In the middle of the shop, four refrigerated meat cases were arranged in the form of a square with the display windows of each case facing the inside of the square. And as I walked around the cases, I saw nothing but their plain white backs and white sliding doors with blood dripping from their handles. I must have circled the cases three times before I noticed that at one corner of the square, the cases weren't touching each other and allowed a passage of about eighteen inches to the inside of the square. I squeezed through, and oh my God! The first thing I saw as I looked into the meat case was a line of black faces which had been cut off from the rest of the heads stacked one behind the other like pork chops. And Felton Kirby's face led the line! Next to the faces rested the front portion of several rib cages, some of which were still bleeding. And as I looked around, I saw black arms and legs stacked up like chicken wings and I saw breasts, penises and testes piled in a bloody bucket like giblets.

I looked up at Mike who was smiling at me from the other side of the cooler. "Are you ready?" he asked.

"I certainly wasn't ready for this," I answered. My stomach churned slowly as I spoke.

"Then you shouldn't have stepped into the square," he said.

He pointed to an opening in the floor and bade me to look in. As I did, an icy draft hit me in the face. The cavernous room beneath the floor must have been refrigerated to near freezing in order to create a draft that cold. But what shocked me even more than the cold air was the fact that the room, which encompassed as much space as a warehouse or barn, was lighted to near daylight brilliance. And from my vantage point in the ceiling of the room, I could see the whole sickening operation. That room was the slaughter house, and it looked immaculate. Modern, efficient machinery took care of the whole operation. Once the bodies were hooked by their heels on a conveyer cable, one machine decapitated the bodies and drained the blood. A second machine gutted the bodies, and the last machine cut off the limbs, quartered the torso, and collected the parts for display. The killing area was the only place where blood stained the floor. And even then for only a few seconds until a flushing mechanism washed it down. The strangest part of the whole operation, though, was the way the victims came in to be killed. They were smiling! The damn fools were smiling and walking one by one into the killing area by themselves. One chick-- a fine chick with a big bushy natural-- walked up before the executioner who wore a long black silk dashiki just like the one Mike wore, took off all her clothes, and with a perfectly straight face, waited for the man to stab her with an eighteen inch saber. The man drew the blade back and with one hard under-handed swing, caught the young woman so hard in the stomach that her heels left the floor and half the saber protruded from her smooth, brown back. And as she curled forward over the handle of the knife, and blood gushed from her wounds covering her legs and gathering in a big puddle on the concrete floor, her legs buckled and she slumped to her knees. Then with blood running from her mouth, she looked up at the man and smiled for a few seconds before she dropped over and quivered dead.

I looked up at Mike who was still smiling down at me from over the meat cooler.

"What is this place?" I shouted.

"You'll see when you get down there," he answered.

"I'm not going down there," I said. I heard a spray of water, and I knew that it was the flushing mechanism washing the woman's blood down a drain. It sounded like a toilet being flushed.

"Yes, you are," Mike said. "You volunteered when you stepped into the square."

I didn't bother to argue with him. I leaped straight back through the opening between the coolers. And as I did, I noticed that three more dudes had come from somewhere, and they were trying to catch me. I recognized one of them as the same man who stabbed the woman. I had to get away. But I was trapped in a corner. As they closed in, I started digging into the walls with my bare hands and the walls turned into ginger bread and the crumbs felt like sand beneath my fingernails. The wall fell away around me as I lunged for freedom with big chunks of ginger bread bouncing off of my head and face and shoulders like sponges. I was free! I was free! I had escaped and was running down an alley in the Casbah. Lillian sat huddled in a jellaba begging for alms, her hair caked with grime and matted to her head. Soon the alley became a series of roof tops in Detroit, and I was jumping from roof to roof, and they were still behind me. I kept running harder. Sweat dripped from my face and arms, but I kept running. Sweat ran into my eyes and burned and blurred my vision, but I kept running. There were more of them now, and they were getting closer. They were all around me. The only way out was to jump to the building on my right. But it was too far. I was tired, and I knew I couldn't make it, but I jumped anyway. I fell. I landed on my face on the cold concrete floor. And as I felt my blood oozing into a big puddle around my broken body, I heard water splashing over my legs. I couldn't feel it because my legs were numb, but I heard it, and I knew that the flushing mechanism was on and washing my blood down a drain.

I struggled to get up before the water reached my head. I felt a clamp on my shoulder trying to put me on the conveyer cable. I struggled. I tried to scream, but my throat was paralyzed. I struggled harder. Then I heard Ida calling me from down a long corridor. Her voice got louder and the clamp on my shoulder yanked harder. Then I opened my eyes and saw Ida standing over me with her hand on my shoulder.

"Your breakfast is ready."

"Wow!" I said, "What a dream!"

"You can eat anytime you want to."

"Wow," I said.

Ida left the room before I got a chance to tell her about the dream. But maybe it was for the better because I still didn't have an excuse for being late yesterday.

I took a shower, got dressed and left without saying another word. In fact, I didn't even see her again before I left. But I heard her in the kitchen. And as I pulled the door closed, the smell of burnt toast stung my nostrils.

V

I stopped at a drug store on the corner of Thirty-fifth and Shields, and called Amelia.

"Oh, it's you," she said. Her voice sounded animated.

For some reason I had expected her not to recognize my voice. I was glad when she did.

"Are you coming over?" she asked.

"Yes."

"Good. I'll be waiting."

"Do you have anything to eat?"

"Other than me, you mean?"

"Other than you."

"Only some cereal."

"I'll bring some eggs."

"Good," she said, "they'll give you stamina."

I picked up some eggs and pan sausage at the store across the street and headed north. All the while I was driving, I kept seeing Mike's young face peering at me from over the meat cooler and hearing him say, what you don't see and believe today, the honky will show you and make you believe tomorrow.

I thought about Lillian and wondered if *Seine Kinder* could protect me from Mike and his goons *and* from Mighty Red.

I got to Amelia's place and went upstairs. When I reached to knock on the door, I noticed that it was slightly ajar. I walked in.

A man with silver-gray hair parted in the middle looked at me, his wide set, pale blue eyes blinking. "Who is this?" he asked Amelia, who was standing next to him.

I knew who he was, because he had the exact same kind of bony, angular nose that Amelia had, and the same colorless complexion. Judging from the light gray plaid suit and white shirt he wore, I suspected that he might be an executive of some sort. The suit fit him too well and looked too neatly pressed to have come off a rack. I reasoned that it had to be tailor-made. Only an executive would bother or could afford to have a business suit tailor-made.

"He's my new lover," Amelia said. "His name is Al."

The man's neck stiffened. His face turned red. He forced his hand out towards me. "Hello, Al," he said, "I'm Mr. Walker, Amelia's father." His voice was devoid of emotion, a monotone. I took his hand. It felt as limp as wilted lettuce.

Amelia continued with the conversation that they were having before I walked in. "I don't know how you found out about the run in I had with Angelo yesterday," she said, "but I don't want your help or your lawyer's help in court next month."

"Be reasonable, Honey," Mr. Walker said. He had forgotten all about me. "I can get you out of this with no trouble or embarrassing court appearance. Let me help."

"No!"

Mr. Walker shook his head and looked down at the floor. He flexed his toes up in his shiny cordovans.

"Ok," he said, "but if you need me, . . ."

"If I need you, I'll call you," she said. She paused. "Did you bring my allowance?"

"Yes," he answered.

He reached into his inside jacket pocket, pulled out a white sealed envelope, and gave it to her. Then he glanced at the gold watch on his arm. "I've got an appointment with the dentist this afternoon," he said.

"I have to go. Nice meeting you, Al." His voice returned to the monotone.

"Same here," I said.

He left.

"Why didn't you let him help," I asked.

"I don't want his help," she answered. "He thinks money can buy anything, even me and my love. But I hate him. I only want to see him on Saturdays when he brings my allowance."

"But he can help you."

"And give him the chance to prove the strength of his money and influence? Never! Besides," she continued, "I don't sell my love, I give it away."

With that, she grabbed me around the neck and kissed me. This chick was weird, but I liked it. I stuck my tongue in her mouth and she sucked it hard. We kissed until spit began to run down the side of my mouth and my tongue ached. I drew away and wiped my mouth with the back of my hand. She squeezed me close to her again with her chin resting on my shoulder.

"Make love to me, Al," she said, "hard love. Make love to me until I scream."

I didn't answer. I just blew the loose hair away from her ear, then stuck my tongue in it and sucked it. At the same time, I pulled her dress up and stuck my middle and ring fingers into her pussy. She moaned. Then she leaped up and slung her legs around my waist and locked them pinning my right arm to my side and jabbing my fingers so deep in her hole they hurt. Then she came all over them. Damn, she was hungry. Maybe too hungry. I began wondering whether or not I would be able to satisfy her. Suppose my dick wouldn't stay hard? I got scared, really scared. I carried her into the next room, the circus.

As I carried her, she leaned back so that I had to brace her around the small of her back with my free arm. With her eyes closed and her mouth hung limp, she pulled her dress, a loose hanging green and yellow polka dot mini, over her head and slung it into the corner. She must have pulled her bra off with it, because before the dress landed, she leaned forward again and stuffed a breast into my mouth. I remembered Ruby's magician act.   Do women practice getting undressed so quickly? Amelia's flat nipple tightened and got hard as I sucked it, and she flopped her head around and around, and side to side as if her neck were broken. Her hair covered my head and shoulders. Quivering, she came again.

She loosened her legs around my waist and slid to the floor pulling me with her. We knelt facing each other. I still had my fingers in her as she began unbuttoning my shirt. After undoing one button, she snatched the shirt open and broke the next two. I looked at her, and she smiled wickedly. I took the shirt off. Then pulling me close to her again, her moves slow and deliberate, she bit me. This girl was weird! She gave me a hicky so high on my neck that I couldn't possibly hide it with my collar. She smiled a wry smile that pulled her lower lip tight across her bottom teeth as she lay back with a pillow propped under her behind. She nearly laughed as I entered her and moaned.

From the orgasms she had already reached, she was sloppy wet inside. I could hardly feel the sides of her pussy as I began thrusting forward, but I didn't stop. I wanted to pump that smile off her face. I worked up a sweat, and she sweat, too. Our skin began to stick. But I still didn't stop. My dick ached. Soon I dropped onto her panting body exhausted. We simply lay there breathing and we smelled of sweat and come and spit. I even dosed off for a minute or two before she asked, "You didn't come, did you?"

"No," I answered. I rolled off of her and onto my side.

I looked at one of the sketches hanging on the wall. At first I thought it was simply a mass of small dots arranged in a circle which was shaded on one side and highlighted on the other. But staring at it as I was, it began to take on form. Then I realized that the drawing had been taken from a huge blow-up shot of a nipple, and that the dots in the drawing had been grain in the photograph. It gave a striking effect; in that, in the drawing much of the highlighting was done by omitting part of the subject. It gave the appearance of being incomplete. But when I realized what the drawing was, all aspects of it, including the omissions, fell into place. The whole experience was like watching a flower blossom in my head. It looked like the kind of picture she would have, weird.

"Has this drawing got anything to do with the psychiatric state you mentioned yesterday?" I asked.

"No," she answered with her eyes still closed. She knew without even looking which drawing I was talking about. "That drawing and realizing what it is is like having a satori, a burst of knowledge. But my condition is such that I experience alternate periods of elation and depression. When I'm up, I'm really up. Like this, I'm bright and bubbly and exuberant. Then at other times, I'm like the rest of the place, gray and drab and gloomy. I won't even talk to people." She paused. "I'm getting better now, though. A few years ago when I was still with my parents, I even tried to kill myself once or twice. I don't get those urges anymore, and that means I'm progressing."

"What brought on this condition?" I asked. I didn't know what a manic-depressive was, and I hoped that, by getting her talking, she would tell me enough about it so that I would be able to talk about it and not let her know that I didn't know.

"A boy," she said. "A boy named Melvin Clark." She paused again for a moment, then continued. "My parents live up in Winnetka, and they are the typical white, Anglo-Saxon, upper- middle class, Protestant family with all the white, Anglo-Saxon, upper-middle class values and aspirations. All of my life, I had lived the sheltered existence of the benevolent little white girl scout helping old people and selling girl scout cookies. Well, when I graduated from high school and enrolled at Northwestern University, my father gave me a speech about how proud he was of me and how much of a young woman I was becoming and how much faith he had in my judgment and knowledge of right and wrong. That was six years ago.

"In my sophomore year there I met Melvin. He was a young, black philosophy major with a rap so strong that I was enrolling in philosophy classes just to have an excuse to be near him. We used to spend hours after classes just talking about life and what we each wanted from it. Then we started going out together, to art exhibits first, then to movies and coffee houses and pot parties. We were great together, and I loved him. He loved me as well. Like any natural man, he asked to make love to me. I remembered my father's speech, and I told him, no. He was very understanding about it. He must have known that I was a virgin and that I was scared. A month or so later he asked me again. I asked him to let my think to over. He agreed, and like a fool, I went and consulted father who told me to wait until I got married. Then father told me to bring the fellow home to meet him. Oh, was I naive! I agreed and brought Melvin home. Why did I do that? Melvin had told me that it would be no good. But, no, my father trusted my judgment, and I talked him into going. He stayed for about twenty minutes before he made up some excuse about having to study for a test. When he left, my father hit the ceiling. He didn't want me to see Melvin again. And how could I even consider him in the first place? I cried and told him that I loved Melvin. But he didn't listen. He locked me in my room for two weeks and had me withdrawn from school.

"I hated him after that. I was determined to see Melvin. So, after father allowed me to go out again, I went straight to the campus and found Melvin. But he was with another girl, a black girl. I told him that I loved him and that I would let him make love to me if he still wanted to. Do you know what he said? He said that he needed a woman, not some little girl who had to ask her father who she could give her hole to.

"That really broke me up. I locked myself in my room for another two weeks after that. I cried every day and night, and refused to talk to anyone, even my friends. Then I cut my wrists. When I shouted out to Father what I had done, he broke the door down, and rushed me to a hospital. And the next three years of my life I spent visiting psychiatrists and attending group therapy sessions.

"Last year they decided that I should leave home, become independent. I did, and now father supports me while I indulge in sex with every black man I can find. He hates it. He hates seeing me with only black men, me, his little lily white girl scout. But I love it. And I love to watch him squirm."

"Are you seeing me just to spite your father?" I asked.

"Well, that's the excuse I use," she answered. "But my shrink tells me that I'm punishing myself for not screwing Melvin when he wanted me. According to him, all my lovers are symbols of Melvin whom I still love."

"Then I'm just another stud that you're running through its paces, is that it?" I tried to sound indignant.

"Yes," she said turning away from me. "But I am a good trainer, and you do like the workouts."

Goddamn this chick! I smacked her on her butt, and told her to get on her knees and bend down.

"Oh, so you're ready to assert your masculinity again, are you?" She climbed onto her knees and cupped her head in her hands on a pillow.

"Damn right," I said. I slid my dick into her pussy and rammed it so hard her knees almost left the floor. I rammed again and again. She giggled. I stopped.

"Why did you stop?" She said, "It was beginning to feel good."

I slid out slowly.

"You're not giving up, are you?" she asked.

As my dick head slid out, I shoved it in again as hard as I could.

"Oh!" she cried and lunged forward with her head down like a horse pulling a plow in rocky ground. Every muscle in her body tightened, and her toes grew taut as they gripped the floor. I gripped her by the sides of her pelvis bone. I gripped her so hard, my fingernails dug into her flesh. I wanted to hurt her. It made me feel good to hurt her. I watched pigeons once making love. The male with his thick, shiny purple throat danced in circles and cooed. When the female stuck her tail feathers in the air, the male pecked her viciously on the head, his red eyes flashing. Then he jumped on her back and dug his claws into her feathers as he made love to her. He liked hurting her. It was part of his nature to enjoy her pain. It was part of mine, too. Amelia's pain was my pleasure, and I liked it. I jabbed her hard and steady, and she cried, "Oh! Oh! Oh!"

After I came, I flopped over on my side feeling light headed and weak. Amelia leaned down and kissed me all over my face. "I love you," she said. Her voice was tender. She cuddled my head in her lap, and her thighs and stomach felt soft and warm on my face, even motherly. "You must be hungry," she said. "I'll fix you something to eat."

I groaned approvingly, and she got up and went into the kitchen.

"Can I help you?" I asked.

"No," she answered, "I want to wait on you hand and foot."

Within minutes she had the sausage on and frying. The whole house smelled like Grandma Daughter's kitchen. In a few minutes more, she returned carrying a plate smothered with scrambled eggs and crisp brown sausage and golden toast. I sat up and crossed my legs under me to eat. Boy, was it good! I must have been a lot hungrier than I had realized, because I nearly gobbled my food down. Those eggs! She had cooked them in butter with diced onions and green pepper and oregano. I loved it! Amelia lay directly in front of me and smiled as I ate.

"Aren't you eating?" I asked.

"I'm not hungry."

When I finished, she took my plate and I lay flat on my back with my arms and legs sprawled out. I felt good, and I closed my eyes to enjoy the feeling of euphoria.

I don't know how long I lay there cat napping, but when I waked up, Amelia lay hugging my feet with the soles pressed against her breasts. I wiggled my toes. Her breasts shimmied like cups of Jell-o, and she smiled. She got on her knees and sat back on her heels as she rubbed her fingers across the tops of my toes. She leaned forward and lightly sucked two small toes on my right foot. It tickled, but I stifled the urge to smile. She scooted forward between my legs and kissed me on the insides of my thighs. My dick began to swell. She lifted it up out of the way and put my testes, drawn up tight and wrinkled like a bean bag, tenderly into her mouth and sucked them. My dick stood straight up. She worked her way up and licked that, too. But not long. Just long enough to get me worked up. She kissed her way up my stomach pausing a moment to stick her tongue in my navel, then sucked my nipples. By now I was as hot to trot as a three-year-old colt. But I controlled myself. I lay back and enjoyed. She crawled forward straddling my hips and waist, spread her pussy with two fingers, and slid slowly down onto my dick. Then she sat up and moved her behind from side to side until she got a good fit. She wasn't as wet inside now. She felt snug and warm. In fact, it even burned a little when she slid down. As she moved around slowly, it became more and more comfortable.

This position was good for about a minute, until I felt the hint of a climax coming. Then I pulled her down and flopped over on top. She had been right about those eggs increasing my stamina. I worked in and out of her so long that even I was surprised. I didn't even get tired as before. By the time I came, I was so worked up for it that I felt as if I were spitting all my insides into her. She simply lay back and received me, soothed me like Joan of Arc or somebody. I was in actual pain, and she loved every minute of it. She held me close to her, and I enjoyed the warmth and softness and the smell of her body and hair.

We didn't say a word to each other for the rest of the time I was there. We both knew that I had to leave, and I guess since neither one of us wanted to mention it, we just said nothing. I simply got up, put my clothes on and left. I'm not sure I even looked at her again after I got off of her. It was as if I was holding her one minute and driving down Lake Shore Drive the next.

When I got home, I walked in with the collar of my coat turned up. Ida sat in the middle of the couch with her legs crossed and her hands folded in her lap. "I'd like to talk to you when you get your coat off," she said. Her voice sounded sweet.

I went into the bedroom before I took my coat off. I changed shirts, then looked at myself in the mirror. The spot was red and round with well defined teeth marks on two sides.

"Did you hear me, Al?" Ida called.

"I heard you," I answered. I knew something was wrong. She had been making short, snide remarks to me all week, then all of a sudden tonight she wanted to talk. I knew she wanted an explanation of my whereabouts for the last couple of days. What could I tell her? Simple! The cold truth. I would tell her all about Amelia, the shirt, and the mark on my neck. In fact, I would walk out now with my head high flaunting the mark. Then she would *know* where I had been. I remembered how weak and indecisive I felt when Ruby found out about Frieda. This time, I was going to be strong.

But suppose she didn't want an explanation. Suppose she was simply trying a new tactic to get an El Dorado. I decided not to expose the mark until I knew for sure what she wanted. I put a couple of band-aids over the mark, and went into the living room.

"Hi," she said smiling as I walked in.

"What do you want?" I asked.

"What happened to your neck?"

"I cut myself shaving."

"You nearly slit your throat, didn't you?"

"What do you want to talk about?"

She hesitated. then she said, "I went to the doctor today."

"And he told you that you were crazy."

"Not that kind of doctor, dummy. I went to a gynecologist."

"Don't call me a dummy."

"I'm pregnant, Al. And let's not quarrel."

So that was it, the reason behind the sweetness.

"I know I've been a bitch to live with the past few months," she continued, "but you don't know how much I've wanted a baby." She looked at me with an expression I hadn't seen in a long time. Her eyes looked like puppy eyes, big and sincere with complete openness and honesty. It looked as if the old Ida were back.

When I first met Ida, I was living in a two room, cold water flat on Van Buren Street on the near west side. I moved there after leaving the abandoned three-flat at Seventy-seventh and Lake Shore Drive, and I was enrolled at the University of Illinois at Chicago Circle Campus. My apartment was walking distance from school.

Ida was in an art appreciation class with me. We got to know each other because we were the only two blacks there. Before long, we were spending time between classes together. At first, I didn't see anything special in her. She was good looking, and her performance in class was above average. But for some reason, she didn't begin to interest me until one of our talks when she told me that she was an orphan.

"My mother died giving birth to me," she had said, "and my father killed himself that night."

"He killed himself?!" I had said incredulously.

"That's right," she had answered, "hanged himself in the bathroom."

She told me that she had lived in foster homes in Ohio until she got accepted at the University of Illinois. She now lived in a dormitory that she assured me was much like the foster homes in which she had lived most of her life. She had no friends. No one she could talk to or confide in. As a result, our talks in the afternoons meant a lot to her.

I asked her once how life was in foster homes, and she used one word to describe it. Poor! "People take in orphans for the money they get from the state, not because they love children. She said the competition for extra bits of food and clothing was very keen. I suppose that that was what I had expected to hear, because I could see the evidence of deprivation in the way she ate, which was so incongruous with the way she looked. It's odd the way people associate good looks with lots of money.

Ida's skin was the color of roasted almonds. Her face was lean with high cheek bones and a pointed chin, and her large brown eyes looked as if they were placed on a slant like cat's eyes. But when she ate, she ate as if she believed her food might be the last morsel on earth. She took large bites, chewed sparingly, and cleaned up all the crumbs by moistening her fingers, blotting the crumbs up, then licking them off. I got the distinct impression that as a child she never quite had enough to eat.

And she was greedy, not to consume, but merely to have. At buffets, she always overloaded her plate. Then she felt guilty when she couldn't eat it all. She compulsively took two of any free samples offered to her, and she stockpiled items like deodorant and cottonballs and soap whenever she found them on sale. Her redeeming characteristic was her honesty. She was like Mama in that respect, honest in a simple, uncluttered manner. "I can't help it," she had always said. "I always feel like I'm going to run out of everything."

It was her honesty that drew us close together, that gave our talks depth and meaning. I had always been too uncertain of myself to express myself openly. But not her. She had always been candid and unashamed.

I learned just how open she really was about two months into the school year. We met in the student union between classes as usual. But rather than sit and rap about class or religion or life as we usually did, she stepped squarely in front of me and said, "I want to move into your apartment with you."

I was dumbfounded. After all, she had never before even hinted at pursuing any kind of relationship between us. And I suppose my facial expression conveyed my inner feelings, because she repeated it. "I like you," she said, "and I want to move in with you. I want to get out of the dormitory. I want to be closer to my best friend." She then looked me squarely in the eye and waited for me to respond.

It was in February that she told me she was pregnant. I felt then as if the final tie between us had been formed. I think that's when I first realized that I loved her. Before then I had liked her, admired her, even envied her for her spunk and courage. But when I learned that she was carrying my child, and that despite all that had already happened to her in her life she wasn't making any demands on me, I knew that she was the woman for me. Or maybe in my heart of hearts, I longed to recapture the feeling of family I had had with Ruby and Gwendolyn. Whatever my motive, that June after school let out for the summer, I got a hair-cut, put on my dark gray three-button roll, and got a job selling for the American Biscuit Company. Ida wasn't showing yet, so she was able to get a job as a salesgirl at Marshall Field's. I didn't mind because I knew we would need some extra money for the baby bills.

Along about that time too I began wondering if maybe Ida wouldn't want to make our living together legal, so I asked, "Dig, do you think we should get married?"

"If you want to," she answered.

"I only asked because I thought you might want to."

"I know," she countered smiling, and we got married that following Monday at city hall.

Early August was when our first tragedy struck. She was in the bathroom getting ready to go to work. She couldn't have been in there more than five minutes before she moaned, "Al!"

I had never heard her cry before, but the way she called me then, I knew that she was about to. I hopped out of bed. When I got to the bathroom, she was standing in front of the face bowl looking down at the water streaming down her gapped legs and puddling on the floor. If there was any one time when I was glad to have a company car, it was then. I took her straight to Mt. Sinai Hospital where they rushed her to the labor room. In less than an hour, it was over she had given birth to a four pound, still-born baby girl.

That proved to be the turning point in our young marriage. At first, she started buying clothes at Field's where she worked, and I figured she was trying to soothe the pain of having lost the baby. But then she bought a new Chevy Camaro automatic with vinyl top, AM-FM radio, tape deck, wide-oval tires and air-conditioning for only two hundred dollars down. I don't know how her credit check passed, but it did, and her notes were well over one hundred dollars a month. But the car and the clothes weren't enough. She started stealing from her employer. She didn't know that I knew what she was doing and that I didn't believe her stories about catching all the good sales or using her 20% discount. But when she came home with two mink coats, one brown and one silver, I had to step in and stop her. I don't know why I never tried to stop her before. I guess I felt sorry for her and tried to justify her actions in light of our dead child. Now things were getting way out of hand. So, one morning at breakfast I said, "Ida, there's something I want to talk to you about."

She smiled pouring coffee from the percolator she had stolen. "Do you?" she said. "Good, because I want to talk to you, too."

"About what?" I asked.

"I want to move," she said.

"Where to?"

"Lake Meadows Apartments."

"Lake Meadows Apartments?!"

"Yes," she said, "Why? What's wrong with Lake Meadows Apartments?"

"Nothing," I answered, "except that it might be too expensive." The real reason was that I wanted to stay out west near the university. I had planned to go back that fall if I could.

"Oh, we can afford it," she said, "We make enough between the two of us to afford it easily."

"Well, I think it's a bad idea," I answered, and I bit into a piece of toast. Then I said, "Now to what I wanted to talk about. Those coats have to go back."

"Back?" she said, "Why? they don't cost much with my discount."

"Even with your discount," I said, "we can't afford those coats. Besides, I happen to know that you stole them."

She didn't say anything. She just looked at me, then at the crumbs around the toaster. She blotted a few of them up and licked them. "Ok," she said, "you take them back."

"Good deal," I said. "And don't steal anymore, because you might get fired."

"Ok," she said pushing the crumbs into a neat little hill with her finger.

I took the coats back that afternoon. And the next morning at breakfast my eggs were hard, my coffee weak, and my toast burned. I thought it was because she had had a bad morning, so I didn't make anything of it. But when my breakfast was over cooked and burned the next morning, too, I asked, "Have you forgotten how to fry eggs?"

"No, Dear, I just had a bad morning." she used a snide tone, paused a moment, then asked, "Have you thought any more about us moving into Lake Meadows?"

Then I saw it. She had asked me that same question the morning before. She was blackmailing me. Still I said, "Ok, I'll make a deal with you. We can move if you promise to stop stealing."

She agreed. And in the dead of winter with the wind swirling out of the north at ten degrees below zero and fifteen miles an hour and with my hands so cold I could barely move them, we moved to Lake Meadows.

The apartment we moved into was a three room arrangement consisting of a living room with a picture window and view of the sister building, a bedroom with the same view, and a kitchen with no view at all. Naturally, she wanted new furniture for the place, so we went to Field's the next day and charged over four thousand dollars worth of home furnishings: two wool shag rugs, one mint green for the bedroom, the other Aztec gold for the living room; a Swedish leather couch and two round wicker chairs; a stereo hi-fi console with fifteen inch woofers; two brass pole lamps for diagonal corners of the living room; an ebony bedroom suite consisting of a king size bed, dresser and chest of drawers; and a color portable television set. It was all ultra modern. The place looked like a page from *Better Homes and Gardens*, 1990. And I have to admit that even though our furniture bill would be one hundred and fifty dollars a month for the next three years, I liked it. It used to turn me on just to walk in the front door and see that front room. And, too, breakfast was perfect every morning.

Our marriage seemed to be running smoother as well. We bought a book on sophisticated love making techniques, and tried a new position every night that we made love until we settled on two or three favorites. My favorite was entering her from behind, dog style, a position I later used on Amelia countless times. Her's was a cross-legged, side position. And, of course, we still kept the old stand-by missionary position. It was the Christmas of that year that I gave her the white, rose print robe because she needed it, and the diamond ring-- which I couldn't afford when we got married-- because I loved her.

On New Year's Eve, we gave a little party and invited some of our friends that we worked with and their spouses. It was a hit. Every weekend after that for nearly six months, we partied with that same crowd. In the middle of that summer, our clique cooled off as fast as it had fired up. Mary and John Jefferson were the first to break away. He accepted a new job with an insurance company in California, and they relocated there. Then Jill and Tom Simmons, after having an argument at our place over who loved whom the most, got a divorce. They discovered that neither one of them really loved the other one at all. The Kirbys, Felton and Lois, began spending their weekends organizing rallies for some civil rights group, and didn't have time to party anymore. That was it. The clique was dead.

Ida's first readjustment to our slower social life came in the form of a new hair-do. Up until then, she had been wearing her hair much the same as she had when I first met her, in a long, lilting, jet black natural that seemed to become translucent around the edges. But when the clique died, she changed her hair to one of those styles with the big looping curls on top. I hated that hair-do, because it made her look cheap, brassy. She seemed to like it, though, so I never said anything to her about it. One day she even asked me, "How do you like my hair?"

"It looks like hell," I told her.

"What do you mean, it looks like hell?!" she shouted. "I suppose you think you could do it better?"

Obviously, she was just trying to goad me into an argument. I ignored her. Then she really turned it on, "You black bastard! You can't tell me my hair looks like hell and get away with it." I wondered what ever happened to all that poise and dignity she had seemed to have. Could she have been putting me on all this time with an act? I remembered the act I had put on for Ruby's party.

"I hate you, I hate you!" she shouted.

I wondered too what happened to that honesty between us?

"You're an inconsiderate pig," she shouted.

"If you didn't want to know," I said, "you shouldn't have asked."

That stopped her. I was surprised, because she looked at me with slow blinking eyes as if remembering how it used to be between us. Then she went quietly into the bedroom and closed the door.

Then one morning about a week before the second moon shot as I sat down at the breakfast nook and sipped my coffee, I noticed it was weak. She hadn't set my plate before me yet, so I had a little time to sit hoping maybe the eggs and toast would be all right. But, sure enough, the eggs were hard as door jams. This was too much. "Ok," I said, "What the hell is it this time?"

Apparently, I didn't sound as mad as I thought I had, because without one moment's hesitation and with an innocent tone of voice, she said, "I want a new car."

"But you just bought a new car last year," I said.

"I don't care," she said, "I don't like it, and I want a new one.

"But it's not paid for!"

"I don't care. I want something I like. I want an El Dorado."

"An El Dora. . .! Then I caught myself. Surely, she wasn't serious. I didn't even bother to answer her. In fact, we hardly said more than five words to each other again until a week later on the morning of the moon shot. All during that time, all my meals were either burned, watery, or over salted.

So now, sitting in the living room after having just spent most of the this evening with another woman, and watching Ida metamorphose back into the sweet woman I had married, my feelings were mixed. I liked the way Amelia made me feel, but I loved Ida. I listened with an anticipation that bordered on anguish.

"The ultimate fulfillment for me as a woman," she said, "is to bear a child. And when I lost the first one, I directed all of my energy to material goals to make me forget. I don't want to lose this one. We had a beautiful relationship once, and we can have it again. I'm going to really try. I won't steal anymore, I won't bug you about a new car, or anything. I want us to make it, Al. And I want you to help me make our marriage work."

Goddammit! Why couldn't she have told me this yesterday morning before I met Amelia? What did she expect me to do, turn all my love and consideration on and off like a faucet?

"Will you help me, Al?" she repeated.

I hesitated because I was unsure of what to say. Then I asked, "Do you want the same honesty we had before with each of us putting everything in the open?"

"That's the only way I'll have it," she answered.

I knew she had no idea of the painful truth I was about to tell her. But knowing her, it wouldn't matter. She would want to hear it, anyway. I was just about to say, I've been making love to another woman. The words were already in my throat when I decided not to do it. I simply wasn't confident enough in myself to make a confession like that without looking and sounding sheepish. I was obligated to tell the truth if she asked, but not to volunteer it. And since my confession might also imply a willingness to give Amelia up, I didn't want to do it.

"Ok," I said instead, "I'll help you save our marriage."

She smiled. Her brown skin looked soft in the fading light from the window. She looked me straight in the eye and asked, "Where have you been the last two days?"

I turned my eyes away to avoid her gaze. This was it. I had to be strong.

"Felton called here about two hours ago and asked for you," she said. "I also found out that you didn't get to his house until ten o'clock last night."

What was I afraid of? All I had to do was tell her where I had been. Whatever happened after that just happened. I wasn't going to give Amelia up. That was simply out of the question. So there was no reason for not telling Ida the truth. I did exactly that. "I've found a girlfriend," I said.

"A girlfriend or a mistress?" she asked. Her gaze into my eyes remained steady.

I reached up and slowly pulled the band-aids off my neck. She didn't bat an eye as she looked at the bite mark. In fact, she was so cool that I wondered whether or not she recognized what it was.

Then she said, "She must have been good."

"She was," I answered.

"Are you going to stop seeing her?"

Ruby had asked me that same question. "No," I answered. "I'm going to keep you both."

"Does she know you're married?" she asked.

"Yes." Then I asked, "What did Felton want?"

"He wanted you to come back to his house tonight and bring me with you."

"Do you want to go?" I asked. I hoped she would say no, because I didn't want to sit through another one of Mike's lectures.

"I might," she said. "Are they having a party or something?"

"No, they're conducting a class on current events relative to blacks in America."

"Oh?" She asked, "Who's teaching it?"

"Felton's cousin, Mike."

"Is it any good?"

"It's interesting," I answered, "but I disagree with a lot he has to say."

"I think I'd like to go," she said.

Damn! She would want to go. "Ok," I said, "We'll leave at nine-thirty."

By now it was dark. I turned on the television set hoping to catch the news or a special progress report on the moon shot. I was in luck. A special report had just started, and they planned to show some live scenes from space. I sat down to enjoy, to take pleasure in the technological progress gained through years of pain and toil and study by mankind.

"Are you hungry?" Ida asked.

"A little. But I'm not in the mood for anything burned or salty."

"It won't be," she said.

VI

The lecture at Felton's house went pretty much the same as the one last night. Only this time I sat in back, and kept quiet. Every now and then as Mike talked about how much honkies hated niggers and how niggers were such fools for continually believing the lies of love and brotherhood told by honkies, I sniffed the faint smell of Amelia's pussy still lingering on my fingers. Soon, Mike neared the end of the session. I could tell that Ida had taken in every word he had said. The muscles in her smooth jaws flexed lightly as she listened and looked at the pictures of charred, mutilated black bodies taken somewhere in Mississippi. And for the first time since she lost the baby, I saw the glint of tears welling up in her eyes. She had really fallen for Mike's story.

They had a discussion period after the lecture just as they had last night. But Ida said that she was tired and that she didn't want to stay. I was thankful for that. I was in no mood to argue with Mike on point after point in the presentation.

Ida didn't say a word until we were nearly half way home. For a while, I thought maybe she had forgotten her promise and had reverted to her tactics for pressuring me into buying an El Dorado. But then she asked, "On which points didn't you agree with Mike?"

"On a number of points," I answered, "but primarily, I disagree with the premise that white people are out to systematically exterminate black people in this country."

She didn't answer.

"Did you believe what he had to say?" I asked.

"Every word."

"Then you're a fool," I said. "that jive about the gas train isn't true. It can't be. And all that other crap! It isn't true. Besides, where did he get all that information? Were his sources reliable?"

"One of his sources was a government document," she said.

"My butt!" I countered. "He just said that to make what he had to say sound important."

"Well, I believed him," she said, "and I still do."

That was all we said for the rest of the way home. Just as well, too. Because I didn't feel like arguing.

When we got home, I parked the car and got out. Ida got out, too, and discovered that she didn't have her purse with her.

"You probably left it at Felton's house," I said. "We can get it tomorrow."

"No," she said, "I have to have it tonight. The doctor put me on some pills which are in that purse, and I have to take one before I go to bed."

We drove all the way back. I told Ida to wait downstairs in the car while I went up and got her things, but she wanted to come, too. We both went back upstairs. It seemed silly both of us fetching one purse.

All the other guests had gone, and Felton, Lois and Mike were alone when we walked in.

"We came for Ida's purse," I said.

"I know," Lois said, "We found it on the floor after everybody left. Come on in. I'll get it for you."

She closed the door behind us, and went into the bedroom.

"Why don't you have a little taste before you go?" Felton said holding a bottle of whiskey up for me to see.

Mike sat back on the couch sipping a whiskey and water.

"Just a shot," I said, and walked towards the bar.

Just then someone pounded on the front door so hard, my pulse quickened. "Open up," he said, "it's the police."

I wondered where they had come from so quickly. I know they weren't around when Ida and I came up. They must have been in another apartment. Mike sat up and started looking around frantically. I guess he didn't hear who the man said he was, and thought that it was somebody trying to break in.

"What's the matter," I said, "It's only the police."

Felton looked scared, too, as he signaled Mike into the kitchen. What the hell was going on? Was everybody here out of their minds? It was the police; we were safe. Yet, Ida cringed by the wall; Mike and Felton fumbled with the lock on the back door; and Lois fumbled around trying to dress Felton Junior. This place looked like a loony pen.

Then the police broke the front door in. They obviously had the wrong house, but unless somebody told them, they might hurt someone by mistake. Clearly, it was up to me. And I was up to the challenge. I approached the first one through the door. He was a big man with fine lines etched at the corners of his thin lips and eyes.

"Look," I explained, "there must be some mistake."

He didn't stop to listen. Using his forward momentum as added power, he hit me in the mouth so hard that my head snapped straight back as far as it would go. In that one split second as his fist connected, I thought my neck was broken and my whole face crushed. I don't remember hitting the floor, but that's where I woke up, face down with a knee in my back and my right arm being twisted so far around that my hand reached the back of my head. I could almost feel an ache in my chest where my ribs had been broken when Lillian's car hit that tree on the road to Frankfurt.

I couldn't see much from where I was, only the purple outline of roses against the royal blue background of the rug on the floor. It's funny how the seemingly random pattern of a rug is in reality a complex geometric design. But I heard everything. The man on top of me shouted orders. "Get those two in the kitchen! And these women, too! Bring the women!" I heard Ida scream, "Let me go! Let me go!" Felton Junior cried, "Mommy, Mommy! Make them stop hitting Daddy, Mommy! Make them stop!"

My arm felt as if it were being torn from my shoulder. And I think I heard that creep kneeling in my back chuckle under his breath.

I cried out, "You're breaking my arm!"

He hit me again, this time in the neck with the side of his hand forcing my face hard into the floor. The purple roses faded into the royal blue background, and the noise around me drifted into silence.

When I woke up again, the big cop was dragging me out of the squad car in front of the station. My shoulder and neck and face ached. My mouth was swollen and tasted of blood. I wanted to touch my face to check the swelling, but my hands were cuffed behind me. The metal cut into my wrists as I squirmed.

They pushed Ida, Lois still carrying Felton junior, and me in front of the desk sergeant. That's where I began my protest. "Sergeant," I said, "I want to file a complaint against this officer for illegal entry and arrest."

"What are they charged with," the pock-faced sergeant asked.

"He's charged with attacking an officer," the big cop said, "and they're all charged with obstructing justice."

"What?" I yelled, "Charged with attacking an officer?" Boy, I was mad! Two days, and two fucked up cops! I was batting an even one thousand. I continued, "This dumb clown kicked the door in and . . ."

"But," the big cop cut me off, "in view of the fact that it was late and they were probably tired and didn't realize what they were doing, I won't press charges."

"You won't press charges?" I shouted, "You don't have any charges to press."

"Be cool," Lois said, "before they put us in jail, too." She was right. I shut up. But I was still mad.

The big cop took the cuffs off of me, and the pock-faced sergeant said, "You can go now."

We left the station and took a cab back to Lois' house, and saw her upstairs. I went into the bathroom and looked at myself in the mirror. My lip had felt big and grotesque. Now I knew that it looked that way, too. It was swollen to nearly twice its normal size, and as I pulled it up with my finger-- I couldn't lift it up on its own-- I saw that my teeth were all bloody. I washed my mouth out with some water and went back into the living room.

Lois and Ida sat talking on the couch. Ida asked why they did it, and Lois answered that they had been after Mike for a long time because of his revolutionary teachings. "The only reason they let us go," she said, "was because they were only after Mike." It seemed that they had arrested him a couple of times in the past on trumped up charges and warned him to be cool. But he didn't stop teaching. Lois said that he was really dedicated, and that we were lucky we got a chance to hear him. I didn't say anything. She said that she feared that this time he would be charged with possession of dope, and jailed. And Felton, too. "You don't know these pigs, Al," she continued, "You never seen them jump out of squad cars and beat two or three dudes up on the side walk at high noon for no reason other than because they looked suspicious. And they put them in jail without bond on phony dope charges. No,

Al," she said shaking her little head back and forth, "you just don't know these pigs."

I knew that she was not exaggerating. This wasn't Nazi Germany, but the recollection of that big squint-eyed cop busting in the house and knocking me flat on my behind quickly substantiated the notion that it could be.

We talked for fifteen or twenty minutes more before Ida and I decided to go. After making sure Lois would be all right there alone, we left.

We said nothing to each other all the way home. I suppose we were both thinking of what a price we had to pay for forgetting a purse. As long as I had known Ida, she had never forgotten her purse. Why had she forgotten it tonight of all nights?

When I woke up the following morning, I felt as if I had been drugged. I was in the same position in which I had gone to sleep, and it took a conscious effort to even open my eyes. As I blinked them slowly, they pulled at the tightness in my face and lips. I tried to yawn, but it hurt too much, so I cut it short. Then I tried to raise up. But as soon as I tightened the muscles in my neck, I cut that venture short, too. I didn't even try to roll over, because I knew my shoulder was sore. In fact, it had even ached as I slept. I simply lay there blinking at the white ceiling.

Ida, who was still in bed next to me, said, "You know, Al, I think I'm going to quit my job."

It took a minute to work up the energy to ask, "Why?" My voice sounded hoarse, and it cracked a little. I was really in bad shape.

"I'm going to join the movement," she answered.

I didn't say anything. Last night I began to see the urgency of Mike's lecture, but the notion of joining some movement seemed far-fetched.

"What do you think of the idea?" she asked.

"I'm not sure," I answered. I wondered if I should go back to Germany for *Seine Kinder*. After all, if I was going to risk my life for a group, I might as well be the leader. "What groups do you plan to check out?"

"I don't know," she answered. "The Black Legion has a store front office on Thirty-fifth Street. Maybe I'll start by just going down there and seeing what they're into."

I blinked at the ceiling for several more seconds before she said, "Think about it, because I think maybe I want us to join together."

I said that I would think about it. She got up and went into the bathroom to clean up.

For some reason, the notion of joining a militant organization-- which I'm sure is the kind of organization she had in mind-- didn't appeal to me even when considering all that had happened to me the past couple of days. I had run into a streak of bad luck, that's all. I couldn't judge every cop by the two I had met.

I reached over to the night stand for a cigarette. As I did, the phone rang. It was Lois.

"Al," she said, "Felton just called. He and Mike have been charged with possession of controlled drugs, and they'll need a lawyer when they go to court Monday morning at ten o'clock. Do you know where we can get a good one?"

I told her that I didn't know of one, but that maybe I could get a recommendation from a friend, and that I would call her later this evening. Then I called Amelia. Her father had some lawyer friends. Maybe one of them could recommend a good criminal lawyer.

"Hi, lover," she said, "Are you about ready for another session?"

"Not today," I answered, "I got into a fight last night, and I'm beat up pretty bad. I called to find out whether or not you know of a good criminal lawyer."

"Why do you need a lawyer? Did you rob somebody?"

"No," I answered, "a friend of mine got picked up on a dope charge and they go to court for a hearing tomorrow morning."

"I don't know," she said. "Why don't you come on over, and we can talk about it."

"Not today, baby. I hurt so bad, I might not even get out of bed. But call your father. He might know of somebody, and call me back later."

She said that she would. When Ida finished her shower, she served me breakfast in bed, and everything was perfect. The eggs were over light, the bacon crisp, the toast brown, and the coffee strong. It's too bad I couldn't enjoy it with my mouth busted up the way it was. After breakfast, she wheeled the TV set into the bedroom for me to watch. When the football game came on, I watched most of it, though I dozed a good deal of the time. The Rams played somebody and beat them 27 to 10. Roman Gabriel threw two touchdown passes. During the football score board program, Amelia called me back. She told me that her father couldn't recommend anyone who would handle the case for less than three hundred dollars cash in advance, and another three hundred in two weeks, so I told her to forget it. Then I called Lois and told her that I couldn't get any recommendations. That must have been around three-thirty or four o'clock, because shortly there after, I got up and wheeled the TV back into the living room to watch it. I watched the news of the Apollo 12 moon shot until it was time to eat dinner. We had roast beef, mashed potatoes and gravy, squash, a salad, and hot rolls and butter. Once again, the meal was perfect. The roast beef was red and the mashed potatoes were smooth. By the time we were ready to go to bed, I felt as if I had been as pampered as a prize winning pussy cat. Ida had really turned over a new leaf.

Then came the morning. Monday mornings for me were usually bad, but this Monday was worst than usual. Or at least it would have been because of the stiffness still in my shoulder and neck, and the swelling in my face. But again Ida saved the day. She got up early and put some coffee on and had a cup ready when I got up. After a hot shower and a good breakfast, I felt almost good.

It took ten minutes longer than usual to get to the office that morning. I had to drive slower than usual to allow myself more reaction time in case I got into a tight spot. I certainly didn't want to have to jam on the brakes in my condition. Fortunately, I had left fifteen minutes earlier as well.

Joe greeted me as I walked in. His phony electric smile was turned on full current forcing his cheeks to stand plump and red, and causing his fully exposed teeth to sparkle. But as usual his pale blue eyes were dead. "Morning, Al," he said, "looks like you've had a little accident." He looked straight at my mouth, and his eyes almost came to life. Or maybe they just looked as if they almost came to life because he blinked them twice in rapid succession.

But the fact is, I believe he was glad to see me bruised up. It was common knowledge that Joe had put up the most resistance to the American plan of hiring black men as salesmen. He had held out as long as he could. But one day a few years ago a white salesman got shot to death in one of his black districts and none of his other salesmen would service those stores. He serviced them himself for about a month until three boys about fifteen years old cornered him outside the same store where the other salesman had been shot, and took all his money. The very next day, he hired Felton.

"I walked into a door," I said, and headed for my desk.

I finished my orders from Friday, and turned them in. I wanted to get a good start today. Today marked the beginning of a four week push on the 8 ounce round cracker stack-pak and subsequent contest, and with first prize being a midnight blue, all wool blazer and a gold wrist watch, I wanted to try to build up an early lead. With all the stores I had in the black areas of the city, I could win this contest blindfolded. Black people seemed to buy more of these crackers than any other kind we made. The reason was because they were cheap. They're only nineteen cents a box, and because black people don't have much money to spend, they buy in small quantities. But in so doing, they establish a costly habit, in that they buy that size all the time, even when it costs more to do it. In white communities, the people buy the 16 ounce size most often, and take advantage of the savings that go with buying the larger quantity. But not black folks. I've seen black people reach over the 16 ounce size out of habit and pick up two of the 8 ounce sizes and end up spending an extra nickel. This contest was made to order for me, and I was determined to win.

I went to the loading dock which was situated in the back of the building, and picked up my weekly supply of promotional materials: displays, coupons, special deal forms, etc., and loaded them into the back seat of my car. On Mondays, my district was usually on the southeast side of town. But because of the contest, I decided to go west to the Blue Pigeon Super Mart first. BP would order a hundred cases with no sweat. And if I rapped some, he might even buy a hundred and twenty-five cases.

When I walked in, BP was dumping a bushel basket full of plastic-covered carrots onto the produce counter. His legs were so short that he had to stand on his little toes for additional leverage. "What's happenin', BP?" I said walking towards him.

He turned his head around. "American Cookies! What are you doing here? Today's not Friday."

"I know," I said, "But I made a special trip to sell you some thirty-eight eighty-three's on a deal." 3883 was the code number for 8 ounce cracker stack-paks.

"How much is the deal?" He asked as he arranged the packages of carrots in neat rows.

"We're offering you fifty cents a case off."

"Good," he said, "I'll take two hundred cases." He finished arranging the carrots, then wiped his hands on his already dirty apron. "I can put them on sale for seventeen cents a box and clean up."

"That's right," I said writing the order. He surprised my by ordering that many cases, and I wanted to get the order filled out and have him sign it before he changed his mind.

"Niggers really eat up some 3883s," he said, "I believe they live off of them. 3883s and water." He chuckled.

He had probably had a little nip this morning, and was feeling good.

"That's right," I said still scribbling. "One ounce of 3883s contain 30% of the minimum daily requirement of niacin and vitamin A as set by the U. S. Government."

That was a pitch I sometimes used. But it was true. It said so right on the package.

"Man," BP said, "You know as well as I do that those crackers don't contain a damn thing."

I smiled and gave him the order form to sign. I smiled because I didn't want to disagree with him after getting such a beautiful order. But my smile must have drawn his attention to my mouth.

"Who smacked you?" he asked, signing the form.

"A cop," I answered.

"For what?" He gave me the form back.

"Nothing," I said.

"You're lucky he didn't snuff you out," he said, "He would have done that for nothing, too."

"I know," I said filing the order away in my briefcase.

By lunch time, I had sold another thirty cases. I had already sold enough to win the prize, and I hadn't even been to half of my stores. Some of the stiffness was gone from my neck, although my shoulder still ached.

I called Felton's house to see if Lois had heard anything about Felton's hearing. There was no answer. I was surprised that Joe didn't ask about Felton this morning, and at the same time, I was glad, because I didn't feel like explaining why Felton was in jail.

The rest of the day went pretty fast. I made six more stores and sold a total of fifteen more cases.

When I got home, I saw Ida's Camaro in the parking lot. When I got upstairs, she, Lois and Felton were sitting in the living room. They didn't say anything as I walked in. Felton sat leaning forward in one of the round wicker chairs and staring at his tightly folded hands. Lois sat on the couch staring into the carpet, and Ida stood up slowly and walked towards me. "Mike is dead," she said, "They killed him in the station."

"What?"

"That's right," Felton said from the corner. "The pigs vamped on Mike right in the station."

"How do you know?" I asked, "Did you see them." My mind was dazed. I still couldn't believe Mike was dead.

"I didn't see them do it," Felton said, "But Saturday night they took us in the back of the station together, and put us in separate cells. I wondered why they put Mike and me into the paddy wagon by ourselves. Now, I know. They had planned to kill us both. But they spared me for some reason. They even let me have my one phone call. But when one of them took the stand today and said that Mike had been killed while resisting arrest, I nearly fell out. Then they dismissed my case on lack of sufficient evidence."

"But are you sure he's dead," I asked.

"We're sure," Ida said. "Lois called me from the station after Felton's hearing, and we all went down to the county morgue and saw him."

Well, that was it. I sat in the other wicker chair near the door. BP sure knew what he was talking about when he said that that cop would have snuffed me out for nothing. I suddenly felt as if the whole legal system in this country were a joke, a game played for the amusement of some at the expense and pain of others. Mike was dead. And why? For telling the truth as he saw it, and no other reason. I sat silent with the others now. There was nothing to be said. Mike had said it all in his lecture. What you don't see and believe today, the man will show you and make you believe tomorrow.

We sat there for a good twenty minutes before the phone rang. And because I was closest to it, I answered it. It was Joe. "Hi, Al," he said, "How are you?" I knew he had something on his mind, because he rarely phoned me at home. Whenever he did and started off with, "Hi, Al, how are you?" it was a sure sign of trouble.

"I'm fine, Joe," I said, "How are you?"

"Fine, fine." He hesitated. "Eh, Al," he said, "We've received a registered letter today from Mr. Arnold Steinberg, Attorney at Law, who is representing a Mr. Louis Angelo. They're suing American Biscuits and the Universal Insurance Company for ten thousand dollars in some personal injury case. Do you know anything about this?"

That damn Angelo! He sure didn't waste any time getting the legal wheels in motion. "Yeah," I said, "I had a little run in with Angelo Friday after work. He claims I hit him with my car."

"Did you?" Joe asked.

"Hell, no!" I said, "But the creep must think that he can get away with an out of court settlement or something."

"Why didn't you report it?" Joe asked, "You're supposed to report all accidents."

"I didn't consider it an accident," I said. "I didn't hit him."

"Well, did you at least fill out the accident card in the glove compartment?"

"I did better than that. I wrote out all the details of the incident in composition form just in case he tried something like this."

"Good," he said, "We might be able to beat this thing. Did you have any witnesses?"

"Yes," I said, "I had one. A girl named Amelia Walker."

"Good! Do you have her phone number?"

I gave it to him, and told him that I would bring a copy of the details to work with me in the morning. I hung up.

Ida said, "You know, Al, before you came in, we were discussing my joining the Black Legion. I think I'm going to do it."

Felton looked at her. "Right on, sister." He shook his head from side to side slowly for emphasis.

"Are you and Lois joining, too," I asked him.

"We already have," he replied. "I plan to quit my job tomorrow and work for the movement full time."

"How are you going to get money?"

"If I have to, I'll steal it," he said. "But we won't be needing much money anymore. We're giving up our apartment and all unpaid furniture, and moving into a cheap little place a few blocks from the legion office."

"Are you quitting your job, too," I asked Ida.

She looked me straight in the eye, "Yes."

The next couple of days were a period of transition for our families. Tuesday morning, Felton came to the office, told Joe to mail his check to my house, and he quit. When Joe tried to explain to Felton all he was giving up by quitting, Felton told him to kiss his black ass, and walked out. Wednesday, he and his family moved. In the meantime, Ida quit at Field's. She simply called them and said that she wasn't coming back. Then she got a natural. Her hair was on tiny blue rollers at first, then she lifted it into a big bouffant do. When I brought it to her attention that her new hair-do was no more natural than the old one, she said that it would have to do until her hair grew back out.

Thursday night, we waked Mike. All of Mike's family came as well as half the Chicago membership of the Black Legion, some wearing blue Levi jackets, some wearing army green field jackets, all wearing black berets with a little silver or gold four-pointed star pinned in front.

We all viewed the body at least once. He was dressed in a brown worsted suit and white shirt, his eyes and lips sewn tightly closed. I had known that dead people rarely looked like themselves. Grandma

Daughter certainly didn't look like herself when she died, and Mike was no exception. His jowls were too fat as if the cavities in his face had been over filled. His once black skin looked lighter as if powder had been used to brighten his complexion. And that same powder left his skin mat instead of shiny, dry instead of moist. Just over his left eye, his forehead looked sunken as if the bone structure had been reset.

His funeral was Friday morning. I couldn't go to it, because I still had to work. But Ida told me that a lot of people were there, too, and that the pastor of the church Mike used to go to when he was younger and still with his parents gave the sermon. According to Ida, the Pastor-- Reverend Sydney Johns was his name-- remembered Mike as an intelligent, sensitive young man with an over active curiosity. Reverend Johns seemed to imply that Mike's over active curiosity was the cause of his death and that some questions go better unasked, go better left to God. But Ida disagreed with him. She told me that she believed all questions eventually have to be asked, and that the questions posed by Mike concerning the future of black people in this country were long overdue. I wondered what Amelia would have to say about the notion of askable or unaskable questions. I saw then how convenient her non-existence theory was, because she could simply deny the existence of all questions, askable or not. It saved one the problem of philosophical decision making. That in itself, I suppose, could be construed as good. More likely, it was just a cop-out.

I spent a lot of time with Amelia the next few weeks. With Ida spending twelve to fourteen hours a day at the Black Legion office, my time was pretty much my own. I'm sure Ida knew I was spending time away from home, but she never asked how much, and I never told her. In fact, we rarely discussed my girlfriend at all.   I asked Amelia during that time if she had heard anything from the American Biscuit

Company concerning the Angelo case, and she hadn't. So I dismissed the matter. I assumed that Joe gave all the information that I had given him to the proper people.

Most of the time Amelia and I spent together, we spent making love. In fact, our whole relationship was deteriorating to a physical plane. Or maybe that's where it had always been. But for awhile, at least, I used to like to think of our relationship as meaningful. Now it was just screw and suck and lick and screw. I screwed her everyday after work, and sometimes I stopped by her house during my lunch hour and screwed her. I screwed her every weekend. I screwed her in the pussy, in the mouth, between her titties, between her knees, between her hands, everywhere. We were like dogs. One week, I don't think I said one word to her all week. I just walked in six days straight, screwed her, and walked out.

Once in a while, Ida would ask if I had screwed Amelia that day. I would say yes. "And now you want to screw me?" she would ask. And I would roll onto her body, and she would let me in.

VII

On the second Friday in December, American Biscuits had their 1970 kick-off meeting in the King's Room of the Regal Hotel on Michigan Avenue. It was an all day deal. But because none of the salesmen had to go to any stores that day, most of us were happy to be there. Or maybe we were just looking forward to the cocktails and American kick-off banquet. In either case, we were happy.

The King's Room of the Regal Hotel looked as big as a barn. The ceiling and walls were painted such a brilliant shade of white that it looked almost as luminous in there as it did outside. I resisted the expectation to hear a toilet flush. Thick beams crisscrossed the ceiling at regular intervals, and were lavishly ornamented with plump, white apples and silvery leaves. Paintings of Cupid and weightless lovers in green gardens with rolling white clouds and blue sky in the background filled the three big squares formed by the ceiling beams, and crystal chandeliers hung one from each end of the beams along both sides of the room. A balcony ran around both sides and the back of the room, and the railing along the balcony seemed to creak under the weight of the fruit and leaves and Cupids. Silver curtains hung in the alcoves along the walls, and light fixtures that looked like albino mermaids doing swan dives from the tops of the alcoves with light bulbs crowning their heads cast additional light into the room. The place looked like a palace; hence, I suppose, its name, the King's Room.

Only at the floor level were there any signs of a convention. But there were plenty of them there. A twenty foot red silk banner with the words "The United States of American" inscribed in silver glittering letters hung behind the speaker's lectern, and countless red, white and blue posters and streamers that read "AMERICAN BISCUITS" hung along the walls and on tripods flanking the exits. So great was the contrast between the upper and lower portions of the room that the overall effect was like juxtaposing modern America with Renaissance Italy.

Before long, Jonathan Schmidt, president of American Biscuits, took the stand. "Ok, men," he said, "let's be seated and get this meeting under way." Everyone in the room shuffled into their seats, and the hum of conversation and short bursts of laughter dwindled to a dead silence.

Schmidt was a short, fat, bald-headed man in a blue shark skin suit smoking a long, olive green cigar. This was the first time I had ever seen the man in person, because his office was in the main office in New York. But I'd heard about him. Mainly I had heard that he was a strict disciplinarian. He stood erect causing his stomach to stick way out in front of him. His stomach looked as if it were so heavy that he had to lean back for better leverage in order to ease the burden of carrying it. It was round, round like his head which reflected the light from the ceiling. His pink jowls and double chin flexed as he munched his cigar. He looked like a symbol of authority despite his clipped stature, and his voice helped to reinforce his image. It bellowed as he spoke. "Today, men," he said still clutching the green cigar in the corner of his mouth, "I have the honor of presenting Gold Star awards to those men whose performances this month have been outstanding. It's not often that I agree to present these awards, because as a rule they're given to mediocre salesmen to prevent having a stock pile of gold stars. But not this time. This time I have personally gone over the records of these three men, and I am convinced that these men are more than worthy of the awards."

I had to hand it to him, this man carried himself and spoke with true confidence. Joe told me Schmidt's success story when I first started with the company. In fact, it was probably company policy to tell this story, but it was still interesting. It seems that Schmidt had made it up in his mind when he was a teenager that he would not allow his height to interfere with his success, and then had stuck by his decision. With constant practice, he slowly converted his shortness from a drawback into an asset. In order to succeed in a tall man's world, he had to be better at his job. His co-workers and superiors knew it. They reasoned that he had to be one hell of a salesman in order to gain the customers confidence enough to sell the customer more than he wanted. They were right. He sold his way from a salesman to a supervisor in five years, and to president of the company in fifteen. Even as he called the names of the gold star recipients and they came forward to receive the awards, they seemed to be walking slightly bent over as if they were ashamed of being tall in the presence of this short but dynamic man among men.

Schmidt continued as the three men returned to their seats, "Let's give them all a big hand for a job well done." He clapped, and we all followed suit.

Next, Schmidt gave us a run down of the amount of additional sales we had made throughout the country in 1969 over 1968, and then told us how well we did in the Midwest and in the Chicago area. It seemed that nationally we were ten percent over 1968 in dollars, but only five percent over in tonnage. That meant that we were not selling cakes and crackers at a rate fast enough to keep pace with the growing population. We were falling behind. Worse, the midwestern area, and Chicago in particular, fell below the national average.

Then he told us that he wasn't worried, because next year we would do better. He knew we would do better, because we were all go-getters who would jump at the chance to go on a two week Caribbean cruise, first prize in a new incentive program for the first quarter of 1970. "That's right," he said, "an all expense paid Caribbean cruise." He sounded like a late night talk show master of ceremonies introducing his guests. We applauded. If we were worked up about the first prize trip when he mentioned it, we were even more worked up after he showed us a slide presentation of all the high points of the cruise. It was in full, living color showing palm trees and sandy beaches and white villas on the bay and black limbo dancers and everything. In each scene, there was a man, whom we assumed was any typical American businessman, doing something new and exciting, or quite and relaxing. He fished awhile, danced awhile and drank beer all the while. Then he slept, sunbathed, and swam. A woman accompanied him, and we assumed she was his wife. The clod wore the same outfit for the whole trip so that we would have no trouble recognizing him. He wore red and green striped Bermuda shorts with an orange and blue flower print shirt. He was quite conspicuous.

The rest of the time until lunch was taken up with facts and figures on projected sales and growth of the company, mass media advertising, new products and packages, and a new bonus program. It was impossible to remember much of it though, because we were bombarded with so much information. Besides, it was after lunch that the real force of the convention came to bear. Schmidt stood before us still clutching his cigar, and said, "Gentlemen, now we come to the part of the program we've all been waiting for. The presentation of new merchandising material for the American salesman in 1970." His voice sounded almost reverent. "The theme for next year will be 'The United

States.'" He gestured to the two veiled tripods flanking him. "Here we have six brand new posters that we can put on display in the stores to help sell our products, and they each exemplify a united state, or a state of being united." He pulled the veil off the first tripod revealing a full color, 18 by 24 inch lay-out of brown sugar cake and yellow ice cream. "American Cake and Ice Cream," he said, "The first united state!"

We applauded.

He unveiled the second tripod. "The second united state, peanut butter and American Crackers!"

We applauded again.

The third united state was stacked behind the first one. "Cake and coffee!"

By now, I was getting tired of clapping, but Joe, who sat next to me, still clapped enthusiastically.

"Crackers and soup," Schmidt said for the fourth one.

At this point, Schmidt removed the third and fourth states from the tripods and exposed two blank white posters. "Something's wrong," he said, "I know we had six posters here. What happened to the other two?" He winked at us, then looked behind the blank posters. "Oh, here they are," he said. Then he looked out at us. "I guess most of you know that I pretended to lose the last two posters just to regain your attention. I didn't want any of you to miss these two babies."

The fifth united state was so elaborate that it made the first four look like snapshots. It was a picture of cookies and milk done in iridescent whites and browns, and trimmed with sparkling silver foil. The poster received a standing ovation. Joe was so moved by the sight of that poster that he nudged me nearly ten times. "Look at that, Al," he said, "Posters like that are what keep us on top." He clapped and whistled as loud as he could. "That poster set up by our cookies will boost our sales by fifteen percent."

Now, I like boosting my sales as much as the next guy. And I do like merchandising material such as good display posters which help me sell more. But Joe was ridiculous. I simply couldn't work up that kind of enthusiasm over a poster.

By now, Schmidt was about to uncover the last of the six posters. I could tell by the way he was hesitating that this was going to be the ultimate in advertising art. Right then, I had a hunch. I knew what the final united state was. Schmidt uncovered it, and I was right. There in iridescent orange and white and trimmed in shimmering gold, star-studded foil stood the final poster. Cheese and crackers. Wow.

It took nearly fifteen minutes for the cheering to subside. All the while I had the distinct feeling that I was attending a high school football pep rally rather than a American sales convention. Joe even worked up a sweat cheering, and smelled musty when he sat down.

Schmidt held his hands in the air gesturing for quiet. "Now we're going to pass out copies of a study," he said, smiling a toothy grin, "that was conducted by the Blue Peacock Food Stores showing the growing emphasis on local merchandising. This study proves that posters like these and shelf talkers sell more product."

The studies he passed out consisted of five type-written pages covered with graphs and tables which explained by what percentage local merchandising material increased sales. The thing that I noticed first, though, sat right in the middle of page two. It was a table showing the average weekly volume of their stores in different neighborhoods. It read:

HIGH INCOME		YG SUBURB		BLUE COLLAR		NEGRO	
$	PCS	$	PCS	$	PCS	$	PCS
38057	99311	38025	95071	37596	95162	38059	90181

What struck me was the fact that more money was made on fewer sales in the Negro community than in any other group.

I told Amelia about the study later that evening.

"Well, there must be a reason for it," she said, "They wouldn't just charge black people more for no reason."

"That is exactly the point I'm trying to make," I countered, "They *are* charging us more for no reason."

I even showed her the copy of the study that I had been given along with the calculations I had made. She wasn't impressed.

"I don't believe it," she said.

As soon as she spoke, I recalled the argument I had had with Mike. Here I was giving Amelia facts, and she wouldn't believe me. Mike had been giving me facts, too, and I wouldn't believe him. What a fool I had been! What a fool!

I got so mad at myself thinking about it that I made myself sick. I began getting cramps in my stomach and the more I thought about it, the worse the cramps became. What's more, I had expected Amelia to believe me without question, just as Mike had expected me to believe without question. I was telling the truth. Maybe Mike had been, too. The cramps in my stomach became more and more intense.

The following Monday, our traffic cases came up in court. It had snowed the night before, and everything that morning looked new and white and clean. Joe knew when my court date was, so I didn't bother to call in. I simply picked Amelia up, and by ten o'clock, we were in courtroom number three in Traffic Court where Judge Jesse Carter, an old man with thick white hair and whose right eyebrow seemed perpetually cocked higher than the left one, presided. Amelia's case came up first. The court clerk, a big black woman with long straight hair and yellow horn-rimmed glasses, called out, "Amelia Walker." Amelia and Officer Angelo approached the bench.

"She is charged with speeding. Is that correct, officer?" the judge asked looking at Angelo.

"Yes, sir," Angelo answered.

I had forgotten that Angelo's nose was so flat and that his raspy voice sounded so nasal.

The judge then advised Amelia of her rights and asked if she wanted a continuance. She declined. Then he asked her, "How do you plead?"

"Not guilty."

"Good! Case dismissed."

As the judge spoke, Angelo's mouth dropped open and he teetered visibly. "What?" he shouted.

Amelia looked shocked, too, but she didn't say anything. The judge repeated, "Case dismissed." He struck his gavel sharply, and Amelia and Angelo left the bench.

"There was something fishy about all this," she whispered sitting back down next to me. "Don't knock it," I told her. The fact is, I was glad to see her get off so easily, because I took it as a sign that I would get off, too. The clerk called my case, and I approached the bench along with Officer Wyler, the beady-eyed policeman who had returned to the scene of the accident with Angelo. The judge asked Officer Wyler what had happened. Wyler answered, "Judge, as you know, the man is charged with hitting an officer with a moving vehicle. Now, I wasn't present when the accident occurred. But when I got to the scene of the accident, Officer Angelo was in such pain that an ambulance had to be called to take him to the hospital."

"Your Honor," I cut in, "this man is lying."

"Quiet!" the judge snapped. "Go on," he said to Wyler.

"That's about all, your Honor. I gave the man a ticket."

"But, you Honor, I have a witness!" I asserted.

"I told you to be quiet!" Judge Carter pondered a moment pulling at the hairs in his raised right eyebrow. Then he asked me, "Did an ambulance come for Officer Angelo?"

"Yes," I said, "But . . ."

"That's all," he cut in. "Guilty as charged. The fine is two hundred dollars. See the clerk for payment arrangements."

"But, your Honor, I have a witness."

"Next case," he shouted, and struck his gavel.

I was so nonplused that my head started aching as soon as Amelia and I left the courtroom. There haven't been many times when my head hurt. So few, in fact, that I didn't even remember the last one. But this one I would never forget. It felt as if my whole head were pounding and threatening to pop my eyes out at any minute. My temples beat hard causing a ringing in my ears, and the back of my neck felt as if I had been wearing a yoke. Two hundred dollars! And I didn't even get a chance to plead my case. What topped the whole rotten deal was the fact that Amelia got off without even saying a word in her own defense. Not one word!

I must have been driving too fast on the snow-packed roads, because Amelia squirmed in her seat. "Al, slow down some."

"Shut up!"

"Don't take it out on me."

"Why shouldn't I?" I shouted. I knew that there was no reason why I should, but I wasn't going to back down. I started grasping for straws. "Your father probably did it," I said.

"Did what?"

"Paid the judge off," I shouted. I don't know whether I believed that or not at first. But as I pursued the idea, it became more and more plausible. And the more plausible it became, the more I began to believe it. "He never did like me," I shouted, "and this was his way of burning me."

"What?"

"That's right," I said. "He was afraid we would get married."

"Why would he think that?!"

"Because I've been screwing you longer than any of your other studs."

She didn't answer.

"And he's no fool," I continued. "He knows that I'm at your house everyday, sometimes twice a day. Why shouldn't he think it?"

She still didn't answer.

"You haven't done anything to cause him not to believe it. In fact, I think you want him to believe it. You're not punishing yourself. You're punishing him."

She jerked her head around, and looked into my face to see if I was serious. "That's right,"I said, "punishing him for not having the faith in you that you thought he had. You want him to believe that you're going to marry a nigger, any nigger at any minute. The very thought of a nigger son-in-law pains him to his soul, and you know it. You know it, and you like it. He's nothing but a spineless prick!"

"Don't you say that about him," she hissed through gritted teeth as her eyes narrowed and her face grew crimson.

But I was worked up, too, and I didn't care about her getting mad.

"Not only that," I continued, "but you're nothing but a cheap, filthy, dick-hungry whore."

And, good Lord! What did I say that for? That woman jumped on me with ten fingernails and all thirty-two teeth. We were both lucky that there were no cars parked on the street we were on, because I couldn't see a thing with her sitting on the steering wheel scratching at my eyes. Before I knew it, the car was sliding and bouncing up onto the curb with the right wheels. The force of the initial jolt saved me. It threw her off balance enough so that I could push her off of me and smack her. I suppose that if I had taken the time to think about it, I wouldn't have done it. But I didn't think. I simply lashed out with the back of my right hand and caught her full in the mouth and again in the eye. That didn't stop her. She kept on clawing at me. I felt small for being so brutal with her.

The car was stopped, so I opened the door and stepped out. My foot slipped on the hard packed snow. I grabbed the top of the door with one hand. With the other hand clutching the collar of her coat and half of her wild, flying hair, I dragged her into the street. She slipped and fell to her knees. It didn't take me lone to figure out that by yanking down on her collar and hair, I could keep her off balance and sprawling in the snow. So I yanked every time she tried to get up. I yanked and dragged, yanked and dragged. Before long, we were ten feet or so behind the car. I let her go and, without lifting my feet too high off of the ground lest I slip and fall, eased back to the open front door. She tried to catch me, but in her frenzy, she was unable to get up. I put the car in gear, and with the wheels spinning snow and slush all over Amelia still slipping and cursing in the street, I pulled slowly away from the curb.

I felt ashamed of myself for leaving her in the street that way, but in a way, she deserved it for being such a hypocrite. After all that jive about hating her father, she came to his defense a little too fast to suit me. It was as if she had fed me a line to make me think of her as interesting or unique.

I headed west from there on Armitage. When I got to my district, I stopped and ate lunch and cleaned up my face. I sustained two deep scratches under my left eye and teeth marks on my right ear. Both wounds bled a little. I cleaned them up with a wet handkerchief, and after eating, I started making my stores. After all, I still had a contest to win.

In about my fifth store, I received a call from Joe. He was fit to be tied. "Get in here this minute," he shouted.

"But I haven't made all my stores."

"You won't have to worry about that," he said, and slammed the phone in my ear.

This was bad. Any time a supervisor of sales tells a salesman to stop selling and come to the office, well, the situation at hand is more than just serious, it is catastrophic.

From where I was, it only took me about fifteen minutes to get to the office. Joe was the only one there when I walked in. "What's up, Joe?" I asked. He stopped what he was doing and looked up at me. For only the second time since I've known him, Joe's eyes were alive, vivid. In fact, they were piercing. It was as if he could see straight into the center of my mind. Before he said even one word, his fat baby face turned red, as red as Amelia's had when I called her a whore, maybe even redder.

"I'll tell you what's up," he said slowly and deliberately. "I've just gotten word that you beat up some woman on North Clark Street, and ran over her with the company car."

"What?"

"The poor woman's father called and said he had two witnesses that would swear it was you they saw."

Now I saw it all. That man *was* out to get me. Then a deeper realization hit me like a shot. Mighty Red! I had been found. My knees began to quiver. Was Joe somehow in with them? I had to act as if he were not. "I didn't do it, Joe," I said.

"Well, how did he get your license number and a perfect description of you and the car?"

"From his daughter," I said. "I've been screwing her for nearly six weeks, so she should know my description inside and out."

Joe's whole body quaked visibly. He must have known that she was white.

"Did you beat her up this morning in the middle of Clark Street?" His voice sounded strained.

"Yes," I said, "but I didn't run over her with the car."

He didn't say anything for a long minute. Then he asked, "did you beat that rap this morning in court?"

For a split second, I thought he was changing the subject. Then I realized where he was leading. I didn't even have to answer. He knew the answer from the way I hesitated.

"You didn't, did you?" he said. Now he wasn't mad anymore. In fact, he smiled. His eyes still looked as vivid and alive as blue gas flames, and his voice was calm. "Well, did you?" he asked again.

"No," I answered.

He paused a minute. "This looks bad, Al. Another conviction involving you and a pedestrian could cost you your license. And even if it doesn't, the company might let you go anyway."

"Why?" Why, indeed, was I even asking why? There was no way I could keep this job if Red knew who I really was.

"We like for our men to be stable, family men," he said.

"I am a stable, family man."

"Not with a girlfriend on the side, you're not."

"Everybody who works here has a girl on the side."

"That's right," he said, "but the company only knows about yours. With this in mind, the company is suspending you until it reaches a decision as to whether or not to terminate you."

"When will that be?" I asked.

"Next Monday. In the meantime, you're still eligible to come to the Christmas party this Saturday if you have a way to get there."

"We'll use the wife's car," I said.

I went straight to the phone booth across the street from the office, and called Amelia. Was she one of them, too?

"What are you trying to do to me?"

"Hi, Al," she said.

"Hi," I snapped, "what are you trying to do to me?" She didn't answer. I could hear muffled voices over the receiver, but I didn't know what they were saying. She must have had her hand over the mouthpiece. Then she said, "Hi, Al," again.

"Who's there with you?" I asked.

"Al," she said, "I love you." Her voice sounded overly sweet and sincere. "I love you, Al, please don't reject my love." She started crying. "Melvin," she said, "please, don't reject me again. I love you, Melvin." She was crying hard now. "I love you, Melvin! I love you! I love you."

Then a sharp thump came over the receiver. She must have dropped the phone. I heard her father in the background saying, "it's Ok, Amy. Everything's going to be Ok."

"No, it's not," she shouted at him. "You've taken Melvin away from me again. Father, how could you?

She was *not* one of them.

"Now, Amy," he said, "you lie down and relax."

I guess she did what he said, because in a few moments, he was on the phone talking. "Listen you," he said, "This is a sick girl. And if you don't stop seeing her, I'm going to make some real trouble for you."

"But you already *have* made real trouble for me," I said.

"Not like I'm going to," he chortled.

Amelia must have gotten up again. "Where are you going, precious?" he asked her.

"To the bathroom, Father," she said in the distance.

Then he returned his attention to me. "Have I made myself clear?" he said.

"You're one of her minions, aren't you?"

"I beg your pardon. I hardly equate being a concerned father with being her minion."

"But you do admit to paying off the judge and to calling the company I work for with that cock and bull story about me hitting your daughter with my car."

"Yes," he said, "I'm responsible for the whole thing."

I heard the toilet flush in the background.

"So you know," he continued, "that I can make some more trouble for you if I want to." He paused, then he shouted, "Amy, what have you done? Oh, my God!" He hung up.

What in the hell could she have done?! I called her number right back, but it was busy. I kept trying. When I finally got through, no one answered.

I took the bus home. The ride gave me time to think. Should I drop out again, go back to the abandoned house? Suppose Mighty Red wasn't behind all of this. Suppose it was all in my head. Suppose, suppose. I needed another sign.

I didn't see Ida's car in the parking lot, so I assumed she was at the Black Legion office. When I got upstairs and unlocked the door, the phone started ringing. I rushed in and answered it. It was Mr. Walker.

"Al," he said, "Amy has slashed both her wrists." He sounded as if he had forgotten about all the trouble he had threatened to make for me. He sounded as if we were old friends. "And she wants to see you," he said. "Will you come?" He paused. "Please."

"What hospital is she in?"

"Grant," he said, "Room 402."

"I'll be there."

VIII

When I got to the hospital, Mr. Walker was sitting in the lobby waiting. He got up to greet me as I approached him. "Al," he said, "am I glad to see you." His handshake was cold and limp. "Amy's been asking to see no one but you since they operated on her. She seems to think she failed you in some way this morning. What does she mean she failed you?"

"I don't know," I answered.

He put his hand lightly on my shoulder as we got on the elevator. I pushed the fourth button from the bottom. At room 402, a nurse coming out told us not to stay too long, because Amelia was still drowsy and would want to sleep. We said that we wouldn't. Once inside, Mr. Walker led the way. "Look, Amy," he said, "Look who I brought to see you."

"Get the hell out of here," she whispered as he approached her bed.

"But Amy, honey, look who I brought."

She turned her face away from him. He stood by her bed a long moment looking down at the floor, then he turned slowly and walked out.

I waited until he had closed the door behind him before I said, "Hi, Amy."

She looked at me. Her thin face was sunken and pale; the thick bandages around her wrists looked cold and white and clean and new. A bottle of clear plasma hung over the bed with a thin tube running from it to the bend in her left arm.

"Hi, Al," she said, "I'm sorry about this morning. I didn't mean to make you get mad."

Her eyes blinked slowly as if her eyelids were thick and heavy.

"That's Ok," I said, "it wasn't your fault."

She looked up at me with water gathering in her eyes. Melvin," she said, "please, don't leave me, again. Please, don't leave me, Melvin."

She sniffed a few times, then her eyes seemed to focus on something or someone behind me. I looked around but the door was still closed.

"Melvin," she said, her voice getting weaker, "Don't leave me. Don't leave. Don't leave me."

She fell asleep still whispering her pleas to Melvin. I left the room.

Mr. Walker was standing at the nurses' station with his back to me as I came out. I didn't want to talk to him, so I hurried to the elevator. Luckily, it was just stopping at this floor. I hopped on, and went down.

I didn't go straight home from the hospital. I didn't want to sit there alone thinking about Amelia and the sorry shape she was in thanks to Melvin, her father and me. I went, instead, to the Black Legion office where Ida worked. I wanted to tell her about today. It's strange, but now that it was over between Amelia and me, I felt a sense of relief. I felt as if everything was going to be fine. I knew now that I never loved Amelia. I had been just screwing her because she was there with her legs open. And she was too mixed up to love me. She loved Melvin. She was just using my dick and imagining that it was his. But now it was all over. I was free.

The Black Legion office as I walked in looked more like a poster and slogan salon than an office. At one time, it had been a store. But now all the shelves and counters were gone and the walls and floor were freshly painted light blue and black, respectively. Posters of clenched fists, Oriental and African soldiers holding rifles high over their heads, and freedom flags hung all around the room at eye level, and slogans like, all power to the people, and, off the pig, hung just above them. The place was empty of furniture except for one desk near the door and nearly a hundred folding chairs stacked neatly along the back wall. Ida was alone at the desk.

"Well, look who decided to visit." She looked happy to see me.

"Right on," I said.

"Why aren't you out slaving for the master?"

"I've been suspended until a decision is made regarding my possible termination."

"That's good," she said. "I wanted you to quit, anyway."

I smiled at her.

"So this is the office." I unfolded a chair by her desk and sat down.

"This is it," she said. "But you came at a slow time. you should have come last week when Otis Bell, the regional minister of propaganda, was here. He gave an interesting talk."

"On what?" I asked.

"The value of the black revolutionary movement."

"And what did he say was its value?"

"Well," she said, "he refreshed our memories on some of the things Mike told us that night at the Kirbys' place, and suggested an attitude to take towards the information based on the possible end results if the information is true. In other words, the information Mike gave us may or may not be true, a point that Felton says you brought up at Mike's first meeting. But Otis said that that in itself didn't matter. What did matter was what black people *believed* was true relative to the actual truth. And there are four possibilities. First, if the information that the white man plans to exterminate blacks is false, and black people didn't believe the information anyway, then no harm is done. If the information is false and blacks believe that it is true, still little or nothing results. If the information is true and we believe that it is true, then we may be able to avert a disaster by being prepared. Only when the information is true and we think it is false are we in real trouble. That one condition we must prevent. Do you see his point?"

"Yes," I answered.

"And the prevention of that one condition is justification enough for the whole movement."

We discussed a little longer the alternative conditions as Otis Bell outlined them, and reaffirmed the need to avoid condition four.

Then Ida asked, "Why are they firing you?"

I told her that they found out about Amelia. I also told her that I had failed to report a serious accident I had had with Angelo.

"I'm glad," Ida said, "because maybe that'll help us get our thing back together." She hesitated a moment. Then she said, "I've made some changes, Al. I've begun to realize that the honky has the whole system stacked against black people, and that we'll never get an equal share of the action."

"Don't allow yourself to be consumed by hatred," I said. "You can fight your enemy, even kill him, without feeling the hatred."

I wondered where that notion came from. It sounded like something Grandma Daughter would say. I knew it was true although I couldn't remember having heard her say it.

"I can't," she said.

"Try," I said.

"I think you should quit, anyway," she said.

"It's too soon," I answered.

"The only reason you got this job was for me."

"I know, but it's still too soon."

"Suit yourself," she said, "but I know we could live quite well on very little money if we move back to an apartment like the one on Van Buren and give up the junk we've bought."

She was right. I had never wanted this lifestyle, anyway. I called Joe to tell him that I was quitting.

"Oh, hi, Al," he said when he heard my voice. "I was just about to call you."

"About what?" I asked. I was suspicious of his intentions. His voice sounded too friendly. He sounded as if he were about to ask a favor, but was ashamed to in view of the fact that he had just suspended me.

"I-- uh-- talked to Glenn Young, my supervisor, and-- uh-- I told him your story," he said, "and he suggested that I-- uh-- put you back on until the decision to fire you or not is reached."

Joe sounded too uncertain about his story. It was as if he were improvising it. I called him on it. After all, I had nothing to lose, because I wasn't going back. "You're lying, Joe," I said, "you didn't have the authority to suspend me in the first place, and now that you can't make it stick, you're trying to get me to crawl back."

"Aw, c'mon, Al," he said. His voice turned sincere. "I'm in a jam. C'mon back to work."

I must have struck a lucky punch, but I wanted to be sure. "I was right, wasn't I?"

He hesitated. Then he said, "Yeah, Al, you were right. Glenn went over the early returns of the contest results and saw that you were way in front of the pack and recommended you for a gold star award for your enthusiasm."

"A gold star award?"

"Yeah," he said. He sounded dejected, "Glenn reckons you've already sold more than most of the salesmen in our group will have sold in two months. He's proud of you. You've made us all look good."

"Did you tell him that you had suspended me?"

"No."

"Well, you had better, because I'm not coming back."

"But, Al," he said, "I don't have anybody who can work that district. We won't make quota if you quit now."

"Sorry, Joe." I hung up.

I told Ida what Joe had just said. "Joe may even lose his job behind it," I added.

"No way," she countered, "as soon as the big honky finds out that a black man got suspended a week for nearly no reason, the little honky will get the gold star award for saving the company a week's salary."

"You're not trying," I said.

Ida didn't crack a smile.

I spent the rest of the day sitting around the Black Legion office with Ida. Occasionally, one of the members would come by to pick up some leaflets and buttons, or a local resident would stop in "just to see what the office looked like." But for the most part, it was quiet. Only one strange thing happened all day. At least, I thought it was strange. A brother wearing a long, black leather coat and a black knit cap down over her ears stood taking pictures of the office from across the street. But when I brought it to Ida's attention, she said, "Oh, him. He's an FBI agent. He takes pictures of the office and the people in it every Monday. That's one of the reasons so few people have been here today."

"How do you know he's an FBI agent?" I asked.

"We invited him over one day and asked him."

The following morning, I called the admissions office at the university to have them send me an application for readmission.

It was strange having no job and nothing to do all day, but I enjoyed the hell out of it. All we did was call the bank and tell them to come and get their car. We called Field's and told them to come and get their furniture. We called the telephone company, the gas company and the light company and told them all to discontinue service at the end of the month. That was it. We didn't even know where we were going to move, but it didn't matter. I suppose we both knew that we could stay a few weeks with Felton and Lois. But we didn't mention it. Instead, we enjoyed the exhilarating feeling of carefree financial recklessness.

I saw Amelia only once after that, the following Thursday morning. I suppose I went to see her just to reassure myself that I was making the right move.

When I asked the nurse on her floor how she was doing, the nurse told me that she was experiencing periodic fits of extreme depression. During these fits, she refused to talk to anyone, refused to eat by herself, and shat on the floor. Her doctor had recommended that she be committed to an institution, and her father had already signed the papers. She was to be committed the following Monday. I looked into her room for a short moment and saw her naked sitting cross-legged in the middle of the floor staring out the window. She didn't see me as I peeked in, because her back was to me. I made as little noise as possible. I simply looked at her long hair hanging down her back and her white, smooth thighs. I felt only pity for her. Could it be that pity was all I had ever felt for her, pity and lust?

On the way to the exit, I got the sign I needed. He wore green scrubs and a stethoscope, his dark hair slicked straight back on his melon-shaped head. He was pushing an empty wheelchair around a corner, and he was half my height. I cut my eyes to see him better, but he was already gone.

The bank and Field's repossessed all our things-- or rather all *their* things-- the same day we called them. The apartment was nearly bare. It's funny how material things can control people's lives and at the same time make the people feel as if they were in control. But walking into that house and seeing only the concrete floor and four bare walls made me feel a sense of independence that was truly gratifying. I knew now that I could come and go as I wanted, and that I had to answer to no one but myself. I also knew that I was through running from Mighty Red.

I had a lot of free time now. Ida wanted me to spend it in the Black Legion office working for the cause. "The revolution needs people to do its bidding," she said one morning as she prepared to leave.

"Does it?" I said. I knew that it did, but now that I was faced with the possibility of becoming one of those people, the statement lost its force.

She didn't know it, but I was already fighting a revolution. I was fighting a revolution in my head. My soul, my very existence was asserting itself, making itself known to me. I didn't want the needs of anyone or anything, even the revolution, to infringe on the progress of my personal revolution. And I could feel the rightness of what I was doing down to the center of my gut. Thinking back, I remembered having the same gut-feeling the day I told Lillian no and left Paris for Chicago. I wondered how long this revolution had been going on.

I suppose the notion of wood sculpting was a product of my inner being asserting itself, or maybe it was just a product of having a lot of spare time. Whichever it was, I picked up the hobby. It was hard at first. I couldn't seem to let myself go. I wondered as I worked whether or not my sculptures would be good. I worried about them looking weird. After all, they were nothing more than two-by-fours-- one was a four-by-four-- set on end with chunks cut out and holes, big ones and little ones, drilled in at various angles. A good sanding job and a couple of coats of varnish completed them. On the third one, I seemed to get carried away with cutting and drilling. I wasn't conscious of what the finished piece would look like. Rather, I concerned myself only with the act itself. The finished product surprised me. I liked the first two I had done, but they looked contrived. They looked as if I had been trying to create a profound looking abstraction. And I had. But not so with the third one. The third one looked genuinely profound. For at least an hour after it was done, I sat on the floor staring at it. Had this come from me? Was I really there? The image of Amelia sitting on the hospital floor flashed through my mind.

I had time to read all of Ida's health and yoga books as well. So this was where Amelia had gotten the idea of breathing exercises. I started standing on my head for five minutes three times a day. Christmas came, but it was no big thing. We didn't buy cards or gifts for anyone.

We found a kitchenette apartment on 35th Street about two blocks from the Legion office, and we moved into it on the 28th. It was exactly what we wanted, one big room with a closet-size kitchen and toilet, unfurnished. It cost only forty dollars a month, roaches and all. We didn't have to sign a lease. It was great. Of course, the roaches were a problem for awhile, but we fixed them. After we scrubbed and painted every square inch of the place, I went to the hardware store and bought some Death Brand Roach and Insect Killer. This was good stuff. It was expensive, but worth it. It came in a paste form and had to be spread with a brush around all the baseboards, around all the doors and windows, around the stove-- or in our case the hot plate-- around the sink and pipes, and around all the bathroom fixtures. When we finished, the place was like a fortress. Not one roach entered our place and lived. Not one. After we bought a mattress, a couple of secondhand chairs, and my sculpting tools, the room was perfect. The floor space was plenty large enough for both of us to do our yoga postures without getting in each others way. And the light in the ceiling cast more than enough light to read or sculpt by.

Life was beautiful. I went to school every day, and made more and more sculptures. I made so many, in fact, that on Ida's suggestion I displayed some of them in the Legion office. I was reluctant at first, because I didn't want my works on public display. But after nearly filling up our whole room with wood sculptures of all shapes and sizes, I decided to display some of them just to make some more space.

During that time, too, Ida began to protrude in front. Her clothes were no problem, though. She wore only loose-fitting African dresses anyway. Because she was pregnant, the variety left our love making. We had to rely exclusively on a side position so as not to put undo pressure on the growing fetus.

And, God! I loved Ida more and more every day. When Ruby died and Gwen was sent back to the world, I felt a hole in my life that I thought could never be filled. I remembered the day I got released from the hospital and Gwen marched on my lap chanting "Daddy, Daddy, Daddy." Ida was filling the void.

I don't know whether or not I had felt this same sense of growing love the first time she got pregnant, but I sure as hell felt it now. Just looking at her growing heavy with my seed caused me to shutter sometimes, and I would have to stop what I was doing and give her a hug, and holding her would make me feel whole.

Before long, Ida began to get pushy about me joining the movement. "Al," she said, "Join the Legion. I want us to be in it together."

"I don't want to join," I said.

"Why?"

"I'm not ready, that's why."

"But we need you," she said.

"Need me for what?"

"To help us wake people up and prevent that fourth condition."

She was right, but I still had my own revolution to fight. "I'm not ready," I said again.

That answer held her for about a week. Then she started again. "Al, please, join the Legion."

It wasn't that I didn't approve of the Legion. I did. I just didn't like the idea of joining when I wasn't ready. My new freedom of mind compelled me to do what I wanted, nothing else.

"No," I said, "I'll join when I've gotten my own thing together, not before. If I never get myself together, the Legion won't need me, anyway."

"But we *do* need you," she said. "We are the grass roots people. Why don't you want to be one of us?"

"I *am* one of you. I just don't want to join the Legion." She sounded like Lillian. The man who would not be grass roots people.

I had always known that fate could sometimes prepare a person to do things that he would not have prepared himself to do otherwise. But I had never expected it to happen in this case. Despite all that had happened to me involving the police, Joe and Mr. Walker, I still wasn't prepared to devote any of my energy towards the revolution. Circumstances changed that. Since Ida was getting bigger with the baby, it became necessary that she spend less time in the Legion office. Lois took over her job. One week after she did, disaster struck. Ida and I heard an account of the incident the following morning on the radio and later went by to view the scene. I even consented to be interviewed at the scene on national TV. But the night it happened we were both at home.

It seems that through photographs supplied by an unidentified source, the local police were able to determine on which evenings large meetings were generally held in the Black Legion office. On one such evening they conducted a raid in order to break up a major dope peddling ring, or so they said. The occupants of the office, some ten men, five women and three children, resisted arrest. All but one six month old baby were killed in the ensuing gun battle. The police lost one man in that raid. According to an eyewitness, a big man with nappy, rust-colored hair came charging out of the building right into the gunfire. He was armed with a wood sculpture. The police filled his body with bullets, but he apparently lived long enough owing to his massive size to club one of them to death. The report withheld his name pending the notification of the next of kin. Felton, Lois and Felton Junior were all at that meeting.

Ida took it hard at first. I suppose I did, too. But I told her that death was nothing more than a transition from one world into another, and that death, all death, even one's own, should not be feared, but merely accepted as inevitable. It helped ease the pain, but only a little.

That night, I dreamed. In the dream, I'm hovering in space. And the earth as I sail in closer is black as if silhouetted against a white sky. On the edge of the two dimensional horizon far, far away, I see several tiny silhouetted figures vacillating-- jagged, knobby figures like little twisted, leafless trees-- olive trees maybe-- jerking slowly from an electric shock, or like tightly wound strands of elastic rubber unwinding slowly and releasing tension in bursts. I sail slowly in on the twisted figures. As I do, the figures begin to look like heaps of ants fighting on the edge of a black cardboard circle. But as I close in, they turn into hundreds of three dimensional men with hard, bulging muscles all dressed in army fatigues fighting one on one in a well-illumined, three-dimensional, sandy, barren field. The sun burns hot directly overhead, and thick sweat oozes out of the men's pores.

I zoom in on a seemingly random pair of combatants. But as the face of one of the men becomes clear, I begin to realize that my choice was not random. His face shines with sweat, and his olive drab fatigues look wet under the arms, across the back and around the collar. The man is me. And I'm fighting to stay alive. The man I am killing wants to stay alive, too. But he's not as strong as I am. My arms are too powerful for him. In fact, my arms are so strong that I've twisted his arms around his neck, and I'm choking him from behind with them. The side of his face is red from blood forced into his head. And the blood in his face slowly turns purple. I realize now that the quivering, jerking release of tension I had seen from space was one man in each of the couplets succumbing finally, suddenly, and in total exhaustion to the strength of the other. I continue to twist and turn my opponents arms, and I hear his cartilage and bone rupture and crack. By now, he is helpless. I force his face down in the sand with one hand; the fingers of my other hand stay locked around his knotted arms. He gasps for air. I know now that the men on the field are not two armies fighting each other as I had thought. Rather, each fight is personal, a personal fight with a stranger. And at the end of each struggle, the war for that victor is over even though the war on the field goes on.

My opponent begins to strangle on the sand that clogs his nose and mouth. He lurches desperately in an effort to get air. To humiliate him to the fullest, I unbutton my pants and stuff my hard, black penis into his stiff, pale rectum. I can sense that he wants to cry out from the pain, but he can't get air enough even for that. I pull a knife from the scabbard at my side. As I feel myself begin to orgasm, I reach around and slide the knife blade slowly, very slowly, under his rib cage and into his pounding heart. He lunges back to avoid the knife; I lunge forward to force my penis deeper. His thick blood spurts. And as he dies, my semen spurts. His body quakes with a spasm of death; mine quakes with one of bliss and elation.

I can see in the end that the man isn't real. His blood, his pounding heart, the stink of his rectum are all an illusion. And in the end, I am free.

That morning, I thought about Grandma Daughter, and remembered that I never found the book with the picture of the sphinx. Then, I began to realize what the quarternary of the Magi meant: KNOW, DARE, WILL, KEEP SILENT. It meant that any man could be or have anything in the universe by simply knowing what he wanted, daring to have it, working towards it, and keeping quiet about it so no one would work against it. Moreover, one could want it all, be it all, be God. One could be absolutely and infinitely free, transcend the laws of man as well as those of nature. Then I saw it and knew it. Not only was I *a* King, related to Uncle Buddy King and Grandma Daughter King, I was *the* king. Through the spirit, I was Al Pearsons; I was all persons; I was one with God; I *was* God. The man in the green Mercedes had been right. In one blinding flash, I knew that I could do anything I wanted to do without the fear of or fact of rebuke or reprisal on the other side. I saw a passage scribbled on a men's room wall once, right over the urinal. It read, "Nothing in Itself is Honorable or Shameful, Just or Unjust, Agreeable or Painful, Good or Bad. It is Opinion which Gives Things Quality, as Salt Savors Meat." I knew what I had to do.

I didn't regard the plan I came up with after the Black Legion raid as a plan of revenge. It was more, much more. This was to be the final victory over Mighty Red. I don't know why I told Ida my plan, because originally I hadn't wanted to. But I suppose I figured she had a right to know, especially in the event the plan failed. She surprised me by saying, "I'm going, too."

"No," I said, "it'll be too dangerous."

"You won't be able to stop me," she said. "You'll either make me part of your plan or I'll see to it that it fails."

There was no way she could stop me, and we both knew it. But her spunk was what I had loved in her most. Besides, if the plan was going to work, it would work with or without her being there.

The next morning, I took two hundred dollars from the final pay check I got from American Biscuits, and went to see a man to whom Felton had once introduced me. The man wore a process and wire frame glasses, and owned a pawn shop on 47th Street. He was also a fence for most of the local stick-up men. From him, we bought a Remington Automatic with rounds for me and a .22 caliber Springfield Automatic with rounds for Ida. They were both stolen guns. Afterwards, we bought a gallon of gasoline, and we put it in four coke bottles with corks and rag wicks.

It's funny how easy it is to do something once you have made up your mind to do it. I showed Ida how to use the Springfield, not from the shoulder, but from the waist. And if she did as well in wet fire as she had done in dry, she would be able to kill easily at close range.

We spent the rest of the day going over the details of the raid. Two of us in on it would almost guarantee its success.

That night around three a.m., after we had gotten a few hours sleep, we put the guns and bottles in the back of the cheap little Volkswagen we had bought a month or so before, and headed for the West Side. I knew of a little police station out there in a semi-industrial area where there would be no passers-by to witness and few policemen to encounter. That station was our target.

An alley ran right alongside the station, and at about three-thirty, that's where I stopped the VW. I left the engine running. We had studied the plan so well that we worked with a minimum of conversation. We put on nylon gloves to prevent us from leaving any fingerprints. We loaded the rifles. I carried the bottles in a paper shopping bag to the outside doors of the station where I set them down. Ida walked slightly behind me carrying her loaded Springfield.

I had expected that I would be scared. And I was. But it was a cold scared, as if I knew that I would die, but as if I didn't care. My mouth felt bone dry, and I know my hands would have been moist were it not for the nylon gloves.

 I looked both ways down the street. It was deserted. "Are you ready?" I asked Ida. She nodded yes. Her lips quivered. She squeezed them tight together. This was it.

I opened the door, and peeped in. The desk sergeant, a gaunt man with large brown eyes and thinning hair, stood up and asked, "May I help you?" He was fully exposed from the waist up. Another officer who was seated by the desk with his back to the door turned to see who I was. His eyes were brown, too. But being a younger looking man than the desk sergeant, his hair was thick and long on top. They were both wearing their uniform blues. I looked at them for a long second. Then

I stepped in, leveled the Remington at the desk sergeant and fired twice. Two small holes appeared in the sergeant's shirt over his heart. He dropped. The younger officer jumped up and reached for his revolver, but not fast enough. I emptied the Remington into his chest. The force of the bullets striking him slung him backwards against the wall, and as he slid down, a thick red streak appeared on the dull gray paint behind him. Just then, a third officer opened a frosted glass door on the other side of the room. It was Angelo. I instantly recognized that nose, flat and crooked. He didn't even have to speak for me to remember that his raspy voice sounded so nasal. Ida shouted, "Al!" And for just a second, I thought she knew who I really was. Maybe it was the way she pronounced the 'l' that fooled me, but I thought she called me Noel. She pointed the Springfield at him and fired. The bullet struck him in the shoulder. It only slowed him a little as he reached for his gun. "Quick!" I shouted, "in the head!" Ida fired three quick shots. The first one thumped through the glass door to his left and behind him. The second one landed in the door frame to his right raising a thin cloud of dust and plaster. By now his gun was drawn and he fired one round which whizzed through Ida's thick fluffy natural. Her third shot plunged into his left eye kicking blood and bits of flesh into its wake. "Oh!" he said almost casually and his right knee buckled and he dropped the gun. A puddle of thick red blood gathered around his head when he hit the floor. Ida dropped the Springfield and stared at him. I remembered how clumsily he picked himself up after he had fallen dodging Amelia's car. I half expected him to do it again now.

The rest was easy. I reloaded the Remington in case we needed it on the way out. Then I lighted the bottles of gasoline, and threw one into each corner of the room. The fire roared as we left.

Once outside, I set the Remington into a garbage can in the alley. We got into the VW, and drove off. We didn't see one passer-by driving or walking. Our escape was complete. A few blocks later we heard one fire siren in the distance. I palmed myself the way Grandma Daughter used to do.

We must have driven fifteen minutes before we even looked at one another. Pain was all I could see in Ida's lean black face, her wet eyes looking at me, her stiff lips, her quivering chin.

"Well," I said trying to console her, "it's over." As I uttered the words, I became aware of a double meaning for them. Granted, the raid was over, but so was something else. The revolution in my head was over, and I had won. I was a new person. I was now capable of doing whatever I wanted to do, and not be hemmed in by amenities and laws. I was free, autonomous. But along with my new freedom, there came a new responsibility. Before, I was able to point to things outside myself and blame them for my failures. No longer. Now I was completely responsible for all my own actions, and was prepared to pay the cost of making them.

Ida still looked at me. But her expression of pain was gone. Her face looked blank, emotionless except for her eyes, which were forced wider open than normal. She looked at every part of my face from top to bottom and from side to side. But she didn't speak. She simply looked, and left me to wonder what she saw.

She miscarried that night, in the cold, leaning against the car, arms quivering, great bellows of vapor issuing from her nose and mouth, vomiting at first from the fear and stress of having just killed a man, then continuing into dry heaves, her body wrenching, lurching, tearing, bleeding deep inside.

The next day, I watched the news. The show led with the story of a police station being attacked and burned to the ground last night. No suspects were in custody. Then there was a short piece on the state's attorney and police chief being accused of authorizing the raid on the Black Legion office. The two incidents were believed to be unrelated. The story got international coverage. They replayed the interview of me standing in front of the Legion office. There were folks behind me with signs, one of which read: "No Justice, No Peace." I had seen this clip several times before, but for the first time, I caught a glimpse of a man standing behind me at the edge of the picture. He carried a sign visible for only a second or two before the cameraman shifted the angle, and cut him out. The sign read: "His Children are coming." That was it! On national television-- indeed, international television-- the *coup de grâce*. Lillian would be proud.

IX

Go in and out the window;
Go in and out the window;
Go in and out the window;
Sweet Mary came today.

Across the way in the parking lot, I'm one of three boys spinning tops. We've drawn in chalk a large white circle on the black pavement. And as one of us spins his top in the circle, the others try to break it.

Eddie and Richard Bunton are twins. They are short and skinny with sandy colored hair. They never break each others tops. Only mine. But they're lousy shots. I'm a good shot. I break their tops a lot. Today is not my day. Today they are lucky.

My top is new and fat and bright yellow. It is already cracked in half. I want to cry, but I can't. Not in front of Eddie and Richard. I play it off.

Their big sister, Sadie, spins a diabolo on a string. It's easy to tell they are all in the same family. She has the same skin color and sandy hair, the same sagging eyes, the same buck teeth. She pulls each end of the string up and down and the diabolo spins, balanced like a gyroscope. She yanks the string taut. The diabolo sails into the air over her head. She catches it again on the string. How long did she have to practice that move? Then in one fluid motion, she bends forward with her tightly curled fists together, and yanks herself over backwards as she raises up on her toes and snatches the string tight again. The diabolo zooms into the air and disappears in the perfectly crystal clear deep blue sky. It must have come down in a tree, because Sadie stuffs the string into her pocket and walks away.

One kiss before you leave me;
One kiss before you leave me;
One kiss before you leave me;
Sweet Mary came today.

The robot writes in the dirt with a stick:

As a
soft and balmy
wind blows
tender
through the leaves
of
stately trees
and the blades of sunburned grasses,
so the tuned of the earth tip-toe
through white marble mansions
and festering slums--
unaffected.

I notice a fat little boy walking towards me. He is wearing a full length, black silk cape, one like a magician might wear. "Are you the one?" he asks brandishing the gun even closer, close enough that I could snatch it away if I wanted to.

"What difference does it make?" the robot asks.

"If you say no, you live."

"Even if the no is a lie?"

"Even if the no is a lie," he answers. "I don't want to make you a martyr."

I can feel the leaves and branches of the cottonwood tree piercing my formlessness as I leak between the molecules of the robot's skull and ascend in a circle of soft, creamy light. From my vantage point above the tree, I see a Chinese woman wearing a purple, silk Manchurian jacket. As she steps slowly through the grass with her knees bent and her arms draped in front of her as if they are resting on an imaginary fence, her posture resembles that of a praying mantis. She is about twenty-eight, and the ends of her waist-length silky black hair wave in the breeze as she moves. Her dark almond eyes stare off at the horizon. Her delicate pearl-like face is calm. She squats down on one leg holding her balance by extending one arm behind her. Her other arm snakes along the leg outstretched in front of her as she slowly shifts her weight. She rises up and pauses on one leg like a crane standing in tranquil water, her other limbs poised yet relaxed in front of her. She looks as if she is expressing herself in a sign language of the deaf. She makes no sound as she moves.

I see cumulus clouds far off on the eastern horizon. They look like the rolling hills of some fairy tale kingdom. I can hear Grandma Daughter in the distance humming an old gospel tune. The robot writes. It writes its life, and it must write fast before it is gone. It takes a deep breath and exhales slowly. With clinical precision it says, "I am the one."

And as I ascend towards the clouds, I hear a muffled burst. I watch the robot slump to the ground bleeding from its side, and hear the staccato, innocent, almost childlike sound of a single pair of feet running along the pavement that leads out of Rainbow Park.

About the author

Larry Redmond is a native of Chicago, Illinois. He graduated from Hyde Park High School and served in the U.S. Air Force. He did his basic training at Lackland Air Force Base (AFB) in San Antonio, Texas, then went for further training at Goodfellow AFB in San Angelo, Texas. He was stationed in Darmstadt, Germany, for three years working in intelligence.

After a short return to the U.S. where he worked at several odd jobs including six months as an assembler for an electronics company near Mt. Vernon, New York, he spend 15 months traveling in Europe where he hitch-hiked from Lapland in Scandinavia to Morocco in North Africa working along the way at a variety of jobs from farm hand to factory worker to dishwasher to carpenter's assistant, mainly in Sweden and Germany. His travels have taken him to Oslo, Norway; Copenhagen, Denmark; Amsterdam, the Netherlands; Paris, France; Cologne, Germany; Barcelona, Spain; and Tangier, Morocco.

Upon his return to the United States he attended the University of Illinois at Chicago, where he majored in Philosophy and minored in English. He did further graduate work and later attended the John Marshall Law School, earning a Juris Doctor degree. He has also done graduate work in Computer Science and Telecommunications at De Paul University. He has worked in Chicago and throughout the United States as a computer consultant designing and implementing fault-tolerant application in a wide range in industries from banking to transportation to manufacturing. He has worked as a criminal defense attorney representing high-profile death row inmates, several of whom were released pursuant to DNA testing. He has been active in third-party politics.

He has also found time for a full and rich family life, with seven children and three grandchild. His hobbies include physical training and martial arts, African and Conga drumming, and yoga and meditation.

He currently works and lives with his family in Chicago.

Visit on-line at www.LarryRedmond.com for other books by Larry Redmond